THE DEVIL IN THE BOTTLE:

THE TRAGEDY OF JOSEPH ("JACK") SLADE

Carol Buchanan

Carol Buchanan Books
KALISPELL, MONTANA

Carol Buchanan /Carol Buchanan Books
280 4th Ave. WN; PO Box 1655
Kalispell, Montana 59901
https://carol-buchanan.com

Publisher's Note: This is a work of fiction. Names, characters, places, and incidents are a product of the author's imagination. Locales and public names are sometimes used for atmospheric purposes. Any resemblance to actual people, living or dead, or to businesses, companies, events, institutions, or locales is completely coincidental.

Book Layout ©2013 BookDesignTemplates.com

Ordering Information:
For details, contact the publisher at the address above.

The Devil in the Bottle/Carol Buchanan. – 2nd ed.
ISBN 978-0-9864203-3-7

NEVADA CITY

MARCH 8, 1864

1.

As yet only a trouble to the air, like the tremor in the saloon's dirt floor felt through his boot soles, laughter edged close into Daniel Stark's hearing. His rifle, lying across the bar, shivered. Putting a hand on the stock, he tried again to explain to the saloonkeeper why he would pay a heavy fine if the miners court found him guilty. "The rules spell it out, Charley. The head of your sluice can't be more than ten inches in diameter."

For all Charley Baer's broad German face showed, Dan thought, he might as well talk to the beer barrel. "This new brewing, you will like it, I think." Charley eased the spigot back, wiped the overflow off the glass, and set it down to wait for the head to settle. After that, he would pour more, wait, and pour and wait, and at last would allow Dan to drink. The glass stood so close to Dan's right hand he might have been fooled into thinking it was ready now, but he knew better. Charley wouldn't thank him for drinking before the head settled. The brewer folded his arms across his tree trunk of a chest. "So maybe my claim, it ain't in Fairweather District, eh? Maybe it's in Nevada District. Maybe the rules is different here. Or maybe they measured wrong." He took the bar rag, wiped a spill off the gleaming oak bar. It had cost a lot to freight that bar up from San Francisco, and he was justifiably proud of it. "When the snow melts, then we see. Ja. When the ice breaks, then maybe —"

Dan lost the rest in a rumble of hoofbeats and raucous laughter. Who was making that godawful racket? Didn't they know there were ordinances now about making a public disturbance? Raising his voice over the ruckus, he said, "By then it may be too — "

A window pane burst. The beer glass exploded, spraying beer and splinters of glass. Charley Baer went down on a scream and a spray of blood. Around the room, men who had been peacefully drinking away the long winter scrambled for cover, tipping over tables, spilling beer, cards, and chips. Dan dropped to the floor, carrying the rifle with him. Rolling over, he levered a round into the chamber. The hoofbeats and laughter faded on up the street. He crawled behind the bar and found Charley bleeding from cuts to his face, one eye full of blood. The other glared. He swore in German, wiped at his face with the rag, switched to English: "By Christ, no more of this we don't have. This we took care of in winter. You go shoot them. Shoot them all. Gott verdammt." Blood smeared his face, poured from his right eye.

"Your eye — You're bleeding." Thinking sure a glass splinter had put out Charley's eye, Dan felt his stomach churn. He clenched his teeth to hold back the bile rising in his throat.

"Ja." Charley wiped the rag across his face, smearing the blood, but he glared at Dan out of both eyes. A jagged cut through his eyebrow ran an inch or so up his forehead. He slapped the rag onto the cut. "Und you also."

Feeling a wet trickle in his sideburn, Dan wiped at it. His fingers came away bloody, and bile burned sharp in his mouth. Gritting his teeth, he rolled to his knees and waited until the dizziness passed, to locate his hat and put it on, wincing as it settled on the cut. Drums thudded in his ears. Hoofbeats coming back? He rocked once on his heels and rose to his feet, rifle in hand, swaying a bit before he found his legs.

Charley stood up, too. Put a hand on the bar to steady himself. "Gott verdamm!" he bellowed. "Diese bastards have my bar scratched. Go, you, Stark, go and shoot the verdammter sonsabitches."

Outside, the air felt oily, as if the day, so ordinary in its beginnings, were slipping from his grasp and he scrambled to catch it, only to have it slide from his fingers. In a space between buildings at the corner of the saloon he spat into the snow. When he straightened, he felt better though his mouth tasted rancid. Picking up a double handful of snow, he filled his mouth, rinsed, and spat. At least it felt cleaner, although he knew his breath stank.

Stroking his thumb across the hammer of the rifle, he asked himself, where are those bastards? The drum thumped in his ears, and the bleeding was probably ruining his muffler. He tapped his thumb on the hammer. Charley Baer was right. They had not acted in the winter, beginning with the first hanging just down the street, to have ruffians come back and disrupt the hard-fought peace.

Across Nevada City's Main Street, a stretch on the road from anywhere to the gold in Alder Creek,

John Lott walked out the door of his store and stood, hands at his sides, as if merely getting a breath of air. Dan nodded to him, and Lott raised an index finger to his forehead. Up the street, whooping and yelling, five or six riders turned their horses. Coming back. People scurried to find cover before merchants and residents drew in their latchstrings and dropped the bars on their doors. A woman let her shopping basket fall, picked up her skirts, and fled up the side street past the Star Bakery. Dan glimpsed red striped stockings as she ran. Downstream, a gaunt man untying a rope on a mule's pack stopped to watch the riders.

At their center, one man rode a bright, blaze-faced chestnut as if he sat on the world's throne. Dressed in a fringed and beaded cream-colored buckskin suit, all the fringes dancing, he lifted his face and bayed to the clouds while the horse sidestepped and swung its hindquarters. The other horses put back their ears and dodged out of the way. The man held the reins and a whiskey bottle in his left hand, as he fired a pistol into the sky with his right. "Halloo! Slade of the Overland is taking the town!" he yelled. "Yippee!"

Joe Slade. Again. He might have known. God damn it.

Controlling his mount with the reins held in his teeth, another rider broke his pistol and brought out a powder horn to begin reloading. The others hollered and fired a few hilarious shots at nothing in particular as they all trotted forward in an untidy bunch.

A ball struck the mule's haunch. Blood spouted from its gray hide. Braying, the animal bucked and kicked both hind feet. The muleskinner sailed backwards, landed on his back, and lay groaning in the street. Tied horses panicked, reared, yanked against their reins, and bolted every which way, slipping and stumbling on rutted ice and melting snow, dragging pieces of hitching rail, trailing broken reins.

John Lott stood unmoving, his empty hands dangling at his sides.

Dan heard: "Shoot them," but whether it was his own thought or Charley's voice from inside the saloon, he did not know. He could end this right here. Six troublemakers, against the seven-shot repeating rifle. A few seconds to solve the problem of Slade and his rampages. The drum pounded in his ears. Damn them. Cock and fire. His thumb tightened on the hammer.

A few seconds to solve the problem of Slade. The smoke would cloud the rest of his life, what remained of it, for it would be murder, and he would deserve what happened next. Taking a deep breath, he took his hand away, stretched his fingers.

He would find a better way.

He slung the rifle on his shoulder and let it ride his back.

Charley called after him, "You give me that thing, I take care of him."

Ignoring Charley, he walked out into the street. He'd be safer – they'd all be safer – if the rifle were not in play. This was Joseph Slade, legendary gunman, legendary murderer. Had he killed more than twenty men? He had not so far killed anyone in the gold camps along Alder Gulch. To Slade, any weapon, especially this one, meant a challenge, and Slade did not back down, not him. Especially when drunk. Midway across the street the drum in his ears changed to a hammer, like a damn blacksmith setting up shop, out of rhythm with the hoofbeats trotting toward him.

The muleskinner cried out, his feet scrabbling as if to gain purchase on the ice and stand up. His mule stopped, stood with its head low, braying its pain.

Slade and his men slowed their horses to a walk, veered toward John Lott, and stopped in a row.

"How do, John." Slade beamed on everyone, his voice cheery. The horse tossed its head.

His followers sat quiet on their restless horses. The rider reloading his pistol poured black powder into the last chambers in the cylinder, capped his powder horn, and stowed it in his coat pocket.

Watching Slade out the corner of his eye, Dan slogged through melting snow toward the groaning muleskinner. Farther down the street, Doctor Byam walked out of his house toward the downed man.

The rider reached into his pocket and brought out a ball that he dropped into a chamber.

"Hey, Stark," Slade said. "How do." He tilted the bottle in a half salute, put it to his mouth.

Pleasantly, he hoped, Dan said, "How do, Slade." He paused, half-turned toward Slade, gauging his temper, the rifle a greater weight on his mind than on his shoulder. Slade didn't appear in a mood to kill anyone this afternoon. Around them tin music rattled from a saloon, the mule brayed, and somewhere a dog barked nonstop. The muleskinner called for help.

Slade's pal freed the rammer from under his pistol barrel to pack the balls down on the powder.

Dan looked up at Slade and thought to himself, a shell in the chamber; all he had to do was cock and fire. He stretched the corners of his mouth to imitate a smile and hoped it was good enough.

Slade returned the smile, his round green eyes like sunshine on a well-scythed lawn.

John Lott said, "You're not coming in here, Slade. Not in your current state of inebriation."

The green eyes lost their happy light, became a dull, narrow green. Moisture – no doubt blood – trickled down Dan's sideburn, but he did not lift a hand to wipe it away. He couldn't bother now about a ruined scarf. Upending the bottle to drink, Slade's lips closed around the bottle's mouth, but he did not drink. He peered around it at the storekeeper, took the bottle away from his mouth. "No, guess not, John." He squinted down its neck and laughed. "Hell. Empty."

Lott said, "Go home, Slade. For God's sake, go home and sober up."

"Go to hell." But his voice was mild, almost absent, and he tossed the bottle into the street. "I need another." Smiling, he touched his pistol barrel to his hat brim in a friendly salute, pulled his horse around so he faced Dan, standing in his way. His pals reined their horses around them.

"Your shenanigans are about played out," said Dan, thinking as the light vanished from Slade's face that he was a double damned fool to talk that way to this man on a bender, but he could not stop himself. "Just go home."

Slade stopped his horse, pointed the pistol at Dan, who tried to calculate whether he had time to bring the rifle around, cock and fire before Slade killed him. Or not.

"Go to hell," Slade shouted. "Nobody gives orders to Slade of the Overland." He spurred the horse forward, as if to ride Dan down, but the animal sidestepped, brushing Dan's left shoulder and sending him staggering sideways, his arms up and windmilling on a tilted world, the rifle bouncing against his side. As he regained his balance, he heard John Lott say, "One of these days, he'll find out he's not Slade of the Overland any more. They fired his ass more'n a year ago." He went into the store and closed the door behind him.

Dan thanked his lucky stars he had not fallen victim to his own rash impulse. He walked on down the street to where a few men gathered around the doctor and the muleskinner. The doctor, a slight man named Don Byam, sat on his haunches to examine him. Looking up to see who came, he said, "Hello, Stark. He won't die, but his shoulder's broken pretty badly." He stood up and gestured to the bystanders. "Let's get him to my house."

Several men stepped forward to help. As the doctor directed, they crouched on either side and worked their hands under him as far as they could, grasped fistfuls of his coat. The sufferer's eyes widened in fear. "For God's sake, don't move me."

Byam said, "We have to. You'd die lying here." To the others: "Careful, now, boys. Stark, you support his head, I'll take that shoulder, easy now, gently, on the count of three." But there was no being easy or gentle enough, and as they lifted him, he screamed once and fainted. "Probably better for him," said Byam as they slogged sideways toward his house a few yards off.

"Oh, shit," said one of the men.

Slade rode toward them. Dan felt spasms along the unconscious man's clothes, as the others took fresh holds on them, or perhaps prepared to let go and find urgent business elsewhere.

Pulling up, Slade said, "This is dreadful, Doctor. I'm very sorry." He fumbled with the reins and his pistol, at last looping the reins over his right elbow and clamping the pistol between his arm and his side, while he reached with his left hand into a waistcoat pocket. "Here, I'll pay for his treatment." He pulled out two tanned and leathery items of irregular shape, longer than they were wide, narrower at one end than at the rounded top. Leaning down, holding the things by their edges, he offered them to Byam.

The doctor gasped, and his weathered face lost a shade or two of color.

Hang on, Dan told him silently. For God's sake don't drop him.

"You see these?" Slade demanded, his eyes merry above his rosy cheeks, his square shoulders shaking, and his voice vibrating with restrained laughter.

Beni's ears. My God, Dan thought. Jules Beni's ears. Slade was pretending to pay for this man's medical care with Beni's ears. Could the stories be true? Had Slade murdered Beni in revenge for shooting him multiple times – sixteen? twenty? – with a pistol and a shotgun, and leaving him for dead? After Slade recovered, he caught Jules, tied him to a corral fence, and shot him – in a knee, an elbow, a shoulder – prolonging Beni's agony by going in for a drink between each shot, while Beni screamed and begged until he died. Then he sliced off his ears for souvenirs. These ears.

"Yes, I see them." The doctor's voice quavered.

"They're legal tender, aren't they?"

Doctor Byam shook his head, his sparse goatee brushing his top shirt button, but he kept his grip on the injured man's jacket around the broken shoulder.

Slade's smile thinned, the roses paled, his brows lowered as his eyes changed from green to dark, and the muscles in his jaws bulged. Even the bones of his face seemed to realign themselves, until his face belonged to someone Dan did not know, a malign stranger. "I said they're legal tender. You agree, don't you?" Even his voice was different, deeper, lower – growling.

His friends sat their horses in a half circle behind him, their pistols in their hands, the fun gone from their eyes, their mouths grim slits in their beards.

Byam stared around at them, swallowed. "I suppose," he squeaked. Clearing his throat, he steadied himself, though his voice was higher than normal, "Yes, I suppose they could be."

Slade straightened in the saddle, put the ears in his waistcoat pocket, switched the pistol to his right hand. He swayed, seeming to teeter on the edge of another explosion.

Before he could tilt the wrong way, Dan said, "Now, if you'll excuse us, we have to get this man to the doctor's house." To the others, "Ready? All right, then. Left foot first. One, two. One, two." For a wonder, they stepped off on his count, and he counted all the way to the doctor's house while sweat ran down under his shirt, and the killing face of a Slade he had never met stayed in his mind, even as they opened the door and sidled down a short hallway into a room where they laid the unconscious man on a long bench attached to one of the walls.

The other men blew out their breath, clapped him on the shoulder, congratulated each other on a lucky escape. "Well done." Byam poured clean water into a basin and washed his hands. "I need an assistant to help get his clothes off so I can set that shoulder before he wakes up. The rest of you can leave, with my thanks." As Dan thought to leave with the others, the doctor said, "You stay. I want to look at your head."

Dan stood the rifle against the wall and sat on the stool, content to wait by the window where the invisible sun brightened the clouds. He laid his hat brim up on the plank floor between his feet. Leaning his elbows on his knees, he gave himself up to understanding that the day had slipped from his grasp when Slade showed the killer side of his nature, the one that the stories told of. Perhaps there were two Slades, the decent, friendly sober man being one. And the other Slade, who came out with the drink. The malevolent stranger. The murderous Slade.

2.

"I've never seen him this bad before." Doctor Byam's fingers worked through Dan's hair as he talked about Slade. "Ouch!" As Dan flinched, he said, "Something's in here." His words were muffled, as if he held something in his mouth. "I cut myself. Hang on, I'll get a forceps." To the two men who waited, he said, "Hold on there. I won't be a minute."

Both men were strangers to Dan, though the one with carroty hair seemed familiar somehow. The other was dark, with thick curly hair and high cheekbones, and skin the color of weak coffee. He looked to have mixed blood of some sort, Indian or Negro, or possibly both. The red-haired man glared at Dan, while the dark man glanced all around the room, his eyes like rabbits hunting an escape.

"Here we go." Byam put a folded rag, formerly a piece of blue plaid flannel shirt, in Dan's hand. "Hold this. Bend your head toward your shoulder. More. That's good. Hold still now." His fingers scrabbled in the hair behind Dan's left temple. "Does it seem to you like Slade's benders are coming faster and getting worse?"

"Yes," Dan said. "His last bender was four days ago."

"Exactly," the doctor said. "Hold still now. Here we go."

11

Biting the inside of his lower lip, Dan sat silent, head tilted. Something scratched him hard. "Hey! Are you trying to scalp me?" Blood flowed fresh and warm along his sideburn, behind his ear. He clapped the rag to the cut and leaned forward. Bright red drops splashed onto the floor.

"Well, look at this." Byam held a long glass splinter so Dan could see it. "That's a nasty hair ornament." He dropped it in a trash can. Dan heard water sloshing in the basin, probably the doctor washing his hands. Byam asked, "What can be done about Slade?"

Sitting up straight, Dan waited for the swirling room to stop, and tried to ignore the bass drum thumping at his temple.

"Shoot him," the carrot-topped man said. When no one said anything, his upper lip curled. "Or hang him. That's what y'all do, ain't it?"

"No."

"Don't give me that. They hung Aleck Carter, the damned vigilanters." His brown eyes glared at Dan. The dark man stared from Carrots to Dan to the doctor, his eyes showing white all around, then ducked his head again, as if studying on the injured man's boot.

"I'd be careful who I talked that way to." Byam ran his thumbnail under the seal on a second bottle of whiskey and set it on a small table that held all his instruments. "Folks are safe here because some weren't afraid to do the necessary that others were too yellow to do."

"It's all right." Dan thought to calm Carrots, but the red-haired man raised his voice almost to a shout. "Of course it's all right. Why wouldn't it be? Why should you-all give a damn what I say? It's a free country, ain't it? Aleck Carter was a friend of mine, damn you. I knowed him in Oregon, he was an honest farmer. He give me my first job, haying in the summers. I say he could never do nothing to get strung up for."

The injured man groaned and bent one knee as if to put the foot flat on the table. To Dan it was a welcome interruption, away from the fate of Aleck Carter. The thought sprang up that was never far away: What if we were wrong about Carter? Few could believe that a good man in one place would go to the bad here, where more gold was available for the taking than most men think of in a lifetime, and wanting gold found the fissure in a man's character and broke it apart.

Byam said, "Here. Take those scissors on that table, and cut his sleeves from wrist to his neck. Injured arm first."

Byam touched the hand holding the rag to the cut. "Move your hand over a little." Doing as he was told, Dan heard a glugging sound and smelled whiskey. A thousand bees stung his scalp. He jerked upright and slapped the pad to the cut again, pressing his lips together to hold in a yelp. "There, now. That should take care of any festering. I'm done. That'll be half an ounce of dust."

"Nearly scalp a man and then charge him for it?" Dan spoke around the pounding bass drum as Byam wrapped a long piece of cloth around his head.

"Balderdash." The doctor dabbled his fingers in the wash basin, shook the drops off. "Why haven't you cut that man's coat off him?"

"I ain't gonna," said the dark man. "Nosuh, not me. He won't like that one little bit. He's a mort proud of that coat. Yessuh. A mort proud."

"You know him, then?"

"Yessuh. Me an him, we met along the trail, at a hog ranch." He shrugged. "He be needing a hand, so I come along."

It could be true. Dan reached for is poke, a deer hide pouch that everyone carried their gold dust in. Holding it on his palm for Byam to take, he thought the two men could have met just as the dark man described, but something in his manner of telling rang a little off key, like a wrong note in a piece of music.

"Looks like you're stuck here, then," said Carrots. "Mind yourself, though." He jerked his head toward Dan. "They lynch people here."

The drumbeat in Dan's head quickened. The room's air was thick, as if woven from too many smells of men, their breath and blood, and long johns unchanged since November.

"I'm waiting," Carrots said. "Well? I say hanging Aleck Carter was murder. What do you say to that?" His face was mottled with pink splotches, and spittle gathered at a corner of his mouth.

The dark man gaped at Dan, and panted as if he'd been running. Byam's hand, outstretched to take the poke, checked in midair. On the cot, the muleskinner took a deep, shuddering breath.

The hell with this, Dan said to himself. If Carrots was here then, what had he done to stop the murders? Or had he looked the other way when good men were robbed of their hard-earned gold? He stood up, and the red-haired man recoiled in sudden alarm.

"A man stood on the scaffold with a noose around his neck and accused Carter of murder, but he had already fled to Hell Gate. No one makes a false accusation at the point of death, when he's about to meet his Maker, and innocent men don't run before or after they're accused."

The high color faded from the red-haired man's face, leaving the stubble on his cheeks vivid against the bleached skin. "That other fella must have lied," he insisted.

Dan ground on past him. His own temper was up. He had done what had to be done to safeguard the honest people of Alder Gulch, and he would not have this man, perhaps a rough himself, second-guess him. He could do that well enough himself. "Besides that, we found evidence that implicated them all in the murders and robberies terrorizing the region." Even in New York he could have won the case on the evidence they had, circumstantial as it was. "I have no doubt. None of us has any doubt they were guilty as sin."

"'We' 'Us'?" Carrots thrust out his chin. "You mean you were one of them? That's right, ain't it? You're one of them damned stranglers."

"Where the hell do you fit in?" Dan took a step toward Carrots, who backed away, fetching up against the table where the injured man lay.

He groaned. His eyes opened, and he licked his lips and muttered, "Where am I?"

Doctor Byam said, "Dammit, we have an injured man here. Dan, put that poke away. You can catch me up with the dust later. But you, Red. If all you can do is goad one of our leading citizens, you can get out. Now."

Dan put the poke back in his pocket. Picking up the rifle, he slipped his right arm through the sling. Staring hard at Carrots, he adjusted his hat around the bandage.

After the stink of that room, the air outside cleared his mind and soothed his face as though he pressed a cool, damp cloth to his eyes. Pausing, he adjusted the rifle's sling strap on his shoulder, let the weapon settle into its place, felt his shoulder muscles respond to the weight. Back in New York, he'd never thought that when he had the opportunity to buy one of Christopher Spencer's new inventions to use as a hunting rifle he would live in a place where it was advisable to carry it everywhere. But that was before Father's – death (his mind recoiling as usual from the word suicide) – before the world he'd grown up in had spun out of his knowing. He felt the rifle's weight as a responsibility on his shoulder, and looked for Slade and his men along the street.

Judging by the noise coming from a saloon farther along and the horses waiting outside, they had taken their hijinks indoors. John Lott, helping to gather up the muleskinner's scattered goods, straightened, and Dan walked over to tell him that the injured man would recover. "My brother and I will hold everything until we can sort out who ordered what. We'll collect the dust for it until he can tend to his own affairs." The merchant eyed the blood stains, the edge of the bandage around his head visible below his hat brim. He said nothing about them. No doubt he'd heard all about it from Charley. "I'll render an accounting whenever he's ready for it."

"Good," Dan said. There was nothing more to be done in Nevada City. The Nevada men would handle any more trouble, and Slade must know he would be a great fool to try them too far. They had pursued Alex Carter and the others, caught them all. Hanged them all.

Crossing Main Street toward the ice-bound creek, Dan took a shortcut between two saloons toward the livery where his rented horse was stabled. As he negotiated knee-high mounds of rubble from the diggings in the creek bed, he smelled frozen waste beginning to thaw. All along, he cursed Slade: Damn you, Slade, damn you, we cleaned up Alder Gulch, we drove the ruffians out, we hanged the murderers in the winter, God knows I tied a noose or two myself. Now that people are settling into peace and believing themselves safe to go about their lives, you ride rough-shod over them? Over us?

Damn you, Slade, bringing this on us. Damn you to hell.

Even as he swore, though, another part of him, like a small boy, wanted to cry. Slade, after all, the sober Slade, intolerant of wrongdoers, an enemy of thieves, was halfway to being a friend, and he did not know how to punish the drunken Slade without hurt-ing the sober man.

There had to be a way, though, there had to be.

3.

The mule, ears flattened, struggled to kick, though hobbles bound its hind legs, and heavy rawhide rope secured its head against a snubbing post. For good measure a very short man held a twitch around its long, soft, upper lip. A second man stood to the side holding the mule's tail straight out, while James Williams, the livery's owner, probed for the ball in the mule's haunch.

Dan stayed outside the corral fence. He was no hand with an angry, frightened mule weighing above half a ton, and he knew it.

"Got it." Williams held up a lead ball at the end of a bloody forceps. "This old boy will be good as new in a week or two." He tossed the forceps toward Dan, who reached up and caught it, an instant later regretting the blood on his leather glove. "Now the hard part." Williams took a bottle of whiskey from his coat pocket. The little man tightened the twitch. Dan's scalp crawled in sympathy with the mule. Williams pulled the cork with his teeth, stepped an arm's length away toward the fence. "Now." The third man let go of the tail and leaped for the fence. Williams poured whiskey into the wound and jumped back.

The mule exploded.

The little man unwound the twitch and scrambled up and over the fence faster than Dan had thought any human being could move. Williams caught the top fence rail, and vaulted over.

Braying its pain and anger to the world, the mule jerked against the snubbing post, made from a medium-sized tree trunk and set deep into the ground. The post shook, the rope halter dropped free. Bucking and braying, it bolted around the corral.

If a man had been close enough, it would have killed him, Dan thought, watching the animal's rage. Mule, you and I both have reason to damn Slade today.

Even as they watched, the mule tired. It stood, legs splayed, and its braying slowed, quieted, and stopped altogether until it stood trembling, sides heaving and nostrils flared to take in more air. "Good," said Williams. "I figured he wouldn't last long at that rate. These critters haven't been fed enough to have much fight in them. It's a long, hard trip up from Great Salt Lake this time of year."

Dan said, "I wonder they made it."

"Or even tried." The little man watched between the top rail and the next lower one. He spat into the snow. "Son of a bitch had to know he'd kill an animal or two trying the passes this early." John Xavier Beidler, who went by his middle initial, X, was the shortest man Dan had ever known, and one of the toughest. From inside the barn, another mule brayed. "Shut up, Bess," Beidler shouted. He rode a tall black saddle mule, Black Bess, that he stabled at Williams's livery, and Dan sometimes wondered how he managed to scramble up into the saddle. "You don't quit that noise, I'll come in there and beat you bloody." He muttered, "She thinks I'll come in and give her some sugar." Fumbling in a pocket, he brought out a twisted paper, put it back. "Maybe later."

They regarded the grey mule in silence. Its sides slowed their bellows action and its head drooped.

"What do you think, X?" Williams asked the little man.

"Might's well." Beidler climbed through the rails, as Williams went over the top, and walked toward the wounded mule, whose head came up, teeth bared, and ears flat. Stopping close enough to the mule to distract the creature, yet far enough that he could jump for the fence and have a chance of escaping, Beidler stretched out his arms. A side gate led into another corral where they had penned the other mules. Lifting the wire loop on the gate, Williams walked it wide, inward to the corral where the gray mule waited, and climbed over the fence. Beidler backed slowly toward the fence, as if he went no place at all, certainly nowhere to bother a mule, felt behind himself for the rails, and climbed through. In the other corral, one mule sniffed the air, picked up a tentative forefoot and put it down a few inches ahead of the other, and so led the other mules, long ears pricked, eyes watchful but not alarmed, into the corral, where they gathered around the gray mule.

A pump stood outside the corral where a rail passed over a water trough. Williams lay one hand on the pump handle and called to his hired hand: "Toss hay in there for them, and fill the trough when I'm done." He hung his hat on the head of the pump, and picked up a bar of rough sage-green soap. Dan took the handle, and pumped enough times to wonder if Williams needed to dig another well. Then water gushed out, splashing both him and Williams.

"Damn shame what we have do to animals to make them healthy again," Williams said over the pump's screech and thump like a mule's bray.

"Yeah," Beidler said. "You think you'll get their board out of Slade?"

"I won't hold my breath." Williams bent, splashed water on his face. "Brrr." He tried to smooth his hair, but when he put his hat on, it sat on the hair rather than on his head and the hair stuck out like a wet shoe brush. "Your turn," he told Dan, meaning that he would pump if Dan wished.

Dan shook his head, and the bass drum, which he had forgotten, was back, beating harder than ever. "He made Don Byam accept Beni's ears as legal tender."

Beidler flinched as if someone had tried to punch him, and the ends of his thick brown mustache drooped. "Damn. Don't he know better?"

"What did he do?" asked Williams. Dan knew he meant Byam.

"He agreed they were legal tender. Anyone would, facing six armed men. Slade, especially. For a minute, I thought he'd shoot Byam's kneecap like they say he shot Beni's." He cocked an eyebrow at X, signaling a question: Were the stories true?

"He never did that. It ain't true. He'd never do a thing like that." Beidler wiped a hand across his face. "At least not when he was sober, he wouldn't." Perhaps hearing the obvious reply in their silence, that Slade was drunk now, and drunk when he killed Beni, he added, "Even then. Look, he was on a spree in Denver, and accidentally shot one of his pals. He stayed around the hospital until he was satisfied the man would get well. Paid all the expenses, too."

Beidler's breathing rasped up from his throat. He scuffed the toe of his boot into the ground. He added, "Slade's a good man. I swear he is."

"Then why couldn't he put the drinking aside for something more important?" Dan thrust his chin out. "Why did he sometimes side with the roughs?" Neither man had an answer.

"Let's go in," Williams said. "I bet you could use something to warm your innards before you start out."

Dan said, "I could at that." Even though Virginia City lay only a mile and a half upstream, he felt the need of something to warm his gullet against the damp chill of March.

At the big barn door, he inhaled the good smells of horses and hay, listened to the sounds of munching, an occasional thump as a horse planted a hoof. In the failing afternoon light, most of the barn lay dark, but he saw that only three horses, his own mount and two others, occupied stalls for transient horses along one wall. Not surprising at this time of year, when snow lay deep in the passes. A buckboard and a green freight wagon were parked along the other wall. In back, despite it being late winter, a pile of hay reached into the shadows.

Williams led the way into his office, a walled-off space barely large enough to swing a cat, that contained a desk, a chair for himself, and two visitor chairs. A two-shelf cabinet hung on one wall. It held brown bottles of liniment, two books, and an assortment of small tools and brushes. He laid the forceps on one shelf, atop a curry comb and a stiff brush. On the opposite wall, a window looked out onto the yard, where he could see custom arriving and leaving, though Dan doubted Williams, a man constantly on the move, would not be content to sit here and wait.

A round black stove stood in a corner, and Williams poked up the fire. A coffee pot sat on the edge of the stove top, and he picked it up and shook it, lifted the lid and sniffed. "The coffee's all boiled down." Seating himself, he gestured toward the chairs. "Have seat." Reaching into a bottom desk drawer, he took out a bottle of whiskey and poured each of them a generous shot in cloudy glasses. Dan leaned the Spencer against the wall beside him and sat down. Williams cocked his glass toward his guests. "Here's looking at you."

"How," Dan sipped the whiskey gingerly, feeling his taste buds shrink from it. Valley Tan was a mix of straight alcohol, tobacco, and water made by Mormons in Salt Lake It just goes to show, he said to himself, in the Gulch men are desperate enough to drink the noxious stuff. Himself included, when necessary, because his own supply of good whiskey was running low.

"How." Beidler eyed him over the top of his glass.

"I've never seen Slade this bad." He swirled the liquid around, watched it climb the sides of the glass and recede. "When he showed Beni's ears to Byam, at first he didn't agree they were legal tender, and then Slade – it was like he changed into someone else." He saw again the malicious stranger peering from Slade's eyes. "Someone evil." A chill draft fingered the back of his neck. "After we carried the muleskinner over to his office, Byam said Slade reminded him of Anton Holter being shot at because he hadn't any money."

After a few seconds' silence, Beidler said, "Holter swore he'd be dead if the charge had been properly loaded. As it was, the ball parted his hair." Crossing himself, a small blur of his thumb across his middle coat button, he added, "God forbid."

The three men sat in silence, each of them, Dan thought, imagining Slade killing someone while he was on a bender. How could they prevent that? Dipping a finger in his whiskey, he rubbed it over the mule's blood on his glove. The drum in his head banged on. "We need a jail."

"No argument there," said Williams.

Beidler snorted. "If we had one, them pals of his would try to stop us from throwing him in it."

"They'd try." Satisfied that the blood was gone from his glove, Dan laid it on his knee to dry.

A silence hung in the air while they considered that. During the winter, when they had broken the power of the criminal element, no innocent bystanders had been killed or injured. Thinking of Red's certainty about Aleck Carter, Dan winced. He hoped no new evidence would turn up to exonerate any of them.

"If he would just control his damn drinking." Williams offered the bottle again, cocking its open mouth toward them, and when both Dan and Beidler shook their heads he corked it and thrust it into the drawer, resting his foot on the edge. "He can, you know, when he's a mind to."

"Oh?" Dan wanted to hear more.

"After we settled that business of the wagon trains, he accepted that I was in charge of the outfit, and I never had a man I got along with better."

Dan had heard this and that about the clash between Williams and Slade, when Williams earned his title, "Captain." Now was his chance to hear Williams tell it. "What happened?"

"He was with a wagon train heading up here, and I was with another one, and we met down around Fort Hall someplace. There were rumors of trouble along the way, and Slade was supposed to be the captain, but he got drunk, and when we met, I don't know who they were more afraid of – armed robbers, Indians, or Slade. We talked it over and decided to join the two trains together for the journey north. Safety in numbers, you know." He swirled what was left of his drink around in the glass and set it on a pile of papers without drinking it. "Folks decided to elect a captain, only Slade said he was the captain and there didn't need to be an election. He was drinking, and generally being a son of a bitch – like he can be – and seeing's I was the other nominee for captain, he got belligerent. I wasn't having any, and after a few more threats, he said we'd decide it later. Then he lay down and went to sleep." Holding the top of the glass, he rolled the bottom edge around the desk top, watching it carefully so as not to spill any of the liquid.

"While Slade was asleep, they elected me, and when he woke up, I told him I was the Captain and he could either work with me or find another train."

Williams looked out the window at the low gray sky. "Like I said, I never had a man I got along with better. We ran that combined train together, and he stayed sober and tended to his duty. He's a good man...." His voice trailed off.

Beidler finished the sentence for him: "When sober."

Dan's head ached, and the whiskey tasted not much better than his own vomit, and he was fed up with Slade and his drunken sprees putting people in danger as if other people had no right to go about their business in peace and safety. He said, "And a brute when drunk."

Once more, the silence came, and this time Dan let it grow, his irritation strong inside him. X studied his boot, where a couple of stitches holding the sole to the upper looked to have pulled loose. "Have you seen him with his wife?" He laid that booted foot across the other knee and picked at the heavy thread, until the thread came loose, to two or three stitches. "When he's with Mrs. Slade, you couldn't ask for a better husband." Taking out a pocket knife, he worked at forcing an end back into the hole. "She's a fine cook, too. I visited them before they built their stone house, and she scared up a delicious meal over a campfire. I doubt I'd get better in New York." He slid his eyes toward Dan, who tucked in a corner of his mouth, acknowledging the joke about his home town. "They seemed like two halves of a whole." Taking both ends of the broken thread, X worked at tying the short pieces off, his stubby fingers deft and delicate. "Of course, I wouldn't know about marriage. I ain't never been in one."

Since setting up housekeeping with Martha McDowell a couple of weeks ago, Dan was learning about marriage, how he was joined with a real person in her own right, who demanded his consideration as a fellow creature sharing his house, his bed.

Williams said, "Good thing Slade keeps his drinking away from her." When Dan raised an eyebrow at him, he explained himself. "She's not in danger from him. He'd never do anything to hurt her." He smiled. "He wouldn't dare. She can shoot as well as any man. Even Slade."

Unlike Martha, whose first husband, Sam McDowell, had been prone to use his fists. If that son of a bitch comes back, he'd better watch out for me, Dan promised himself.

"I don't understand it at all." Beidler worked at making the two short ends into a knot. "When he's sober he's a gentleman. Soft-spoken, good manners. He has a good mind, too, and he's had a decent education. We –" he coughed, cleared his throat "– talk together on all sorts of subjects. But when he's drunk he turns into somebody else. It's like there's two men living in his skin, a gentleman and what you said, a brute, and the brute comes out with the drink."

Dan pinched the bridge of his nose. "So we have only to convince the brute to go home and sober up. Then we convince the gentleman to stay sober."

"That'll hold till I find a cobbler." Beidler tied the knot. "That's it. His friends will talk him into going home." He looked up as Dan rose to his feet. "Easy as pie, I don't think."

"Yeah. I better get back. What do I owe you for the nag's keep?"

"She wasn't here long enough to eat much hay. A pinch of dust."

Dan took out his poke, a small leather pouch, and reached in with a thumb and forefinger. He captured some gold dust and dropped it in a glass Williams held out to him, brushing his two digits lightly together to drop in the tiny bits. Finished, he pulled the drawstring tight and put it back in his inner coat pocket.

"We have to convince him." Williams lighted a lantern to guide Dan's way to the stall. "Some of the boys are getting a little tired of him riding in and 'taking the town,' like he says." He leaned on a post while Dan saddled and bridled the horse, a gentle mare and sure-footed on the rutted track that passed for a road in Alder Gulch.

He knew who Williams meant by "the boys." Mostly living in Nevada City, they regarded Williams as the "Captain," and called him "Cap." But he was tired of Slade as a topic of conversation. Why not talk about the weather? Or how long the gold would last? His head hurt, and he was happy to be leaving Nevada City.

"I hope their patience lasts until we can convince him to stop drinking."

"I hope so, too, but Fitch for one thinks we've been too easy on Slade. He told me we should have dealt with him during the winter along with the road agents."

"Damn it, Fitch is not in charge. The Executive Committee is. We are." Dan pulled the cinch tight, wrapped the end around the metal ring that held it to the saddle. He tested it with two fingers against the horse's sternum, and let down the stirrup.

"I know." Williams walked beside Dan as he led the horse to the big door. "You know Fitch, though. Always has to give you his opinion whether you want it or not."

Dan glanced into the office. Beidler sat bent forward, head in his cupped hands, maybe studying his boot, maybe thinking of his good friend Slade. As Williams hauled the door open, he slid the rifle into its saddle slings and led the horse outside. She pricked up her ears and sniffed the air, whickered softly, the sound deep in her throat that always reminded Dan of a human laugh. As he put his left foot into the stirrup, She danced a bit from sheer eagerness to be home, so that he had to hop after her a couple of times before he swung aboard. The rifle under his right leg comforted him.

"Yeah," he said. "I know Fitch." Raising a hand to Williams, he nudged the mare into a light rain flecked with fat white globs of snow.

4.

Riding away from the creek, past cabins left deserted for winter, Dan came to the main road and reined the mare to the right, around humps of mining rubble buried in snow. She knew her way home, and walked as quickly as the pitted road allowed. He gave himself up to her rhythm, moving with the saddle as if in a boat. Heading upstream toward Virginia City, horse and rider passed windows where mellow lamplight already glowed, though it lacked two hours of sunset. Somewhere a violin screeched out a polka, and a nearby piano competed with a shrill waltz. The instrument's felt hammers needed ruffling, he noted, though that would not help the cracked sound board. From Charley's saloon a deep roar of laughter followed him out of town until the heavy air dampened it. He listened to the saddle creak, the horse's hooves, the unaccustomed quiet. In summer, a man could barely hear himself think over the mind-numbing din – sledge hammers breaking rock, blasting powder exploding, men yelling, the occasional gunshot. Now, a hundred feet to his right, Alder Creek ran under thick ice. Silence ruled.

Except for Slade. Dan ground his teeth.

As he rode closer to Upper Town, as miners sometimes called Virginia City, the mare pulled at her bit, wanting to hurry home to her corral and her evening hay. She splashed into Daylight Creek, and stumbled, all four hooves scrabbling to catch her balance as Dan heard men whooping and hooves pounding

31

behind him. Pistol balls slapped into the water. Ears flat, the horse found purchase in the stony creek bed and leaped for the opposite bank, scrambled for her footing. She lurched, and her head went down so that Dan saw the track as if from the top of a cliff. He gathered the reins, felt contact with the bit, the animal's head came up, and they staggered into a fast, ground-eating trot.

Dan glanced behind to see Slade and his pals riding merrily, drinking as they came. At the corner where the main road turned left and became Wallace Street, the Leviathan Hall hid Slade and his pals from Dan's view, he slowed the mare for fear of causing an accident, although, he reflected, he might as well not bother, as deserted as the street was. On both sides saloons and business establishments waited for spring and the miners' return. In one shop a lonely merchant played patience on a nearly empty display case, while some of the tables in Fancy Annie's Saloon, next door to the store where he rented space for an office, were empty. Instead of crowds rushing about, intent on digging the gold out of the creek bed or miners' pockets, a few men strolled along the boardwalks. Up ahead, where Jackson Street crossed Wallace, a woman came out of the Eatery and paused on the edge of the board-walk to pull her hood over her head and collect the skirts of her dress and cloak in one hand. The other hand clutched a wrapped package. The hood turned his way, but in the thickening dusk, with the wet snow falling, he was just another rider. She stepped into the quagmire of a street, and started across, head down, intent on her footing, one hand holding her skirts out of the snow, the other keeping the package safe.

Martha, going home from her reading lesson.

The commotion Slade brought grew louder. Dan glanced back. Instead of stopping at one of the saloons on the main road, Slade and his bunch rode up Wallace. Dan urged the mare into a faster trot.

Martha stopped, looked toward him bearing down on her, and her gaze went beyond him, and her mouth opened in a silent O. She froze.

The riders behind him hollered and fired their pistols. He dragged at the reins to stop the horse beside Martha. Scraping the rifle out of its slings, he threw his leg over the saddle horn and slid down to land by her, and grab her to him. Shoot! And he would, he'd blast their damned heads off, the bastards, he could do it if they endangered Martha, might anyway for scaring her. His finger felt for the trigger. Slade and his pals galloped by them, shooting into the air, yipping and hollering, their horses' hooves pounding, breath rasping, clods of snow and frozen mud bombarding him and Martha.

"Damn you, Slade, if you hurt my wife, I'll kill you," he yelled, just as another pedestrian shouted: "Slade, there's a woman."

Wrenching his horse about, Slade saw Martha beside Dan. He held up his hand, roared, "Stop."

Slade and his men surrounded them atop their blowing horses. From out of the stores and saloons men came to see what was the commotion. The man who had warned Slade about Martha's presence stood beside Dan as if taking a position on a battlefield. His beard was stained with yellow-brown tobacco juice, and he wore the right sleeve of his butternut-colored officer's coat pinned up neatly below his right elbow.

Dismounting, Slade dropped the reins to the ground and took off his hat. Fat wet snowflakes settled on his hair. He bowed to Martha, flourishing the hat. "I beg your pardon, ma'am. We would not for the world have dis– dis– discommoded a lady." Shamefaced, he stood before her, a little wobbly, waiting for her to accept his apology. "We only thought to have some fun with your husband."

"Your idea of fun," said Martha, "don't translate well." Dan felt her trembling as she held the crook of his elbow, but her voice was steady. "I suggest you return home and become a sober man, rather than frightening people so."

"She's right, Slade." The bearded man in the Confederate officer's greatcoat smelled of chewing tobacco, acrid and sweet at once, and a sharp, wild odor Dan could not identify. "We've had about enough of your shenanigans around here. Go on home to your wife, and stop frightening ladies out of their wits."

Slade straightened his back. The sheepish look vanished. "Begging the lady's pardon, no one gives orders to Slade of the Overland." His tone darkened, and Dan heard the malevolent stranger lurking behind the bland mask that was Slade's face.

He felt Martha's arm stiffen, and a corner of her package dug into his biceps. He must get her away, but how? They were surrounded by the ring of Slade's friends, who glowered down at them from their horses' backs. Damn them all! She should not have to endure this. (Memory flashed a picture: Mother at her embroidery hoop, complaining of her skirt being torn as she attempted to board an omnibus. From behind his newspaper, Father had said, Then call a hansom cab, my dear.)

The bearded man in the Confederate coat glared at Slade. The crowd of men grew. They came out of the saloons, drawn by their eagerness for some excitement to relieve winter's long boredom. In the upstairs windows at Fancy Annie's, curtains moved. He imagined the whores or their clients interrupting themselves for the greater thrill: perhaps Slade would kill someone.

Damn them, damn them all.

The drum beat faster in his temple. He must get Martha clear before Slade shot someone. He took a small step aside, poked the rifle barrel into the mare's side in front of the cinch. The horse moved over, and Martha moved with her, the horse side-stepping, clearing a space with its bulk, and they edged farther from the blossoming quarrel.

"You think you're still running the stage line?" The Confederate took a half step toward Slade, his chin out, his beard jutting forward. "You got no authority here. I wouldn't have you manage a skunk farm." Turning his head a degree or two toward Slade's pals, he added, "Though maybe you are." And spat.

"Yeah? You being the great Major Fitch in Price's Army? That run from Pea Ridge?" Slade's head tucked down, and he peered at Fitch from under the brim of his hat, the pistol in his hand coming up almost of its own will.

"What the hell do you know about war?" Shouting at Slade, Fitch's deep South accent thickened.

"I served in the Mexican War, and my discharge paper proves it. That's more'n you —"

Fitch raised his short arm. "You son of a bitch, I left this at Pea Ridge. This is my discharge."

Slade's pistol pointed at Fitch's head. Between one breath and the next, everything seemed to stop. Only the steady snow plopped down on their shoulders.

Dan imagined blood staining the snow. No. Not again, he said to himself, God forbid.

"Gentlemen." He spoke as if he and Martha were taking their leave of a formal occasion, perhaps a grand ball at the Fifth Avenue Hotel. His quiet tone of voice startled them, turned their heads his way.

"Gentlemen, would you excuse us? Mrs. Stark would appreciate a cup of tea in front of her own fire."

Slade's gun hand, the pistol as yet uncocked, sank to his side. "Oh, drat. Fitch, let's stop this. We'll apologize to the lady and then go take a drink and be friends. What do you say?"

From his expression, Dan did not suppose that Fitch wanted to be friends with Slade, or drink with him, but there was no good way to avoid the invitation, not from Slade, who might drink with a man and shoot him before the shot glass was empty. They made their apologies, and Dan mounted. He reached a hand down to Martha while Fitch laid his right hand over his short left arm to take her foot and boost her up behind him. Once she was settled, he urged the mare away from there, and felt in the animal's eager walk that she wanted to be gone as much as they did.

Something hard dug into his back. "What is that you're carrying?"

Martha said, "The Bible. I was going home from my reading lesson."

His house stood on Jackson Street, uphill from Wallace. When they reached it, Dan lifted his right leg over the saddle horn and slid down, then reached up for Martha. He held her close for a moment, felt her trembling like a sparrow in his hands. "Little Brown Sparrow," he whispered. After a moment, they stood apart.

"I have to tend to the horse," he said.

"You go, and I'll start some tea," she said. "You were right. I could appreciate a drink of tea." Her laugh rang with an underlying sob. "I made sure we'd catch us a bullet. You saved us."

You saved us. He should have been pleased, but for some reason her words rang hollow against the hammering in his ears. Not until he had helped the

stable boy feed and water the horse and had nearly finished brushing her did he understand that he had been
at least partly to blame for putting Martha in such danger, and how different the outcome could have been if
just one ball had gone wrong. He saw again the blood
spouting red from the mule's rump, and his boots
could find no purchase on the barn floor sliding away
under them so that he thumped down on his knees, his
hands out to catch himself from falling. Beside him,
the horse tucked up one hind hoof in a threat to kick,
but he could not rise. After a few seconds, the hoof
came down. The horse lowered her head to the pile of
hay on the floor of the stall. Dan stayed on his knees a
moment more. Slade had not seen Martha, had only
thought to hoorah Dan himself, and he had brought her
into danger when he rode faster to reach her before
Slade did.

He rose to his feet and leaned on the horse, who
lifted her head and looked at him, hay stalks dangling
from her mouth.

God, he thought, if anything had happened to
Martha – how could he live with himself?

5.

Martha McDowell watched Dan'l ride up Jackson and turn right on Idaho, downhill toward the livery. Shivering, she turned to walk up the path to the front door. At the sight of a glow in the two front windows, she paused to get ahold of herself. Dotty must be to home, for a lamp to be lit, and she'd taken the dog inside. Martha could hear him barking. Clutching the Bible, she picked her way along, between the high ridges of snow edging the path. In the dusk, the day's snow melt was setting up to ice over another layer of ice. Feeling shaky, and not anchored solid to the ground, she inched along, sliding one booted foot after the other, not daring to pick them up and take a rightful step.

Joe Slade. Drinking again so soon, harder and more, and him given to killing like he was. And them pals of his, drunk likewise and grinning, waiting to back him up. Dear Lord, what if Dan'l hadn't been there? Or even Tobias Fitch, much as she hated being beholden to him, being a pal of Sam McDowell like he was.

Her foot slipped, and the snowy banks tilted before she caught herself and stood still, trying to banish the thought of McDowell, but once there, he would not go away. Him and his big, fast fist. What would she have done without Dan'l after he left? He'd been a drinker like Slade – no, not just like Slade, on account McDowell drank steady, being more drunk sometimes than other times, but almost never himself, or not the man she thought she'd married. She blamed the war, but truth to tell, he'd always had a rough side and too much fondness for moonshine. She just hadn't figured on what the drink would do to her and the young'uns.

A few feet from the front door she stopped, caught by the lamplight in the windows. This house was better'n any she'd ever thought to live in. Dan'l had bought it for her and the young'uns to be with him, instead of the windowless one-room cabin they'd had with McDowell. She ought to love the house, and wanted to, but couldn't. It was too full of guilt.

They couldn't be a real family, while McDowell was alive, or she could divorce him.

Until then, she and Dan'l were living in sin, and wasn't that a fine thing for the young'uns to know? They'd given their consent, but still it was wrong, much as they all loved Dan'l.

Inside, the dog barked. Timmy told it to hush up, and as her fingers grasped the latch string to draw up the latch, the door opened a crack. She looked up into one of her son's eyes, all she could see of him, before she stepped aside for him to swing the door wide open. "Mam?" He stretched to hold the door and let her come in. As she went by him, she thought how tall he was coming to be. When he got his growth, he might be as big a man as his Pap. He peered out behind her. "Where's Dan'l?" He spoke in a child's voice, so surprising in a boy near five-foot-eight that other boys teased him about it, asking when he would stop talking like a girl. As a consequence, he didn't talk much, being self-conscious as only a boy rising sixteen could be, and blushed to hear his own soprano.

"He's taking the horse to the barn." At the big table in front of the stove, Dotty looked up from the homework she'd been scratching on a slate. Chalk dust puffed up in the lamplight, and when she raised her head, there was chalk on her nose. "You're working mighty hard to make that much dust," said Martha, and answered Timmy's question. "He rode to Nevada City today on a case."

"Oh?" His eyelids crinkled at the corners. "Too bad he didn't ride on a horse." He giggled.

The high-pitched sound teased Martha's face into a smile that burst into a laugh so hard it dropped her onto a bench beside the door, and then it wasn't laughter no more. She bent over the Bible, sobbing into her hands.

"Mam, Mam, don't cry, what's wrong?" The young'uns talked to her, patted her back. Canary, the yellow hound, stood at her knees muzzling her hands and whining.

When she could get control of herself, she blotted her eyes on her sleeve and smiled at them. Her young'uns. What would she ever do without – but life without them was unthinkable. She dammed fresh tears behind her smile, and fumbled in her skirt pocket for a handkerchief to blow her nose.

"Mam." All wide-eyed, her mouth a round O, Dotty asked, "Mam, what's wrong? What's happened?" She sat down beside Martha.

Laying the Bible on her lap, Martha put her arm around the child's shoulders. "Dan'l and I had ourselves a run-in with Mr. Slade."

"Are you-all right?" Dotty gripped her forearm, her shoulder, and laid the back of her hand against her cheek, like she had to make sure her Mam was really in one piece.

Martha drew in a breath, scolded herself, shame on you, throwing a conniption in front of the young'uns that way.

"That —" Timmy swallowed the rest of what he might have said, but his face said it for him. His eyebrows drew together over his nose, and he tucked his chin like he wanted to fight someone. "He's at it again? Already?"

"Yes, he's at it again," said Martha. "Dan'l rescued us. And Major Fitch helped some, too." It pained her some to give any credit to Fitch, not liking him as much as she did. He'd been in cahoots with McDowell, paying his way to prospect for gold in return for a share in the claims if he found some. Grubstaking the miners called it.

The dog barked, startling her so that the Bible nearly slid off her lap. She caught it just as Dan'l walked in and closed the door, pulling the latch string after him.

Now that the sun had set, shadows that lurked all winter in the corners of the room crept out to the edge of the lamplight. "Why are you sitting in the dark?" Dan'l asked. Martha thought how, if he'd been a Southern man instead of New York bred, he would have said, you-all.

"Happens it's where I landed," she told him, and to Dotty, "We could use another lamp lit." The child lighted the lamp standing on a round table between her and Dan'l's chairs. As soon as its glow chased the shadows back, Martha felt better to see the sitting corner she'd made, all cozy for them to sit in, evenings after supper. He'd read to them while she took up some mending. Tonight, maybe he'd read more to her from *Kenilworth*, one of the books he'd brought out from New York.

McDowell didn't hold with reading. Pussy stuff, he'd called it. She was learning to read her Bible, and she knew what he'd say to that: What's a woman want with reading? All you're good for is to pleasure a man when I want you. Then he'd grab a part of her and squeeze. Hard.

What if he came back? Would he kill Dan'l? He was like Slade, uncontrollable on account of the drink, and if McDowell come back and killed Dan'l she didn't know what she'd do, and if he never came back she'd be an adulteress until she could divorce him. The preachers said so, and the Bible said so. She knew the Commandments. The Lord didn't like adultery. Not one bit.

Dan'l took the rifle off his shoulder and laid it across the top row of pegs on the other side of the door, above the shotgun and the revolver, and the derringer. He moved slow and careful, like the run-in with Slade had taken something out of him. Unbuttoning his coat, he cocked his head to look at her, really look at her, like McDowell never did to her remembrance, even in the beginning. "You all right?"

"Mam says that Slade's up to his tricks again." Timmy moved aside for Dan'l to hang up his coat.

"He is that." He eased the hat off his head.

Seeing the stained bandage, the blood-caked hair, Martha jumped up. "What happened to you?" Blood had soaked into his muffler, and she had no doubt his coat and shirt also had blood on them. "Let me look at that." She fairly dragged Dan'l to the washbasin. As she went, she gave orders to the young'uns about supper and fetching her medicinal things, her dried herbs, and tinctures and infusions. She told Dan'l to strip off his shirt, and take his long underwear down to the waist. When he bent over the washbasin, she washed his head, and Dotty held a candle while she found the cut – a nasty thing it was, too – and snipped away the hair around it. And more, him needing a haircut so. The young'uns trotted here and there, doing the needful about their supper and bringing in more water from the pump out back. In amongst it all, Dan'l held quiet with nary a peep out of him though she knew it had to hurt. She grumbled mightily about doctors and their ignorant ways until she had everything cleaned up and the wound sealed under a tincture of woundwort and dogsbane.

When he told them what had happened in Nevada City, Martha thoughts twisted like a rope around her throat: the glass sliver might've cut a big vein, or Slade might've shot Dan'l. How far had the splinter gone into the skull? She banished him to the bedroom to change his clothes – "Everything, mind, I'll have to put everything to soak."

Timmy planted himself in Dan'l's way. "What do you-all mean to do about Slade?"

He meant the men, Dan'l being one, that had cleaned out the gang of murderers and robbers that had plagued the roads since gold was discovered. Folks was safe now to go about their business.

Except for Slade.

Timmy put his fists on his hips. "Well?" Martha held her breath. That was the kind of challenge that had earned him his Pap's fist more often than not.

"We'll have to persuade him to go home and get sober, then persuade him not to take drink again."

"How're you going to do that?"

"I don't know at this point."

The two of them held each other's gaze, until Timmy said, "You could haul him before the Tribunal."

"No," Martha gasped. Whimpering, Dotty sidled close, and Martha put her arm around the child's quivering shoulders. She was as scared as Martha, not knowing how Dan'l might take being talked back to.

Dan'l smiled at them. "Your mother is right. We don't want to try him in the Tribunal. Slade has done nothing to bring him to their attention."

"Them others, y'all hanged them." Martha knew the boy meant the twenty-odd men who were part of the gang

"They either committed murder or armed robbery, or they were guilty of conspiracy to commit murder and armed robbery." His voice was level, talking to Timmy like he was a man deserving of respect, not a boy to be fobbed off with half-truths or told to run away and not bother him. He looked toward her. "Slade has committed no capital offence."

"What does that mean?"

"He hasn't done anything to hang him for. He hasn't killed anyone."

"So he's got to kill someone before you can hang him?"

"That's the law. We can't punish people for something they might do."

For a second or two Timmy stared at Dan'l, then broke away to look at her. Martha read a new understanding in his young features, as if something Dan'l had said meant more than he thought. "That's like Pap, ain't it, Mam?" her son said. "He's a great one for whaling on me 'cause I'd be doing something bad sometime."

"Ain't there nothing you can do?" Martha asked, and when Dotty nudged her and whispered, "isn't," she corrected herself. "Isn't there nothing you can do?"

"Send him to the People's Court, if it comes to that. He respects Judge Davis. The Judge will fine him, but it's doubtful he'll be able to pay. He's about drunk up that small fortune he made bringing down the freight from the Milk River in December. What we can do to stop him from drinking, I don't know, but we'll do what we can." Standing there, his shorter hair damp and clinging to his head, and his torso bared,

Dan'l took his lower lip between his teeth and looked at the floor, a habit he had when he was thinking hard. He'd even forgot he was half naked, though goose-bumps prickled his skin.

What a fine figure of a man he was, Martha thought.

In the silence someone's stomach growled, surprising them into laughter while Timmy's face flamed. Martha said, "It appears like we ought to eat our supper."

Dan'l went into the bedroom to change his clothes while Dotty set the table and Martha tidied up her healing things. She was tucking them into the cupboard when a sudden thought made her pause. Poor Mrs. Slade. How did she manage with Slade's drunken habits?

6.

Hearing a man bellow from the toll gate, Maria Virginia Slade gathered her skirts and trotted toward it, little Jemmy running ahead with the dog. As she rounded the corner of the house, she heard another man's voice, lighter and mean: "What's a little Injin kid doing here anyway? This is a white man's house." In the yard, the dog stood between the boy and two men. She couldn't hear growling, though its upper lip raised to show one long tooth and the fur stood up on its backbone. Its tail curled tight over its back. Jemmy had met men like these before. He stood head down, his toe digging at the ground, fists jammed into the pockets of his overalls. "Answer me," said the man. Jemmy mumbled, "I live here with my mama and papa."

"Where's your papa at?"

"He ain't home." Jemmy backed a step as if the dog pushed him.

"That so?" The man showed his teeth in a wide grin.

Maria thought she'd never seen a man's smile so much like a wolf's. As she walked up beside the boy and put her hand on his shoulder, Maria felt the pistol's weight in her coat pocket and was glad of it. "It's all right, Jemmy. These men just want to pay their toll and go on their way."

The second man nudged his partner, who looked at her with admiration in his small, close-set eyes. He looked from her to the boy, then back to her, and she read the speculation in his face as plain as a book. He thought she was no better than she should be, and maybe worse, a white woman with an Indian man, to get the half-breed child. "How much for the toll?" Neither man raised his eyes above her chest. The man who had teased Jemmy licked his lips. She touched her coat where the loaded pistol in her pocket dragged it down. Through the wool, the hardness of the steel reassured her.

"Two dollars." She kept her face and voice businesslike, almost unfriendly, knowing the generous shape of her body betrayed her to men, even under the man's overcoat she wore on top of the sweater she had knitted from thick wool. She had no illusions about what men wanted from her and how only Joe's reputation protected her from them. If they insulted her, he would come after them, and men knew it. God help them if they did more than offer an insult. No one wanted to be on Joe Slade's bad side. No one wanted his ears in Joe's waistcoat pocket.

Waiting for them to find the money to pay the toll, she hollered silently into the distance, Come home, Joe. Come home. Why aren't you here? For God's sake, hurry home. I need you here. Jemmy needs you here.

Roughnecks like these were like strange dogs. If they smelled fear, they'd be at her, but if she faced them down, they'd go on their way. She thrust her right hand into the coat pocket and felt the butt of the pistol, the revolving chamber, and took courage from the rough carved wood and smooth steel. Just let them try something.

Small Eyes pulled out a notecase and offered her $5.00 in greenbacks. "No," she said. "We don't deal in paper." She was not about to take paper and give change in gold. She was no fool.

He frowned, but returned the paper to the note-case and put it in an inner pocket without a mutter. The one who had not licked his lips handed her a greasy leather poke. "Take it out of there, Ma'am, if you please." He spoke as if she were a lady, but his eyes did not lift to her face.

"I'll weigh it out," she said, pivoting to go into the house.

"I'll come along if you don't mind." Small Eyes took a step, and the dog growled a warning.

Maria spoke to the dog. "Hey! It's all right." The dog turned its head toward her, its upper lip relaxing over its teeth. "Stay with Jemmy."

In the house, a scale stood on a small table, the correct weight ready on one pan, their own poke – a deerskin pouch – beside it. She walked around the table and stood across from him. In here, she could smell him, the acrid smell of old sweat mixed with new, and something else she could not at first name. His odor weighed on her, bringing out a dampness on her palms. She wiped her hands on a towel, thought, Steady, girl. The pistol, handy in her pocket, steadied her as she poured gold dust onto the empty scale pan until the pans leveled.

All the time, he watched her through narrowed eyes, as if counting each flake. When she had finished, she drew his partner's poke closed and gave it to him. When they were gone, she would pour the gold dust into Joe's poke.

"Thank you, Ma'am," he said to her chest. His tongue licked one corner of his mouth and then the other. Lifting his gaze to her face, he leered at her, as if to say he knew what she was, and he was the man to give her something to remember him by.

"Your husband around?" he asked.

"He'll be back directly." Small Eyes stood between her and the door. From the pocket where the
pistol rested, she took out the toll gate padlock key.
Carrying the two together had been Joe's idea: That
way you won't have to pretend when you tell someone
you're going for the key. Damn it, Joe, come home.
She said, "Perhaps you saw him in Virginia City? His
name is Joseph Slade. Some people call him Joe
Slade."

His manner changed. His back lost its pride, and
his shoulders sagged. "He's your husband? Joe
Slade?" He stepped aside for her to pass by him.
"You're Mrs. Slade?"

"Yes. Yes I am."

As she unlocked the chain around the gate, she
rejoiced inwardly. She had scared this – this son of a
bitch just by mentioning Joe's name. Served him
damn well right. The thought of his hands on her made
her want to puke, him and his filthy thoughts smearing
across her day. Behind her, the two men talked, their
voices too low for her to catch what they said.

"Your husband, Ma'am?" asked the smaller man.
"You said Joe Slade?"

"Yes. Joseph Slade. He's in town on business."

They exchanged a look, and Maria read into it
something different, not only the fear his name usually
brought, but a kind of shared secret amusement besides. "Oh, yeah, we seen him."

Small Eyes said, "He's having a good time, him
and his pals. Didn't rightly see much business about
it, unless you count riding his horse into saloons and
shooting out the lamps." Giving her a final leer, he
climbed up on the wagon seat. His partner flapped the
reins on the mules' backs.

She closed the gate so quick it nearly bumped
their tailgate as they drove away. Muttering under her

breath, she locked the padlock and looked around to see where Jemmy might be. He heard strong language enough from Joe and other men. He didn't need to be hearing it from her. Seeing him standing on the step into the house, she made herself smile at him, though she wanted to scream at the wind. Watching the two men lumber away in their wagon, she curled her hand around the pistol's grip. They didn't look back, not even once, but she cursed them in silence until they drove into a mist rising at the crest of the hill and disappeared from sight.

When they were gone, she stood still, unable to stop cursing. She swore at Joe for being absent on another spree, and at his friends in town, those who thought it great fun to drink with him and encourage him, and she cursed those who could not make him control his drinking or – better yet – stop altogether. When her repertoire of cuss words ran out, she started over while the mist thickened into snow.

Turning to go into the house, she peered down the Virginia City road to where it curved around the mountain between their stone house and the town. The snowy wind beat on the wide brim of one of Joe's old hats that came down low on her forehead.

She shouted, "Damn. Damn. Damn. Come home, damn you, Joe Slade."

A small hand tugged at her elbow. Jemmy said, "I'm hungry."

Something in her face, her look, made him shy away like a horse, in one jump out of her reach, one arm raised over his face to protect himself, the other outstretched to ward her off.

She covered her eyes in her hands, but his image stayed on her eyelids, and her curses turned on herself. Had she and Joe not caused him enough suffering? How could she scare him so, and him only a child?

She uncovered her eyes. His wet hair clumped on his neck, and his shoulders rounded.

"Of course you're hungry. We've been working all day. You've worked hard, and you protected me from those men." She walked toward the house, made her voice happy and light and calm, as if she spoke to a frightened colt. "Let's go in and get warm. You're a good boy."

"Really?" He gave her one shining look. At her nod, his back straightened and he scampered ahead of her toward the back of the house. Pretending to watch her footing, she dawdled a mite to let him get well ahead of her and go in first if he had a mind. Instead, he lifted the latch and pushed open the door, waiting in the snow for her to go in first.

Inside, they took off their dirty boots and hung their wet coats on the pegs, his down low so he could reach it himself.

As she poured the dust from the scale pan into their poke, a thought occurred to her. "Tell you what," she said. "Peach pie is Joe's favorite. What say we make one for him, and have it warm for his dinner?" If she made it, surely he'd come home. Surely this time would be different, not like the other times. He'd come home, and stop drinking, and life would be good for them.

She held out her hand, and Jemmy put his small, grubby paw on her palm. "You go get dry, and I'll make us some lunch. We can start on the pie right after we eat." Brushing a wet lock of hair out of his eyes, she added, "We won't have to go out again till it's time to feed the horses and the cow."

They hurried through lunch, and she let him beat the egg and showed him how to measure the flour and water for the crust. She'd thought her crusts were too thick, but Joe had told her: I like a crust you can bite on 'cause it holds the juice. The pie in the oven, to make the time go faster, she pulled out the board Joe had made. It was smooth, highly waxed and polished to make it easy to wipe off the marks of different games.

"I know a game," said Jemmy. He liked to make up games, and invent the rules – sometimes change them – as the game went along. While they played, the snow lashed the house, beat against the stone walls, and Maria worried that Joe would ride home through the storm and be soaked to the skin.

When she took the pie out of the oven, Joe was still not home.

When they had fed the horses, and dashed through the snow into the house, Joe had not come home. His voice did not boom out, "Smells like something good in here."

"I'm hungry," Jemmy said. "Can't we eat? Joe ain't coming home tonight, is he?"

She turned a bright face toward the boy, a face she did not believe fooled him, because it certainly did not fool her when she caught sight of it in the wall mirror. "Wash your hands and help me set the table. If he's not back then, we'll eat, and he can have his supper when he comes home."

Fear whined at a corner of her mind all through dinner, wanting to be let in. She held the door against it, because if she let it in, it would change to a raging wolf and shred her peace. It wasn't fair to hold the pie for Joe, so she let the boy eat a piece. She gave him a cup half coffee and half canned milk as a great treat. After they had washed up, they sat by the fire through the evening. She taught him songs, changing the words to some to make them suitable for young ears.

When he yawned, she said, "Let's sleep in here tonight on the bearskin." She could not sleep alone in her and Joe's bed. Bringing pillows and quilts, she made up their beds before the fire, and tucked the quilts snugly around him because she lay closer to the fire and might block some of its heat. There would not be much sleep for her, she knew; she would wake from time to time and keep the fire up, in case Joe came home in the night.

"Please," she whispered to the fire. "Make his friends bring him home soon."

Sometime later a snarl of fear awakened her. Joe had worn his buckskin suit, his Denver suit, she called it because he had always worn it when he went to Denver on business, during the days when he was Slade of the Overland. She would later hear reports of damage done, and once he had shot one of the friends who had been with him. Each time he came home, he would be sorry, and promise to mend his ways, but he would not or could not stop drinking.

Drink that undid him every time. No matter how she begged him to stop, he would not. Perhaps if she threatened again to leave him, he would stop this time.

No, she had tried that once, and it had not worked. It only made him angry, in a stony, cold way that frightened her: What if she lost him?

She would never leave him, she knew, never. Love was worth the wait.

VIRGINIA CITY,

MARCH 9, 1864

7.

She was in luck, Martha told herself. Coming down to Wallace Street had meant gathering up her courage in her hands like holding her skirts so as not to drag in the snow, but Slade and them had been somewheres else. She had found the cabbages at Morris Brothers Grocers and the potatoes at BAM, the grocers in Kiskadden's Stone Block, and now she would go home with fixings for a good venison stew. Three cabbages not too dry and shrunk. Ten pounds of potatoes not too wrinkled or soft, with enough goodness left to be useful. She would core out the eyes – some of them already sprouting – and cut up the rest into chunks. The sprouts she'd save, let them grow more and plant them outside when the ground warmed up.

Maybe Dan'l would dig up a plot for a garden. Thinking how she'd start it, Martha said, "Good morning" to the grocer and stepped over the mudsill onto the boardwalk.

And stopped.

Somewhere, a man sang in a thick, raspy voice. It had to be a comic song, though she could not catch the words on account of the distance, and on account other men laughed loud enough to rattle the window sashes if they'd been closer.

Slade. Blessed be, where was he?

She wanted to duck back into BAM, one of the three stores, where the thick stone walls would shield her from flying balls. If she went in there, though, she couldn't see Slade's whereabouts, and that she had to know before she crossed Wallace.

Drat the man, that his shenanigans kept her from going where she would. This was like the ruffians in the winter. Just like them.

The air lay heavy and chilled against her face, and the lowering clouds had the colors of pewter, pale and shiny, dark and dull, but all gray. The street, as she walked up to the corner, lay like a river between her and home, a river of muddy snow, garbage, and horse droppings, fed by melting snow crusted with ice from the night's cold. To go home, she had to cross it, seeming wide as the Jordan, or the Styx, that old river between life and death.

At the corner of Jackson and Wallace, she hesitated outside Lydia Hudson's Eatery to peer around, listen for where the song and the laughter came from. Would she have time to cross the street, and head for home before the shooting started? No horsemen in sight, but there hadn't been last night either when she started across. Last night, she thought, with a flip-flop in her chest. Get ahold of yourself, she muttered. Slade or no Slade, she had a family to feed, and a floor to scrub, and a new batch of sage tea to start. Setting her jaw against the reluctance of her feet to carry her into the street, she took a firmer grip on the handle of the string bag and lifted one foot to step over the snow bank.

Boots thundered toward her over the boardwalk. She swung around, nearly losing her balance, to confront whoever it might be. None but Timmy, running hard up the slope, shouting as loud as he could in his little boy's voice, "Mam! Mam!" She had no time to be relieved it was him, when he seized her arm on the run, nearly spilling a cabbage. "Mam, you got to get under cover." He rushed her toward the Eatery's front door as Slade and his cronies rounded the corner at Van Buren Street and loped down Wallace. They reined to a stop in front of Mayor Pfouts's store, called Pfouts and Russell, though no one had seen Mr. Russell yet.

Slade sang, for all the world like he was serenading Mr. Pfouts.

Someone had pulled in the latchstring on the Eatery door. Timmy pounded the side of his fist on it. When he paused to listen for someone to let them in, Martha heard the words to the song plain as anything.

"Oh, Paris Pfouts had a pecker this long," Slade sang, holding an index finger and thumb about an inch apart. "He went to Madam Moll, and it grew a little more." The distance between forefinger and thumb widened a bit, and he whooped and rocked in the saddle.

Martha gasped and covered her ears, but she could not keep out the obscenity.

Slade roared out the next verse: "Moll Featherlegs said, 'Put it here if you can.'" He pumped his middle finger in and out of the other fist, and doubled over the saddle horn, laughing, his face in the horse's mane.

Hooting and hollering, his men fired off their pistols, rode in circles around him.

Albert, the free Negro who worked for Lydia Hudson, opened the door just enough for her and Timmy to slip in, closed it after them, and dropped the bar. Martha sank onto a bench at the front table and set the string bag on it.

She could not catch her breath, and her heart like to jump out of her chest.

"My dear," Lydia called from the back of the Eatery's one room. "I'm coming."

The only light came from a few candles placed to shine directly on their work, at the front, on the small table where Albert weighed folks' gold dust, and in the back kitchen area. There a candle showed a side of beef that Albert's wife, Tabby, chopped into ribs. Her black face and forearms were part of the darkness, the cleaver seemed held by no human hand, but came down on its own, a streak of light breaking through the spine in a steady hush-chunk. Like no other sound in the world, it raised goose bumps, as if Martha heard the soft rip of a pistol ball tearing through human flesh and bone.

Holding a candle to see her way up the right-hand aisle, made wider to accommodate hoop skirts, Lydia Hudson bustled toward them, one hand shielding the flame from her haste. Its upward shine gave her face a ghoulishness so far from her Quaker soul that Martha almost smiled. Lanterns stood dark on shelves along the walls, but kerosene being so dear, and supplies dwindling until the passes cleared, Lydia would not light them until the first customers arrived for dinner.

She squeezed Martha's hand. "Come on back and wait till that scoundrel moves on."

Albert's deep voice rumbled, "I be watching out, Miz Stark. I tell you when's safe." His pale shirt gleamed in the daylight from a hole in the log wall. It seemed he'd begun to make a window, just a hole wide enough for him to see what happened outside. A shotgun kept company with a saw leaning against the wall.

"I'll stay here and watch with Albert, Mam." Timmy wanted to see out the hole, too, Martha knew. About to say something motherly and unnecessary, like Be careful now, or Keep your face away from there, she felt a catch at her heart. Her boy had gained some on Albert in height; his head struck just at the darky's chin. Whatever she'd been fixing to say she'd keep to herself.

Between blows with the cleaver, Tabby nodded to her. Martha smiled. "How d'you do, Miz Rose?" she said, same as she would to a white woman. Not many months since, she'd thought of Tabby first as a nigger, then a darky. In her slave life, Tabby had been a field hand, and a child of hers was sold away before she met Albert. She'd brought with her a hatred of white people, but since they'd fought the plague of typhus together, Martha and Tabby and Lydia, Tabby would smile at her now and then. And now Martha almost never saw or thought of Tabby's color at all.

The Eatery held only two long tables with benches tucked under them. Martha pulled the back bench out at one end and seated herself. Lydia sat close to her, and her friend's nearness comforted Martha.

Albert said, "Oh, Lord. That Mistah Slade, he's shootin' and drinkin'."

Lydia grasped Martha's hand and said, "I think we'll have work at the Recovery soon."

Martha said, "I fear so. Before we're done, I do fear so." The Recovery was a small bachelor cabin where men without someone to look after them recovered from illness – like the typhus – or accidents, and Lydia and Martha, among other women in the camp, helped the doctors by tending to them.

Albert said, "They's men walking up towards him. Vigilantes, I'm thinking. Yes, so 'tis."

"Who?" The question burst out. Martha prayed, Please, Lord, not Dan'l, not Dan'l, let it be someone else, not Dan'l. Lydia's hand gripped hers, and she fastened onto it, tethered herself to it, knowing Timmy's answer even before he spoke, his voice a squeak.

"Dan'l. Dan'l, Mam, Dan'l, he's one of them in front, and that Slade's drawing a bead right on him."

8.

Slade threw back his head and laughed loud to the sky, as if, Dan thought, inviting the heavens to share his joke. One of his followers spoke to him and he reined the horse around without breaking up the song, "Oh," drawing out the Oh until he nearly ran out of air, then filled his lungs, and began another verse that he could not sing for laughing except the long drawn-out Oh. He cocked his pistol and the wavering barrel crossed Dan's chest, wandered back to point at him, the muzzle a round, surprised O: O here we are, O look at death. Slade laughed. Dan's foot slipped, knocked his steps out of rhythm with his heart. The Spencer's stock thumped against the back of his right thigh, reminding him that he carried it, and could bring it around fast enough for men to doubt the outcome between him and Slade. And wasn't that a hell of a thing to know about himself, Slade being such an extraordinarily talented gunman even when more than three sheets to the wind?

Beidler, walking on one side of him, carried his usual shotgun. Fitch, on the other side, carried a hand gun in his right-hand pocket that dragged on his coat. Dan, who was not on terms with the Almighty these days, prayed they would not have to remind anyone that they out-gunned Slade, whose aim vacillated among them.

Slade's enlarged image throbbed on his retinas. Dan's gut cramped; his sphincter muscles tightened.

The pistol's round muzzle wobbled side to side, up and down. It spat a small flame, followed by a circle of smoke like a blown smoke ring: O. O here comes death.

The pistol made a sound like a large housecat sneezing.

Misfire.

The cramp relaxed. He would not disgrace himself after all, but in place of the damp and chilly fear of shame his stomach burned, and sour bile leaped into his throat. He coughed.

Slade's pals laughed, a dog barked, and somewhere a horse whinnied.

Slade fumbled in his waistcoat pocket. Did he search for pistol balls between Jules Beni's ears? Before Slade could find either, the men had closed on him. Dan reached up and took hold of the barrel, warm through his leather glove. His fingers were steady, despite the flickering heat in his neck. "For God's sake, Slade, you could've killed one of us." Slade pulled the weapon from his grasp, shoved it in the waistband of his trousers, and sat weaving in the saddle, eyes sparking with fun, ready to fight.

Dan jammed his hands into his coat pockets to keep from hauling him off the horse and beating the shit out of him. Slade was tough and strong, but damn it, Dan thought, so am I, and I'm taller by half a head. An inner voice warned, Touch Slade and his men will kill you.

"Damn it, Slade," said Fitch. "Go home and sober up before you do kill someone."

"Aw, you know me, fellas." Slade tilted the bottle to his mouth, lifted it away, and peered down the neck. "Shit. Empty." He flung it over his shoulder, careless of anyone behind him. "I was just joking."

A joke? Dan's scalp cut throbbed, and the thin sleet creeping between his hat and his coat collar did not cool the heat rising from his body. Aim a pistol at men and pull the trigger. If it misfires or the aim is off, make it a joke. But if it had not misfired? If the aim had been true?

What then? Would it still have been a joke if one of us had been wounded? Or killed?

No. Slade would be conscience-stricken, like the time in Denver. The hell with that, Dan said to himself. Remorse would move Slade to tears, and be forgotten with the next drink.

X said, "Why don't you just ride on out of here and sober up? Old Copperbottom could sure use the rest, and I bet you could, too."

Slade's eyes slitted like an angry cat's. "You telling me what to do?"

"Nope, not for a minute. Just thinking of Old Copperbottom." X rubbed the blaze between the horse's eyes. "You both look like you need a rest. Why don't you take him home?"

His face clearing, Slade thought about it. "Yeah, maybe you're right." He squinted up at the clouds. "My dear wife will be wondering where I am about now." His face softened, and he rubbed his belly. "I'm feeling a bit peckish, myself." He lifted the reins, and the horse headed down Wallace. "So long, fellas." Bellowed another verse of his song: "Oh, Jeremiah Fox had a pecker this long." Stumbled over his own laughter: "Madam Moll said – "

At a window, a curtain stirred, perhaps one of Moll Featherlegs' girls, or Moll herself, watching.

"Shut up," Fitch roared. His voice had moved battalions under cannon fire. A breeze parted the skirts of his old uniform coat, once gray but faded to the color of a ripe butternut squash.

Over his shoulder, Slade raised his third finger. His friends, tailing him, looked back and laughed, cuffed each other's shoulders as he led them around the corner of Jackson Street, uphill toward the road out of town.

"They're enjoying this," said Dan. "It's like Slade is pulling the teeth of a live grizzly bear."

X said, "At least he's on his way home."

"This time," Fitch said. "You think he won't come back? This ain't the last time by any means. One of these days we'll have to give him what he deserves, or he'll kill somebody." He rubbed the stump of his arm.

"No," said X. "He'll come around. He knows who we are. He's just being a little stubborn."

Fitch snorted and shifted the chaw of tobacco to his other cheek, spat through a gap between his lower teeth. "If he don't know who we are, I am willing to teach him the same way we taught them others."

"No." Dan gripped his hands behind his back to stop himself from lifting up his hat and scratching the cut, that had started an itch along with the throbbing. "We can persuade him to go home. He'll listen to us."

Beidler nodded. "That's right. He'll listen."

"If he doesn't?" Fitch reached his hand into his coat and scratched someplace. "What then? Or what about next time? When do we say enough is enough?"

"He has done nothing except be obnoxious," said Dan.

"Yet," Fitch said. "What if that hadn't been a misfire? If one of us was dead would you do something about him? He's a loaded cannon and it won't take much to set him off."

When he and Beidler were silent, X perhaps scouting among their alternatives for something palatable, in case the worst happened, or to stop it before it happened, Fitch said, "Damn it, we can't let him go on wrecking the town. He's got to be stopped."

"Damn," Beidler said. "It's a hell of a thing, ain't it?"

9.

Throughout, while first Albert and then Timmy took turns watching out the window hole and telling what was happening, Martha held tight to Lydia's hand. She prayed for Dan'l, for none of them to be hurt, for Slade to ride home, to repent of his drunken ways. When the boy said, "God Almighty, he's pointing that pistol at Dan'l," she near to swallowed her heart, it leaped about so. Even him shouting, "Misfire," could not calm it. Not until he announced, "They're riding away up Jackson, they're going home," like he couldn't hardly believe it, did she realize her lips still moved, molding every breath into a prayer. She turned around to look at her son, to ask him if it had truly been a misfire. He came away from the window slit and thumped down at the front table. Silhouetted against the light from candle and window, his shoulders sagged like he'd dropped a heavy burden. "That was too close, Mam."

Lydia said, "Praise the Lord."

Martha could not speak.

"Hallelujah." Tabby held the cleaver high, poised a moment to check her aim, and chopped down through the spine of the animal. Small shards of bone sprayed out as the backbone parted, one section tipping over the edge of the chopping block.

Lydia jumped to catch it and laid it back on the table. Rather than sit down, she took up a large knife and went

65

to carving the ribs into steaks for the evening's dinner. As she worked, she talked. "My dear, last night I was so afraid for thee and Mr. Stark. Albert wanted to go to thy rescue."

It took a second or two for Martha to understand what Lydia was talking about, to haul her thoughts away from the fear, knowing she might have lost Dan'l just then, or he could have been bad hurt. But the Lord had delivered him, like his namesake in the Bible, from the fiery furnace.

When she understood, she said, "No, Albert, you mustn't be putting yourself in harm's way. When he's sober, Mr. Slade does not favor slavery, but no one knows him when he's —"

"Likkered up?" The contempt in Timmy's voice stopped Martha.

Lydia carried on. "It would not be wise to thrust thyself forward, considering how the Confederates outnumber the Union people here."

"The Vigilantes ain't hung no niggers," said Albert.

Tabby gasped. "No. Don't you be saying 'hanging' and 'nigger' together." Her eyes were huge and shocked, and the thought jumped at Martha: Tabby remembered a real lynching, and not them the Vigilantes hanged here. Were her nightmares populated like Dan'l's, with dead men turning on ropes?

Albert strode down the aisle to gather his wife to himself, patted her back, his black hands against the light-colored fabric of her dress shaking with his own frightful recollections.

It was their private moment, Martha thought. Let them be. Rising, she found Lydia had the same idea, and Martha followed her to the front, where she fastened her cloak and gathered up the groceries.

Dear Lord, that some folks would have such visions in their minds their livelong days. As bad as anything the battlefield could turn up, that Sam McDowell made her hear about: that his cannon blasted Union soldiers into red mist, one twelve-pound ball cutting down a file of men. He'd laughed to tell how they took a second to wonder where the missing leg or stomach had got to before they collapsed. He'd weep and rage that the battle smoke was not thick enough, that it blew away too fast so he'd had to see what he'd done. And then he'd look for something to hit.

Was that what Mrs. Slade would have when he got home? The man whose secret rage at himself poured molten onto his family? Or would he spend it on folks in Virginia City, and ride home calm and peaceful until the next time?

"Why are you so quiet, Mam?"

"I can't help feeling sorry for his poor wife," said Martha. "What will he be like at home?" In a dim corner, away from the light, she made out a darker shadow, a woman watching down a long road, her hands gripping each other so hard the nails dug into them, the wind blowing back her long black hair.

"From what I've heard, Mrs. Slade is well able to look after herself." Lydia shook out the ruffles and creases of her black dress. "She rides and shoots as well as any man."

"That don't matter. She has a woman's heart. And liquor does things to a man." Martha pictured Sam McDowell pounding on their cabin door, demanding she let him in though the latch string was out and she hadn't set the bar. In their bed, she had slept as far from him as she could, and she'd learned to sleep almost without moving lest she wake him in the night.

"She'd be better off without him." Timmy's child's voice cracked from his hot anger at Slade. "The Vigilantes oughta hang him."

"No." Martha and Lydia spoke together, and Lydia said something about forgiveness, but Martha, knowing Timmy wouldn't yet hear of forgiving his Pap, let alone any other man that terrorized other folks when he was likkered up, said, "He ain't done nothing to hang him for."

For a long moment they were all silent, listening to the boy breathe like he'd been running. Martha was sure they would hear her heart's hoofbeats plain as anything.

Timmy said, "Then if he'd killed Dan'l just now, or last night when he hoorahed you-all, they could hang him?"

Dan'l – killed? Martha's thoughts stopped.

"Thee must not think of hanging," said Lydia. "It is an evil deed, and one Almighty God cannot condone. Thee must learn to forgive, to love thine enemies, as our Lord did. Forgive and forget."

Before she had finished, Timmy shouted at her: "I'll never forgive Pap, never in a million years, and Slade's another one just like him, abusing folks that never did him any harm. They oughta hang him so he can't hurt no one ever again." With that, he slammed out of the Eatery, his anger resounding in the echo from the banging door.

After a moment, Martha took the handle of her string bag. "I'd best be on home to start tonight's stew." She could think of nothing to say about Timothy's outburst. Truth to tell, she understood how he felt because she felt a little like that, herself, only she knew folks couldn't be hung on account of what they might do, or who'd be safe? As for Lydia's call to forgive and forget, she wouldn't be putting herself in Sam McDowell's way again if she could help it. Forgetting just didn't seem like good sense.

"Thee must be grateful that Mr. Stark is a temperate man," said Lydia. The two friends embraced briefly before she opened the door for Martha to step out.

"Oh, I am," Martha said. "Exceedingly."

She spoke the truth, but it was something she hadn't quite got used to with Dan'l, that he could take a drink or two and leave it, and he was not rough with her, even in bed, where Sam had been roughest. Yet she'd lived with Dan'l only a couple of weeks, she reflected when she had safely crossed Wallace. Up ahead, three men turned the corner on Idaho and were out of sight on the other side of the Melodeon Hall. Dan'l, Beidler, and Fitch? Where were they going? She walked started up Jackson toward Dan'l's house, her thoughts returning to Sam McDowell and Dan'l. In her experience, men seemed to think they had a right to discipline their wives, or take out their frustrations on them, and it wasn't just McDowell. She reckoned the first blow could still come, but if it did, she wouldn't wait for the second one.

10.

They had done it. Slade was going home. Dan's shoulders relaxed until the Spencer's leather sling strap slid down and caught on the point of his shoulder. He, X, and Fitch watched Slade and his pals ride up Jackson, laughing among themselves. Now and then one of them glanced back over his shoulder. Wind gusting from the north blew down the back of his neck, and he thought he smelled a threat of snow. He half turned, his glance crossing Fitch, who stared back, a challenge in his eyes as if to say, Do you think this is over? Because in his own mind Dan did not think they had solved the problem of Slade. It had been too easy, and God knew Slade, even sober, was stubborn. What would they do the next time?

For now, though, he thought to go to his office and review the district rules for water rights, was already considering loopholes and arguments that Judge Davis might not rule against in the suit against Charley Baer.

Staring up Jackson, Beidler said, "Shit."

Dan swung around, the rifle flaring outward so that the strap slid from his shoulder and he grabbed for the weapon to save it from dropping.

Slade's road home began with a right turn onto Idaho Street, then downhill toward Alder Creek, where the road bent again, upstream along the Creek. Eventually it forked, one branch leading toward Slade's stone house, and the other up a mere track to Summit, the highest of the mining camps.

Dan stared, disbelieving, toward the top of the slope. The riders turned left. The wrong way.

Laughing, they rode around the corner of the Melodeon Hall.

"God damn him!" Fitch, perhaps forgetting his short arm no longer had a fist at the end of it, punched the air. They set off after Slade, up the boardwalk. Dan's longer legs carried him to the front, Fitch just behind. Beidler broke into a jog to keep up. On Idaho, they hurried along the Melodeon's wall, past a couple of vacant lots where snow mounded over the sagebrush, to the new street, Van Buren, that paralleled Jackson to cross Wallace downhill from Idaho.

Down the slope, about halfway to Wallace, in front of Dorris's Dry Goods, Slade's boisterous pals milled about, now and then firing a shot in the air, swigging from bottles, laughing and hooting while the horses stepped about, ears laid back, tails lashing.

Slade rode through the low front doorway, lying along his horse's neck, the saddle horn gouging into his stomach.

Dan cursed the rough ground that slowed him down, even where buildings had laid boardwalks in front, this being so new a street that most of the lots were empty. Glass shattered, wood splintered, hooves crashed on planks, half a ton of horse and rider among elegant glass and oak display cabinets.

A man shouted, "No, no, you sons of curs! Get the hell out of here." Sick with déjà vu, remembering yesterday in Lower Town, Dan swore at his sluggish pace.

At last he shoved his way through the crowd, Fitch's swearing in his ear, his foul breath in his nostrils. He took off his hat, swatted it at a horse's nose. The animal shied away, and he heard X's voice: "Make way. Make way. Let us through."

Inside the store, Slade's voice shouted, "You think I won't, then? I'll kill you, you try and stop me. No one orders Slade of the Overland." Wood broke, iron clanged as in a peal of untuned bells, and hooves thundered on the floor. A shot stopped Dan almost under the hooves of a horse trying to back away. He dodged, avoided another rider, took hold of the rifle's stock and forged toward the door only to leap aside as Slade backed his horse out of the store.

Slade turned the animal, and loped downhill, his cheering troop after him. After they rounded the corner on Wallace to ride past John Creighton's store, their noise faded uphill, toward open country. Dan did not think they had seen the back of Slade for long, but that was not his concern now.

They would see about Dorris.

The store owner, normally a hearty man of blunt humor that resonated a bit off in Dan's ears, sagged against the wall. He stared at the devastation, his eyes dark and huge in his blanched face.

"My God, he said he'd kill me. My God." He repeated, "He said he'd kill me." He gasped for air. "He almost did. He pointed that Navy Colt at my head, and then he fired it, at the window. He said he'd kill me. Sweet —, he almost killed me." Dorris's breath came in quick pants, like that of a dog tied too long in the hot sun. He fingered the side of his head.

Turning him gently toward the broken window, a chill wind blowing in, Dan saw a scorched streak through the hair above his ear.

Dan took hold of his upper arm. "He won't kill you. You're all right, do you hear me? You're all right. It's over. Slade won't kill you."

"He like to killed me. He like to killed me."

Fitch slapped his face.

Gasping, Dorris recoiled, stumbled against Dan, who held him on his feet. "What the hell do you think you're doing?" If Dan had not been holding Dorris, he would have slugged Fitch, something he contemplated with satisfaction at almost any time.

"He's shocked. That's how you bring them out of it."

Dorris took a deep breath, struggled against Dan, who let him go. Surveying the wreckage, Dan wondered what could be salvaged. Amid broken display cases, now mere shards of glass and slivered wood, bolts of fabrics lay tangled with spurs and miners' picks. Dan smelled the metallic odor of canned beans; bent and broken cans of peas and milk dripped into torn sacks of flour, through cracks between floor planks. What to save first? He started to pull cans from the flour, thinking to save that first: people would need it, because no one knew when the passes would clear for the freighters.

"How do I start over?" Dorris's voice had the distant ring of a man questioning God. "It's all gone. Everything. I put everything I had into this store. I've nothing now. There's nothing left."

"We'll help you clean up."

Someone offered to fetch brooms, shovels, more buckets. Another man said he had a couple spare lamps. A third said he had an extra display case, if some would help him bring it. Men's voices, a bustle of labor, filled the room. "Don't worry," one told Dorris. "We'll have you back in business by sundown."

"Slade, he'll make it good." The speaker, who was laying pieces of glass in one heap, paused. "He always pays up, you'll see."

Dorris laughed, a high, shrill sound that raised the hairs on the back of Dan's neck. "He paid already."

"There, you see?" With a satisfied air, as if to say, What did I tell you? the man who had vouched for Slade looked around at the others.

"He paid with Beni's ears." Dorris could hardly speak for giggling. "He pulled them out and showed them to me, and said they was legal tender, and when I said they was just bits of gristle, he took out his pistol and put it in my face, and said, 'They're legal tender, ain't they?' And he half-cocked it, and so of course I had to say yes, or get my head blown off. Then he said, 'There. Paid in full.' Then he fired that Navy Colt of his anyway." He touched the tender side of his head.

"He laughed. The son of a bitch laughed." He glared around at the other men. Another man humiliated, Dan said to himself; he thought of Don Byam yesterday. "Damn it, you'd agree too, if you was looking down a pistol barrel."

"Any man would," agreed Dan. "He did the same thing down in Nevada yesterday. He paid Doctor Byam with Beni's ears." He'd laughed then, too. Boys will be boys. All in fun.

Like George Ives. Dan turned up his coat collar. Ives had laughed, too. He had ridden into saloons and stores and shot them up. He had laughed to see the destruction he'd wrought, the ruin of other men's dreams.

Glancing around, Dan met Beidler's eyes and Fitch's, and exchanged a grim nod with them both. Did they think of Ives, too? Bending to the work of saving the flour, he could not shake the idea of Ives. How much did

Slade differ from Ives? He had not demanded loans at gunpoint as Ives had done, but he made people accept Beni's ears as legal tender for the damage he did. At gunpoint. Ives had threatened to murder men if they had no money next time he asked for a "loan." Was Slade another Ives? Surely not. Not to the point of murder, for Slade – sober – was the kindest of men. Ives had taken his mad pleasures in cold sobriety.

But a drunken man was as capable of murder as a sober man.

"We have to talk," said Beidler's voice above him.

Dan straightened. Beidler and Fitch stood together, an unholy alliance if Dan had ever seen one, each as adamant for his cause as a man could be. Fitch, the Border Ruffian and officer in Price's Army. X, who admired John Brown. Under different circumstances they would kill each other over slavery and not much regret it.

Checking on progress, he saw that the others were making quick work of cleaning up. A stack of unbroken cans grew in a corner, piles of broken wood and glass collected near the back window. Other merchants brought more buckets, brooms, shovels, hammers and nails.

As the three men left the store, they met Jim Kiskadden, who owned Kiskadden's Stone Block, coming in with two of his tenants. They all carried buckets, scrub brushes, and brooms. One man said, "Might as well see if they work before I sell them to the miners."

"You watch," said Kiskadden to Dorris, not realizing he echoed an earlier promise. "We'll have you back in business by sundown."

11.

The three men walked down toward Wallace and paused where a new building stood. The boardwalk had been laid, but the window frames had no glass in them. It would wait another month or two before a shipment of window panes came in from Great Salt Lake. When the snow melted from the passes. Dan fastened on that idea as a way to stave off the thought he did not want: Slade resembled Ives. All too well. He did not want Ives's end for Slade.

Corn snow rattled on his hatbrim. The breeze brought Fitch's odor of chewing tobacco and bearskin. The Southerner said, "We can't have this."

"We have got to send him home." Beidler's lower teeth caught the ends of his mustache.

"But how?" asked Fitch. "If he won't go, do we hogtie him and throw him over the back of his horse? We thought he was going awhile ago, but look what happened. He can't be allowed to take the town and ruin men – near kill them any time he feels like it."

Across Wallace on the corner, men worked to put a roof on the new drug store, Rank's Drugs. Dan watched over Beidler's head as a rafter rose on ropes and pulleys. Two men straddled the bearing beam; one raised his hands to guide it into place at his end. Beidler turned to see what Dan was looking at, turned back with understanding in his eyes.

Footsteps sounded behind Dan, and they made room in their circle for Jim Kiskadden. "I'd swear Slade did not fire that pistol deliberately. It went off by accident. I'd swear it. He's not a murderer."

Fitch reared back and laughed out loud, his adam's apple bouncing under the stringy dark hairs on his throat. "This is Joe Slade you're talking about? Who's killed 24 men. Or is it only 20?"

Dan gaped at Kiskadden. "Good God, man, where have you been? Dammit, if his pistol hadn't misfired, he'd have shot one of us right in front of your building."

"He's no killer." Kiskadden's lower jaw pressed outward, his chin jutted out at them. "I don't believe in his reputation. No authority has ever arrested him or charged him with any capital crime." He added, "No woman as fine as Mrs. Slade would marry a deliberate murderer."

No smoke without fire, Dan said to himself. A look passed around the group, a silent acknowledgement of the rumor that said she had met her husband in a bordello.

Fitch snorted. "That's because Ben Holladay protected him. As long as the mail and the passengers came through on time, Holladay didn't ask how Slade kept order."

"No," Beidler said. "It's because he ain't a killer. Not at bottom. He's only killed one man, and that was in a fight back home. He was getting the worst of it and hit him with a rock. It was bad luck the poor fellow died."

Whose bad luck? Dan wanted to ask, but this was no time for levity. "What about Beni's ears? Didn't he kill Beni and slice them off like some damn bullfighter?" He tugged his coat collar snug around his neck, burrowed down inside it, sheltering from the raw breeze.

Kiskadden and Beidler spoke together, but Kiskadden's higher tones carried over Beidler's rumble. "The stories you hear, dammit, are not true." He smacked one fist into the other palm at each word.

"He has the ears." Dan used his courtroom voice, his prosecutor's voice, as if he argued Slade's case in the Tribunal. Beidler's head drew back, and the muscles in Fitch's jaw bulged, as if he accused them of something, but he didn't care. He had to know what Slade was truly capable of. Was he the killer everyone said he was? Or not? "How did he get them?"

Kiskadden answered on one long breath. "Jules Beni was a crook. He managed a division of the Overland, where the town of Julesburg is, but things always went wrong in his district. Hay caught fire, but then there'd be a rancher with extra and Jules would buy it. Horses would be stolen, and the Indians blamed." He drew in a breath like a gasp. "Beni would offer a reward, and don't you know, someone would find them and bring them back." He looked toward Beidler, who nodded. "That's how I've heard it."

From whom? Dan wanted to ask, but held silent, the answer at once coming to mind: Slade.

"Hah," snorted Fitch. "Fine swindle, that was."

The other men nodded.

"Because of all this, the mail went through sort of haphazard, never on time, or it got lost, and the government threatened to cancel the contract." Kiskadden glanced at Beidler for confirmation.

Beidler shrugged. "True as far as I know."

"Finally, management – I mean Ben Holladay – fired Beni and gave the division to Slade. He came in just after some hay burned, and a rancher sold him a replacement stack. Only the whole middle of it was nothing but sage-brush and tumbleweeds."

"What did Slade do?" asked Fitch.

"Went over to the rancher's house with his men and gave the son of a bitch twenty-four hours to relocate be-fore he burned him out. After the rancher packed up his family and sold his stock, Slade burned his homestead." Beidler rubbed his hands together. His knitted gloves had the finger ends cut off.

Kiskadden said, "After that, he managed that division and his own."

"Six hundred miles of road," Beidler said. "Well managed and peaceful. The mail went through on time, and the Overland bosses were happy. Even Ben Hol-laday said, 'Well done.'"

Dan's feet were getting cold in his damp boots. Thinking they were about to stop the story there, he prodded them. "What about Beni's ears?"

A narrowing of Kiskadden's eyes and a slight down-turn at the corners of his mouth seemed to accuse Dan of bad form, a bulldog quality out of place in a gathering of friends. Dan did not care. More was at stake here than Kiskadden's good opinion.

Taking off his hat and turning it around as if inspect-ing it, Beidler said, "Beni didn't love Slade much after that." His voice held a smile that his mustache hid. He put the hat on again, and tugged the brim down securely.

"I'd imagine not," Dan said. "Rather the opposite, I should think."

Fitch said, "Way I heard it, Beni caught Slade with-out his pistol and ambushed him. Shot him six times, then emptied a load of buckshot into him to finish him off, then left him for dead. But Slade didn't die. Eventu-ally, he recovered and Ben Holladay sent him to St.

Louis to get the best treatment. You can imagine what Beni thought when he heard Slade had come back."

"What did Slade do?" Dan imagined Slade hunting Beni down.

"Nothing at first." Beidler chewed on his mustache. "He told people that Beni should stay out of his territory, his division of the Overland, because he would kill him on sight. That worked for a well over a year, but Beni couldn't let it lay. He come back into Slade's territory, and bragged around that Slade had better watch out for him."

"That the way of it so far?" Dan fixed each man with a stare in turn, as though they were witnesses at a trial. Because in his mind Slade's reputation was on trial.

Beidler dipped his head. "So far. Everyone says that Slade didn't go after Beni as long as Beni kept out of his division. But when Beni came into Slade's territory, and bragged around that he'd kill him, Slade couldn't have it. You can see that, can't you?"

"Hell," Fitch said, "even I can see that. Slade had things running smooth and there was Beni threatening business."

"Not to mention those threats came," Kiskadden said, "after what he'd already done to him."

"Here's where things get murky," said Beidler. "But one thing's clear: Slade did not go after Beni. He offered a reward for anyone who brought him in alive. No reward if they brought him in dead."

Dan thought about it. The reward was within Slade's rights, he being the Overland's manager and there being no other law than his own in that 600 miles of Overland road. He might have planned to have Beni taken to the legal authorities in Denver. Somehow, though, Dan doubted it.

"That's all right so far," he said. "We've banished several men with the proviso that they can be shot on sight if they're seen around here again."

He'd expected to hear that Slade had decided to clean up on Beni once and for all, having ample reason. Had he gone after Beni and killed him fair and square, no one would have thought ill of him for doing it, public opinion and the common law of the West being what they were. Jules's popularity had ended when he ambushed the unarmed Slade. No one liked a backshooter.

From the new drug store a man cried out: "Watch it."

Almost as one, the three men swung toward the noise. The rafter slipped from the contraption of ropes and pulleys and crashed down, almost knocking one of the men off the beam. When the noise cleared, he raised his hands, laughing. "It'll take more than a beam and some rope to kill me."

People who had stopped to watch laughed with him. They all knew the joke, especially with him sitting on that beam, but Dan saw nothing funny in it. Nor did Beidler and Fitch, exchanging with him a silent look of shared memory. Again he heard Williams's voice: Men, do your duty. They had obeyed, and Dan would have bet they, too, had added to their nightmares, waking and sleeping, the stench of death. Or perhaps not, being veterans of bloody battlefields where, afterward, piles of human limbs grew higher than a man's head.

The man straddling the beam hitched himself across on his hands and butt toward the tangled ropes draped over it.

Imagining himself in that building, the bodies turning on their ropes, he groped for a way back to the present moment. "What went wrong?" he heard his own voice asking.

"I've heard four versions of this, but what's common in all of them is that friends caught Beni for Slade." Beidler held up four thick fingers and bent down his index finger. "One. They brought him in alive and tied him to a snubbing post – or a fence – in a corral, and Slade shot him in the knees, the elbows, the shoulders —"

"For God's said, stop," Kiskadden said. "That's a horrible story and I don't believe it."

Dan gritted his teeth. He knew the agony Beni would have suffered, the unspeakable pain that froze a man and chilled him worse than any blizzard, sent him shivering uncontrollably, unable to move. He'd known it himself during the winter, in one gunshot to his thigh. Had people stood around and watched Beni being killed by inches?

Fitch spat a stream of tobacco. "The other version's worse. Someone who was there claims Slade would shoot, then go in for a drink, then come out and shoot, then get another drink."

"He was drunk then, too?"

They stared at Dan, the implications dawning on them. Kiskadden shook his head. "No. No. He did not do that. He did not. He would not. We do not have that to fear. Look, the other times he has taken the town, he has not done – he wouldn't. He's a decent man when —" He broke off.

Fitch finished the thought for him. "When sober."

From farther down Wallace, somewhere near the Creek, they heard drunken singing and raucous laughter. Then the sounds faded, as if Slade and his pals rode away.

The man on the beam shook loose the tangled ropes.

"I agree with Jim," said Beidler. "I don't think he'd do that, drunk or sober. I believe, like the other stories

say, Slade's friends brought Beni in dead or he died before Slade saw him, and they cut off an ear to prove
they'd got him. They gave Slade the ear, and Slade said
he might as well have the other one, so he cut that one
off, too."

"After Beni was dead." Kiskadden fixed each man in
turn with his blue-eyed stare, his chin lifted, as if to say
that proved Slade was no monster, that whatever lived in
Slade and came out when drunk was nothing to be con-
cerned about.

Across the street the rafter rose again. The man on the
beam brought one foot up between his hands. Standing
bent over, balanced on his hands and one foot, he put the
other foot on the beam and stood upright, teetering, arms
outstretched for balance. That's us, Dan thought. Balanced on the hanging beam, hoping not to fall.

12.

In the barn loft, Maria pitched down hay for Jemmy to carry to the horses. The rafters were close over her head, and she worked fast as she could, dreading the spiders that might drop down her neck. This time of year, there would be no snakes, but she feared that spiders could last through the winter. Although the roof kept most of the weather off the hay, there were no walls up here because Joe had not had time to build them, so the breeze from the mountain tangled her skirts around her legs. She wished she had trousers like a man. Perhaps she'd cut down an old pair of Joe's to wear for chores. No one could see her up here. She would offend no one's sense of propriety.

Jemmy ran after hay the wind scattered and added it to the piles he made, one for each horse. As horses would, each left his own hay to go after another's, bumping each one who in turn went to horn in on another horse's breakfast.

Jemmy laughed to see them. "Why they do that?" he called up to Maria.

She twisted around to look where he pointed. "Because they're horses. Who knows why horses do anything? No one can figure them out." She aimed the pitchfork at a spot to one side of the ladder. "Watch out, there." When Jemmy had backed a respectful distance away, she dropped the pitchfork, tines down, so it stuck in barn floor.

Holding her skirts out of the way with one hand and the ladder with the other, she climbed down. There had been no tolls yet today, but it was early yet. There was still time, time for someone to be on the road, and time for Joe to come home. She took hold of the pitchfork to pull it out of the ground, but it would not come. She pulled harder, braced her feet wide and seized it with both hands, but still it held fast, stuck deep into the frozen ground under the late winter melt. Moving the handle back and forth, she bent it so far she feared she would break it. Tried again. It stuck.

Jemmy wrapped both small fists on the handle opposite her and leaned against it.

As the boy pushed, she pulled, the two of them working back until the tines slid loose, scraping against stone, so that she stumbled backward and nearly fell. Jemmy let go, though he went to his knees with the suddenness of it and scrambled to his feet, brushing at his pants. His eyes shone with fear, but at what, she did not know. Not her, not this time.

Maria smiled at him. "We did it, thanks to you. I could never have done it by myself." She never could tell why he got so fearful. Had his real parents mistreated him? Joe would never hear of anything like that.

"I bet you're hungry. Let's go have breakfast." She wiped the tines on some hay and hung it in its place. "Would you like some toast? You can help me plan a garden. When the weather warms up, we'll get seed and plant vegetables."

She showed him how to draw out the rows, the principle of planting taller plants like corn to the north so they wouldn't shade the smaller plants like squash and carrots. They were discussing how tall a fence they would need to keep out deer when she remembered. To-night was the Night.

The ballerina, Kate Harper, was coming to town, and the whole town would be there to see her. Joe had prom-ised they would go. He had promised. He would come home in time for them to go to Virginia City. The town – the entire Gulch – had talked of nothing else for weeks. He knew how much she was looking forward to it. He would not disappoint her.

13.

L ooking from Van Buren downhill toward the
creek, Dan watched the clouds shift in the sky
as if jostling each other for space, changing
shape and color according to the angle of the invisible
sun. The late winter light, devoid of shadows, showed
the rough log structures laid out along the street as in a
drawing. He wished he could draw. At one time he'd
thought of becoming an architect, but he lacked something between his eye and a pencil, so he'd taken his love
of geometry and trigonometry to surveying before
Grandfather wore him down to the law.

Now, the buildings along Wallace amused him, accustomed as he was to the substantial brick and stone of
Manhattan. The Eatery, a log cabin no bigger than fifteen feet wide by twenty feet long, huddled next to
Kiskadden's Stone Block, the only two-story building in
town. The lower floor was made of the rubble dug out of
the creek, dumped into a wooden framework, while the
upper floor was of wood. He was not sure of its dimen-
sions, but three stores occupied the lower floor, BAM
and two others. As he stood there, avoiding thoughts of
Slade, wishing snow did not obscure landmarks and an-
gles so that he could be out fixing claim boundaries,
Martha walked out of the Eatery.

Seeing him, she waved and stopped on the corner to
wait. When he drew close enough, he saw her eyes glis-
tening. He had discovered months ago that they had a

luminous quality, and now they shone even more. "You're all right." She laid her palm against his chest as if to feel his heartbeat and be sure.

He covered her hand, felt it trembling against his palm. "Yes, I'm fine. I didn't know you were here."

Holding up the string bag, she said, "I bought fixings for dinner."

He smiled at her. "You'll need time to primp, or have you forgotten tonight is Kate Harper's performance?"

"We're still going?"

"Of course. Slade won't trouble us there." He squeezed her hand. "I'll be home for early dinner, just as we planned."

"Do you think she will be here?" Martha lifted her face to ask the question, and it was all Dan could do not to bend down and kiss it, thereby offending propriety and making Martha out to be something she was not.

A commotion near the foot of Wallace caught their attention. A stagecoach had rounded the corner at a walk, and the driver whoa'd the six jaded horses to a stop in front of the Overland office.

"I think she may have arrived," he said. "We'll have a fine time."

Martha said, "Do you walk down and make sure, and tell us. If she's not to be on the stage, I won't have to primp." She smiled, teasing him. "I'll wait across the street."

"All right." Dan saw her across Wallace before walking down to the stage office.

A gentleman in an overcoat dismounted from the stage and turned to hand a lady out. The crowd gathering around the stage applauded, and she rewarded them with a wave of her hand in its pearl gray glove. Kate Harper had come to town. Dan turned to wave at Martha, standing on the vacant corner, and held his thumb up. She waved back, and he watched her walk up Jackson until another log structure blocked his view.

Thinking he'd have to congratulate the stage driver on bringing her safely through the passes, Dan strode down the boardwalk to Dance and Stuart, the dry goods store that housed the ticket office for the Overland Stage Company.

Slade, riding as if he led a cavalry charge, rounded the corner onto Wallace, and galloped downhill toward the stage. Their horses kicked up winter's debris, spattering the riders, themselves and pedestrians. Dan leaped into a run, the rifle stock thudding against his thigh. He seized the stock, to have it ready if Slade or one of his men should shoot, but Slade veered around the stage to gallop to a wider spot in the road. He wrenched his horse's head around and charged toward his men, who scrambled out of his way as he galloped through them.

Slade skidded to a halt in front of the team, his men following as best they could.

Slade laughed. The stage horses skittered in their harnesses, the coach rocked back and forth as if about to roll away, and the driver grabbed the brake and set it. "Whoa," called the driver, "Whoa. Easy."

The female passenger shrank back. Men shielded her as Nat Stein, the Overland agent, opened the door for her to take shelter in the office. She and her male companion disappeared inside. Men stood in front of the door, their arms crossed, feet braced. Every one of them, like Dan, carried a long arm or a pistol that weighed down their coat pockets.

Stein walked toward Slade, stood in the street confronting him. "You ought know better than that, Slade, dammit. Scaring the passengers to death that way. Now back off. We've got passengers to see to, and the mail and luggage to unload."

Stein was not a big man, being somewhere around five feet six inches, yet he faced up to Slade like many bigger men would never dare to do.

"You know who you're talking to?" Slade didn't quite shout, but his voice carried over the general confusion. "You don't order me around. I'm Slade of the Overland." His face, still bright with fun, darkened into a twilight of wrath, and his brows drew together.

"Maybe you was Slade of the Overland." Stein's voice matched him for strength and carrying power. The noise around them quieted, and men checked their surroundings, looking for a quick way out of the line of fire. "But you ain't no more. You don't run the Overland Stage company here. I do. I'm the agent. You're not the boss of the line in these mountains. I am. Now get out of here. Go home and sober up. I got work to do." With that he turned around, not waiting to see if Slade did as he was told. The men guarding his door stepped aside for him to pass through, and Dan saw Stein's bloodless face and blanched lips, the face of a man expecting to be murdered at any moment, to be shot in the back. The stories people told proved Slade did not bother with the niceties when he wanted to kill someone.

Slade's mouth opened and closed, as if he tried to speak and could not. His face purpled, the veins on his neck swelled, but no sound came out. Finding his voice, he roared, "We'll see who's who around here. I'll have another drink."

And with that, he galloped down Wallace and around the corner of the Leviathan Hall.

14.

As Dan walked into McClurg and Ptorney's General Merchandise, McClurg nodded to him: "Good work today." Replying with a shrug and a shake of his head, Dan went on. McClurg called after him, "At least he didn't try to come in here." Dan opened the rear door of the store, leading into the storeroom, where the partners kept their supplies of merchandise and empty crates and barrels. Here he had blocked out this corner for an office. In New York, Dan would have scorned it as worthy only for brooms and rubber boots, it being not even a room or even a proper closet, having only two proper walls, the outside wall and the wall that separated the store proper from its box room. The other two he'd defined by stacking empty wooden crates labeled Window Panes and Canned Goods and Sundries and Ladies' Boots. He leaned the Spencer against the single-board wall between the storeroom and the main store and rubbed his shoulder to work out a knot in the muscle. Taking the tinder box from his coat pocket, he struck a spark that ignited a bit of muslin, and when he had a small flame, he brought a candle to it. There were only small wooden boxes to sit on; he could not bring himself to order furniture with Father's debt still to pay. With the candle lit, he closed the lid of the tinder box, shutting off air to the little flame. He slid aside the desk top, three planks nailed to crosspieces at top and bottom that had turned out too crooked for a door, as if made by a carpenter either blind or blind drunk.

An odor of salted fish from a tin that had exploded in transit wafted to him as he reached down into the small crate. Holding his breath, he retrieved a whiskey bottle with a string tied around it partway down. He poured a shot into a glass and retied the string at the new level, and replaced the bottle. Shot glass in one hand, candle in the other, he nudged the door over the crate again and sidled behind the makeshift arrangement onto the box that served him as a desk chair. Ramming the candle onto the nail sticking up from the desk top, he took a wad of papers from his inner coat pocket and leaned on his elbows to see them better in the candlelight. The plank top wobbled.

Men's raucous laughter and a few shots came from the street.

Taking a sip of whiskey, he put his hands over his ears, and gave his mind over to saving Charley Baer from losing his claim. As things stood, Charley had only two defenses. One, he did not realize his ex-partner had tried to cheat by using a sluice with a head wider than the rules allowed. That sent more water through and robbed his neighbors upstream of water that rightfully belonged to him. With thousands of men mining four-teen miles of stream bed, water rights were closely guarded.

From next door, at Fancy Annie's saloon, Dan heard men's loud laughter and shouts: "Give us a kiss." "Drinks for my boys." The fast clomp of horses' hooves. A woman's voice shrilled, "Get that beast outa my establishment."

"He's thirsty." Slade laughed. "I'm thirsty, too. Come on, whaddaya got? Beer for me, wine for my pal. Ol' Copperbottom's a good horse. Better'n most people. Hurry it up, there, goddammit."

More laughter from the men.

Covering his ears, Dan tried to think. Two, two — What the hell was two?

"That's more like it. Open it up. Whoa there, boy, drink this. You'll like wine once you get used to it. I need me a drinking pal, these others ain't no good."

Whoops of laughter gusted through the wall on the chill breeze. Dan put his index fingers in his ears. As from farther away, he heard the commotion.

"Hey! Don't back away like that, you good for nothin' cayuse. Hold still, there. Damn it, I said hold it. Drink it, damn you."

Gleeful howls from Slade's men. The horse's hooves pounded the floor like axe blows biting into the trunk of a tree.

A woman shrieked, "Get out of here! Go on, I said. Git!"

A pause in the noise.

Hilarious laughter rose, louder, more raucous than ever.

"Now look what your damn animal did," shouted the woman. "Who's gonna clean that up? Here, you, get the shovel. You, Slade, damn you, take that beast out of here. This ain't no barn. Damn right this scattergun's loaded. Now get out. All of you. And don't come back!"

On their own laughter, the men's heavy boots carried them out of the saloon.

Dan lifted his drink toward the outside wall. Here's to you, Helen Troy. He cocked the jelly jar glass toward her and sipped the scotch. Letting it roll against his soft palate, he tasted its peaty flavor in his throat, felt its warmth slide down his gullet. Now, maybe, he could do some productive thinking about the business at hand. Blaming Charley's former partner had its attractions. Although he couldn't prove it had been the other man's idea, neither could the plaintiffs prove Charley had done it, or even knew the sluice head was larger. Yes, that would be the way to play this hand: Bluff the jury, turn the cards against his client's accusers so they would pay the court costs. Including his fee.

Failing that, he'd break their witnesses. He was good at that. He'd done it before, and the defendant had gone to the gallows.

Yes, indeed. Thinking of how he'd play this defense, Dan finished the two fingers of scotch. He'd walk over to the People's Court and get a court date from Judge Davis, then go to the barber shop and get a haircut. Maybe a bath, too. After all, tonight was a gala night. He owed it to Martha to clean up for it. Having thought of a way to cast considerable doubt on the plaintiff's case against Charley, he felt like celebrating anyway.

Not like Slade, though. Never like Slade.

15.

A voice stopped him. "You got your nose in the air too good to speak to your friends?" Beidler, with Kiskadden, stood in his path.

Dan answered the humorous glint in the little man's eye. "I can't help my nose is up so far. It's along with the rest of my face." Seeing them reminded him of Slade, and he stifled an inward sigh. "I was just thinking."

"Thinking mighty deep, you ask me," Beidler said. "Watch out or you'll think yourself into a hole and fall in."

"Think about coming with us for a drink," said Kiskadden. "We thought we'd have a beer, maybe a game of billiards."

"Take our minds off things," Beidler said.

"Don't mind if I do." A beer would go down well, and maybe he could stop thinking about lost causes. He walked along with them to the Washington Billiards Hall, where a man could get a drink and play billiards for 50 cents.

Beidler pushed open the door. Over his head and Kiskadden's shoulder, Dan saw Slade sitting at a table, drinking and talking with three or four friends. Damn. Too late to remember an appointment and back out, he thought.

Some men at the billiard tables in back were in the midst of a game, and a low murmur of conversation underlay other sounds – billiard balls clacking together, footsteps around the tables, the glug of beer being poured. Rising over the low murmur of men's voices, someone laughed, quickly cut off as if worried that Slade would somehow take offense. Someone spat a stream of tobacco toward a coffee can on the floor, and Dan heard the splat, smelled the acrid odor.

Tension, thick and stifling, lay over the room, portending a storm. Everyone watched Slade out the sides of their eyes; though they talked and laughed and drank and played, they tuned to his note, like violins tuned to a dissonant key.

Noticing the three newcomers, Slade waved them over.

Kicking the leg of the chair a friend sat on, he said. "Bring up more chairs." To another, "Go help him." Obediently, the men arose and drew up more chairs.

At the bar, Dan exchanged pleasantries with the bartender, who watched over his shoulder as Slade held forth to the table and the room at large. "Hope his good mood lasts," said Tomlinson. "I got a good business here, and I ain't of a mind to lose it." Finished drawing the beer, he slid it across to Dan, who said, "I'll pay you for it when we're in the clear." Tomlinson nodded.

The Spencer weighed on Dan's shoulder, unbalancing his trip across the across the sawdust floor as though he carried a ton of gold instead of one beer. Would the time come in this place when he did not have to go armed everywhere? Sitting down, he listened to the others talk about the weather and how they wished for the snow to melt and how a mule train had come in yesterday, and the stagecoach today, so maybe spring was on the way at last. "Unless there's another blizzard," said Beidler. "Fellas who been in this country since '58 tell me anything can happen."

Slade, who had freighted before and after his three years with the Overland, talked about the difficulties of freighting long distances. "It's so damn hard to find water and forage for the beasts," he said. "If you don't know the trail, if it's your first time on a trail, it can be a real son of a bitch. You got to keep the critters healthy enough for working, and sometimes I got to feeling so damn sorry for them when we went long without water or feed. Especially water. Once it was near a week, before we found a watering hole, and it was so foul from other animals that I didn't want to let them near it, but it was at least better'n nothing."

His enunciation was clear, his Illinois accent strong. Dan, who had heard President Lincoln speak at Cooper Union, thought how similar they sounded, except Slade's voice made easier listening than the President's high-pitched, nasal tones.

Slade, telling his story about freighting, laughed. "Next day it snowed, and it snowed the whole damn rest of the way until I began to wish for dry days again."

"A man's never happy, is he?" said Kiskadden. "When we've got it bad we wish for something better, and when it's good we" – his words slowed, inviting them to join in – "wish for something better," they chorused, laughing together.

"Speaking of freight," Slade took another pull at the bottle of whiskey, "I think oxen are more reliable than horses to haul freight."

Kiskadden shook his head. "Nope. Mules are best. True, they're stubborn, but they're smarter than a horse and a damn sight smarter than an ox. A horse will go for you till he keels over, but a mule won't. In the long run you get more out of a mule because he has a better sense of self-preservation."

Beidler took the last of his beer and stood up. "I'll be seeing you gentlemen later."

Slade growled, "Where are you going? Are you afraid? Yellow?"

One of his friends choked in the midst of a laugh, and his face blanched, his lips still holding the shape of his smile. In the back of the room, a cue clattered to the floor.

Slade's pistol, leaping into his hand, leveled at X. The planes of his face hardened, his eyes narrowed and darkened, as if a sidewinder emerged from the shape of a man, fangs lowered to strike.

Beidler's heavy mustache quivered at the ends, but his face wore its friendly expression like a mask over the dawning realization of something new, unwelcome, and deeply disappointing. His close friend cursed him, threatened to shoot him for leaving the table.

The backs of Dan's hands tingled. Keeping both hands on the table, where Slade could see them, certain that if he allowed his right hand to slide a fraction toward the stock of the Spencer the moment's poise on the tip of Slade's rage would break and end in murder.

"I ain't interested in the weather," said Beidler, "and I got things to do. I can go now if I want to. Or stay. It don't make me no never mind."

His voice was calm and steady, his tone calculated to let Slade have it either way, to agree to X leaving or make it attractive for him to stay.

The players and the drinkers, seeing a break they had waited for, left the saloon. At first, they eased their way around the sidewinder, as if to avoid attracting its attention, then when Slade did not appear to notice them, they bolted from the place. Tomlinson's neutral gaze held Dan's attention, seeming to make a silent plan, inviting

Dan into a pact. His hands dropped below the bar. Besides himself and Tomlinson, Dan counted Beidler and Kiskadden against Slade and his pals. They were outnumbered seven to four. Or three, depending on whether or not Kiskadden had a weapon. In a shooting, there was no guarantee that any of them would come out unhurt – or alive.

"We can talk this over later," said Kiskadden, "can't we, Joe?"

Slade looked away from X. "Sure, if X ain't interested, we don't have to talk about it now. It's not polite, though, to walk away like that just because you're not interested in a conversation. Stark, here, he didn't try to walk out just because he could give a damn about politics."

Politics? Who said anything about politics? Dan looked toward X, who nodded as if Slade had said something wise, the Oracle speaking to them from Delphi. His face held no expression.

"Be seeing you, then." Beidler moved toward the door.

Slade called out, not quite an order, but not quite friendly, either, "X, come back here."

Dan forced his right hand to pick up his beer, carry it to his lips.

X walked back the few steps until he stood behind the chair he had vacated. "All right, I come back. What do you want?" he said, not challenging Slade, not poking a stick at the sidewinder.

Slade said, "Take a drink with me. I know there's a good bottle behind the bar." He raised his voice, though the bartender stood only about eight feet away. "You got good whiskey back there, don't you, Johnny?"

"Sure thing, Joe," said Tomlinson.

"What about it?" Slade rose from his chair.

Everyone, Dan included, scraped back their chairs and stood up. How was it, he asked himself, that Slade, who was not a big man, could intimidate a room full of men, some of them, like himself, much bigger and better armed? Was it his lethal reputation, the proofs of which rode in his waistcoat pocket? Was it the Navy Colt he was so 'gifted' with, as one man put it? Was it that he was ever ready when drunk to act out his reputation to the point of murder? He felt his skin growing hot. We are not, damn it, a bunch of outlaws to be subdued for the good of the community. There's no need for Slade to act like this, we're as docile as a house cat. Another voice in his mind countered, Even house cats have claws.

Beidler said, "I'd rather drink than fight, but I'd rather not drink. It's too early in the day."

"It you don't want a drink, why'd you come in here?"

"I came in for one beer, and I had it, and now I'm ready to get on about my business."

They faced each other, Beidler just over five feet tall, and Slade perhaps eight inches taller but neither of them big. Yet each contained the toughness of men much bigger than themselves, as if cannon power came wrapped in a shoe box.

Dan forced himself to breathe deep and slow, because if a fight broke out, the way Slade's companions were spreading out, he could do nothing to prevent someone from being shot. He let his right hand find the stock of the rifle; it felt slippery under his palm.

Slade raised his pistol. "You don't have to drink unless you want to."

Meaning, Dan understood, that Beidler could fight instead, that his choice had only two ways to go, to drink or to fight.

"Mr. Slade, that is another privilege and I don't want to do that either. I won't drink," Beidler said.

Slade ordered Tomlinson to set up drinks up for his friends. "Be quick about it, you slow son of a bitch."

The bartender brought out the bottle of the usual Valley Tan.

That's torn it, Dan thought, considering that Slade's friends stood behind them. Kiskadden had said nothing throughout the situation, nor had Dan, because it was not his business, but something between Slade and Beidler, though he would not let Beidler fight seven men all by himself. If he had the chance, the Spencer could take all of them, one ball for each. If he had the chance, if one man or another didn't shoot him before he had the opportunity to shift his aim from one to the other. In either case someone might die.

Tomlinson brought out a Navy Colt's revolver from under the bar. Pointing it at Slade, he said, "You want a fight, Slade? You can eat the first ball." He had not cocked the weapon, but it stared at Slade, who wilted like a starched collar in a sudden snowstorm.

"Oh, hell," said Slade. "Let's quit this."

"Good idea," said Beidler.

Kiskadden looked around for a chair and sat down on it so hard it bounced a fraction under him.

Dan let go of the Spencer's stock. He braced his legs, locked his knees to stand upright.

Now Slade said, "You can stay and have a drink, can't you?"

"Later, maybe, Joe," said Beidler. "I was on my way to see to Black Bess when I met Kiskadden and we decided to stop in here. I better be looking after her. It's a sin to neglect an animal."

Dan walked out with Beidler. Accommodating his long stride to the little man's pace, towering a foot over him, he wondered who was really the bigger of the two, because he had left the rifle on his shoulder. He had done nothing to help Beidler. Or to stop Slade.

16.

At Jackson Street, they turned uphill. Kiskadden left them to go back to his business. "I'm nervous about leaving it when Slade's in town," he said.

When Dan and Beidler had walked a ways, as if by common consent, they stopped by a house two doors down from Dan's own. He imagined Martha going about her work, perhaps scrubbing the floor because she could not abide a dirty floor, and her standards were as high as his mother's, who did not have to do her own cleaning. He stood with Beidler, breathed in the cold dry air, and thought that damn it, someday his wife would not scrub her own floor or anyone else's. Looking at X from his own height, Dan could not see the man's face, hidden under his hat brim, as he stood looking down. Foreshortened, the hat appeared over large for X's small feet. His fists bulged deep in his coat pockets.

When Beidler lifted his face to speak, sadness lurked deep in his eyes. "He's my friend, Slade is, don't you know? Maybe the best friend I've got around here, 'cept for Williams. Left to himself he'd probably do something completely peaceful, like make money. He's good at business. He's got a fine business head on him, and he's got a herd of dairy cows because he knows how much this place needs milk. All the little children around here. We've talked about how gardens would be a money-maker." The little man gazed down Jackson, past Daylight Creek and Cover Street. Dan thought he might be looking at the hill where the road agents were buried. "You know, it would be nice to make a garden and sell vegetables – carrots, and peas, and lettuces. Beans. Squash." He paused for a moment as if seeing a different life to be led. "My Ma had a garden and she'd let me help in it when I was a little boy. I purely liked the feel of the dirt in the spring when it's just warming up. The smell of it." As if lost in memories of his mother's garden, he was silent another moment before he shook himself as if waking from a dream. "We'd got to do what we done to keep peace here. You knowed I fought against Quantrill's Raiders in Kansas, didn't you?"

Dan nodded. In New York before the war, he'd read how Quantrill and his gang of renegades had ridden into Lawrence, that Union town on the banks of the Kaw, and burned it down and slaughtered nearly 200 men and boys. Beidler had fought them, perhaps had been a Jayhawker, one of those Union men who had raided into Missouri. He used to think that sort of violence unthinkable. But that had been before Father's downfall and – death forced him to seek gold, before he joined in the work the Vigilantes had to do. He had done then what he could never imagine himself doing, but what choice had they? What other means had they to rid the country of criminals in a place where murder was tolerated?

Beidler talked as Dan had never heard him and might never hear him again. This tight-lipped, tough man talked only because, after the shock of his great friend Slade threatening his life, he happened to be here now. Dan had ridden with him, had pulled a rope as X had done, and Cap Williams. That was the reason X bared his soul now. In his own nightmares, waking as well as sleeping, Dan heard the thud and twang of rope as a full grown man hit the end of it. Heard the choking and struggling, smelled the stench when death released the bowels and bladder. Were X's nightmares the same? No one would ever know, he thought. Beidler would never give himself away so again. He could not, Dan understood, considering how a small man had to be much tougher than a big man in order to keep alive in a country of killers. Perhaps he and Slade understood each other, because they had to fight for their lives every day.

But in Virginia City, at least, Beidler had men's respect, if not their endorsement. He had nothing to prove any more.

He pushed his hat back and Dan met his eyes, while the silence trailed out as he thought of something to say. "Country like this makes men do what they never figured on, starting out." What other men, safe in their own minds, knew to be wrong, or evil. "Nobody knows how drink will take him."

"I'm scared," Beidler confessed. "I'm scared he'll kill someone. Yesterday it might have been you. Today it could've been me." He brought a big blue handkerchief and wiped his face. "If a man can meet you and commune with you as a friend when he's sober, and then turn around and mistreat you, or threaten to kill you when he's drunk, or –" X shook his head. "I don't understand it. I just plumb don't understand it. How can you ever trust a man like that?"

"I don't know," said Dan. "I just don't know." Commune, X had said. We communed. Dan thought of the friends he had made in school, had left behind to come West. He did not think he had ever communed with any of them, shared whatever depths of soul the word implied. Communed. What was worse, he asked himself as they turned back toward Wallace, toward the commotion caused by Slade's disorderly presence. To have never had that deep a friendship or to have it and find it betrayed in a fit of drunken pique?

Adjusting the carrying strap of his rifle, he walked along even with the smaller man's pace, watching his footing in the treacherous mounds of dirty snow and rutted, frozen mud.

17.

66"There comes Toponce," said X.

Up Wallace, on a one-eared mule, rode Al Toponce, the French freighter, who stopped his mount as they reached the corner. "Where's Slade?" he asked without so much as a how-do-you-do. A man with a mission, Dan thought.

Beidler's hatbrim tilted upward to reply to the man on the tall animal. "Last we seen him, he was drinking at the Washington Billiard Hall."

Dan added, "Watch out for him. He's more changeable than usual."

"That so?" Toponce eased his butt in the saddle. The mule shook his head, his one ear flapping back and forth. The stump of the other held a thick scab across its end.

This must be the mule whose ear Slade had cut off a week ago, damn him, thought Dan. The son of a bitch might have a reputation for kindness, but only when he was sober. This was a piece of unnecessary cruelty, to an animal minding its own innocent business. It wasn't testimony to Slade's toughness, or his courage, only to a streak of meanness akin to threatening a friend at gunpoint.

Dan wanted to reach out a friendly hand to the mule, but he knew better. The creature might have developed a healthy and immediate mistrust of human hands reaching for its head. How had Toponce managed to bridle the beast?

"I got a message for him from Williams," Toponce said.

"And that is?" Dan asked.

"Williams sent me to tell him, 'Get out of town at once.'"

"That so?" Beidler's voice held only the usual interest.

The mule shifted its feet as if wanting to move, and Toponce stroked its neck to quiet it. "The boys is getting mighty damn tired of Slade and his hooligan ways."

He'd had this conversation with Beidler and Williams just yesterday. Dan said, "We've got to persuade him to go home. That's the first step. Then some of his friends will have to convince him to stop drinking."

Toponce gazed into the distance, up Wallace to where it disappeared into the sagebrush and juniper trees, now reduced to mounds of snow and dark cones against the white. "They've been talking their balls off to Slade for nigh on three months. How long do you think they'll wait while he destroys their livelihood, injures their animals?" His eyes came back to Dan, who wanted to look away. "Till he kills someone?"

Reining the mule around, he said, "The bastard better listen to Jim's message." He flung over his shoulder, "Jim don't want to have to deliver it in person, but he will if he has to."

18.

As Toponce rode up the street, Dan thought to himself that Jim Williams could be a little forceful sometimes, and with the mood Slade was in, he might not back down so easily as he had in their first encounter.

Beidler chewed his mustache a second while he made up his mind. "I'll go along to the billiard hall, and see if I can add to the persuasion."

Paris Pfouts kept his store in a log building substantial by Alder Gulch standards, about the size of the parlor in Dan's old New York home, before Father's – death. It stood near the northeast corner of Jackson and Wallace, and over the doorway, a sign read Pfouts and Russell, although Mr. Russell had not yet arrived in Alder Gulch.

When he pushed open the door and heard the bell clang above his head, Pfouts and Tobias Fitch bent over something that lay on the narrow display table between them. Turned toward him, their faces changed from curiosity to welcome to alarm.

"Anything new?" Pfouts stood up straight.

"Depends on what you call new. Jim Williams sent Al Toponce with a message for Slade: 'Get out of town now.'"

"Ah," said Pfouts.

Fitch shifted his chaw to the other cheek and looked around for the spittoon. When Pfouts pointed toward the front door, Fitch sidled past Dan, who left it open for him as they brushed by each other.

"Is the Judge in?" Dan asked, and when the storekeeper nodded, he said," I came to get a court date for a case involving Charley Baer."

"Oh, Lord, what's Charley done now?" Pfouts asked.

Dan stopped, thinking maybe he'd better come up with a new strategy to defend Charley, and then wondering if this strait-laced Southerner ever let out with a real curse.

Outside, a man yelled, "Shit!" Fitch closed the door. "That'll teach people to think about what might come out of an open door." His grin faded. "So Williams has sent a message, has he? It's about time we thought seriously about Slade."

"Don't you think we've been doing that for the last three months?" Pfouts asked. "Like we didn't have enough to do?"

"He's been a damn nuisance ever since he brought in those supplies." Taking a wider stance, Fitch braced for an argument.

Pfouts glared. "Nobody else could have done that, brought the entire load in from the Milk River after the boat dumped them there. He organized the whole expedition, Lord knows how many yoke of oxen, and wagons, and drove them more'n three-hundred miles up there, loaded the supplies – thank God they were still there – and brought everything back, without any trails to speak of, and past all the hostile tribes. Name any other man in the Gulch who could have done that, and then tell me what would have become of us if he hadn't brought them in? I purely hate to think. We owe him for that. Considering the snow this winter, we owe him our lives."

During this tirade, Alex Davis had come out. "That's right," he said, underscoring Pfouts's speech. "We owe Joseph Slade more than we can ever repay."

Fitch's words slurred around the chaw in his mouth. "Yeah, and he's been charging interest on that debt ever since." Tucking the tobacco into one cheek, he said, "How many saloons and stores does he wreck, and how many balls do he and his pals shoot, and how many people will he threaten with that revolver of his before someone gets killed?" He thrust out his short arm toward Dan. "He nearly got Stark or me here just this morning. If you was burying one of us now, would you think he'd gone too far?"

He could not let them think he was a party to the lynching Fitch wanted. Dan said, "We can't hang a man for what he might do. Even if one of us is killed, it would be ruled accidental death and not murder." He turned toward Judge Davis, leaning against the door jamb. "Isn't that right?" Knowing full well that he was right, he wanted Alexander Davis in this discussion because the other two, Missourians like Davis, and Fitch especially, being a veteran of General Price's army, and a survivor of the disastrous losses at Pea Ridge, like Davis himself, would take it coming from him while they – Fitch especially, again – would not want to hear or listen to anything from a damned Yankee like himself. Especially a non-veteran. The only thing that saved him from their absolute contempt was his participation in the winter's activities, his own position as a prosecutor, his membership in the Vigilantes, the fact that he had pulled his own rope. He had earned his modest place in their esteem as he had earned his nightmares.

"That's right." When Davis stood straight, he matched Dan's height inch for inch, a leaner man, rope-strong, who won nearly all his foot races. "Without evidence to prove malice aforethought, and not committed during a felony, the death of a man in these circumstances is not murder."

"Manslaughter at best," Dan agreed, "punishable by – what? – ten years to life imprisonment?"

"Who knows?" Davis said. "Has anyone yet seen the Idaho Territorial Criminal Code?"

"Not that I know of," Paris Pfouts said. "The delegates haven't had time to get back from Lewiston yet."

Behind his back, Dan doubled his fists. He forced his jaws to relax so as not to grind his teeth from sheer frustration. "Damn Congress," he said. "Those idiots in Washington think they know what to do for the country, but all they want is to grab as much of the pie as they can. What could they have been thinking of, setting up the Territory without allocating a legal code to it? And then —"

Slapping Dan's back, Fitch guffawed. "That's almost the first thing you've said I can agree with. Idiots in Washington thinking they know what's best out here."

"Putting the Territorial capital in Lewiston with 400 miles of mountains between it and us," grumbled Pfouts. "How the hell are we supposed to know what laws the Territory passed when it takes a month or better to travel around the Bitterroots in the winter time?"

"Getting back to our problem," said Fitch, "it don't do us much good to think of ten years in a penitentiary when we don't have one. Or a jail."

"There's a jail in Bannack," Davis reminded them. He meant the small two-room cabin the former sheriff had built behind his office.

"Yeah, eighty miles away," Fitch said. "By the time we rode to Dempsey's, he'd be sober and there'd be no point in jailing him."

Davis shifted away from the doorjamb. "Besides, it's no place to hold a man for more than an hour or two. It has no heat, and someone would have to look after him. Change his bucket, give him meals, that sort of thing."

Fitch said, "So there we are. Right where we were with the others. I say we'll save a lot of grief if we act sooner rather than later."

"No!" Davis almost shouted. "You cannot be party to murder. If you hang Slade, you will all be murderers."

"I agree," Pfouts said. "The best we can do is per—"

Fitch cut off the merchant's statement. He glared at Davis. "You and Pfouts have 'persuaded' Slade all winter. What makes you think he'll listen to you this time? Or any time? We don't get tough with him, he'll think he has us buffaloed."

Davis said, "I will not be party to that line of thinking. Behind that drunken lout is a good and decent man. You cannot hang him."

"That's the hell of it, isn't it?" Dan said. "We can't do anything to punish the drunken lout – as Alex said – without harming the good man."

Fitch seemed not to hear him. He glared at Davis, who returned the glare in full measure.

At last Davis said, "You cannot lawfully hang him absent a trial before judge and jury, with evidence of true murder beyond a reasonable doubt."

"Oh fuck that." Fitch swung around to stare out the window for a moment before he swung back. "You always want to keep your conscience clean."

Dan could stand on the sidelines no more. Much as he sympathized with Davis, even agreed with him on interpretation of the law, he could not join him in his fantasy. "When we asked you to join us in December, you said just that."

"I said then and I'll say now, I will not be a party to extralegal activities, and that's what you all did. It's what you propose now. You acted unlawfully to rid the country of perceived wrongdoers – without due process of law."

"You wanted no action outside of a regularly constituted court." Dan held back his temper, kept his voice low and even, although every pulse beat time against the cut in his scalp, and threatened to overwhelm what shreds of control he could muster. "Your legal principles won't permit it. Am I right?"

"Yes. I said that when you wanted me to join you, and I say it now."

"I agree. If we had such a thing, I'd condemn us as a lynch mob. But we are not. We have no code of laws since Idaho Territory was formed a year ago." He doubled his fist in its glove and pounded softly on the display table to emphasize what he said, as if to pound the reality into Judge Davis's fantasy of the way things were – in civilized places. "No code. No court. Except in Lewiston." He stopped for breath, raised his palm to prevent Fitch from butting in. Pfouts stayed out of this legal wrangle.

Davis said, "This is the Third District of the Idaho Territorial Supreme Court. Chief Justice Edgerton could have held court any time he wished. Why did he not?"

"What court decisions could he have upheld or struck down? There is no appeals court to refer cases to him. There is no lower court whose decisions can be appealed. There. Is. No. Code. Of. Law. There is nothing to try a man by. Nothing. Except the laws of common decency, the Ten Commandments, and the Common Law."

"We all agreed in December to go by the Common Law. Then you hanged twenty-odd men."

"Yes. To both. Because we narrowly survived the Ives trial, as you yourself well know, having been one of his defenders." Holding himself in, because he respected Alex Davis for standing by his principles, no matter how illogical and pig-headed, and because he wanted – God, how he wanted – the makeshift People's Court to work, to hold Slade in check, to hold others like him and worse in check, Dan took another turn of the rope that snubbed down his rising anger. He could not risk ruining the fragile trust between him, a Union man, and Davis, the Confederate, who had freed his inherited slaves but had fought against the Union invasion.

"Hell, we don't even know if we're in Idaho Territory. Maybe we're in Montana Territory, though seeing as how Congress has to wrangle over every comma, that's not likely. Justice Edgerton has barely had enough time to reach Washington yet." The Chief Justice had left in January, to talk to his friend the President about splitting the area east of the Bitterroots off from Idaho and calling the new territory Montana.

Fidgeting and squirming throughout the discussion, Fitch broke in. "Yeah, what were we to do? How could we take those bastards to trial when we had no court?"

Davis's face, that of a well-trained lawyer, showed little of his emotion, but his jaw muscles tightened and his eyes narrowed.

Tells, Dan thought. He'd do well not to play poker with me.

"You cannot go against the law," Davis said. "There is no justification for vigilantism. You, a New York lawyer, should know that. Or is the New York bar more lenient than Missouri?"

"I don't fault your legal training, Your Honor." Dan stifled the urge to sneer at Davis's title. "Or your legal principles. But I do fault your logic. We could not, can not, take suspected criminals to a court of law because until we established your court and installed you as judge, we had no court. And don't tell me you think the miners court, with its God-damn jury of the whole, the mob jury, sufficed. Don't say we could have repeated the Ives trial for all 21 suspects, or I will remind you of the history of this place." Pausing a beat, he said, "Dillingham."

Pfouts said, "The Dillingham affair was before my time here. It happened just after Discovery, am I right?"

Dan, who had arrived in Alder Gulch late in the summer of 1863, looked at Fitch. The one-armed man had been in the Gulch since shortly after gold was discovered. As he laid it out for Davis, Dan found his own thoughts filling in with what Fitch did not say. "Dillingham was murdered in front of hundreds of people right down there on Main Street." (Nothing here then but a few wickiups and maybe a half dozen log cabins, Dan thought. Men sheltered wherever they could, intending to grab as much gold as possible could before winter threatened, and then go home.) "We caught the murderers right then, and tried them in the miners court." (Grandfather would never believe a court of law in a wickiup, brush piled into the shape of a teepee.) "They found 'em guilty as charged." (What else, considering that at least a hundred men saw the murder?) "But on their way to be hanged, some women got to pleading and crying and the jury took another vote." (The jury of the whole, the God-damned mob jury, being everybody

THE DEVIL IN THE BOTTLE | 119

within sight. We had them to contend with it during the Ives trial, too.) "And another. I forget how many, but eventually they commuted the sentences to banishment. The killers rode off, but they come back in two-three days."

Davis's eyes burned blue flames. Fitch held his own, returned glare for glare. "You're saying that's what will happen with Slade. Are you impugning the integrity of this court?"

Fitch lifted his arms a few inches from his sides, let them drop. Dan's eyes watered at the odor that rose like a miasma from his clothes. "Not your integrity, no," Fitch said. "You're a man who sticks to his guns. You wouldn't join us in December, though like Stark said, there was no court then, and no code to uphold in the first place. Well, we have a court now. You're it." He paused, his jaws working furiously on the chaw. A drop or two formed at the corner of his mouth. "If it's up to you to deal with Slade and his bunch, you better take a strong stand."

"Or?"

"There ain't no 'or.' That's it. What law we've got is down to you, backed by us." He swung toward Pfouts. "Ain't that right?" Not waiting for the merchant's reply, he spun back, his eyes raking across Dan, and said to Davis, "You and me, we fought in Price's army at Wilson's Creek and Pea Ridge. I'd like to know how in hell a Yankee Unionist son of a bitch understands the legal situation here better'n you do, and why he's the one to show you what you can't see in a God-damn mirror."

With that, he turned on his heel and stalked out. The overhead bell clamored in Fitch's wake, muffling the slammed door's echo and giving Dan a moment to try to pan his swirling thoughts for something useful to say. When the noise died a little, Davis spoke first.

"With some men, battle leaves a taste for death." He swallowed, though his clean-shaven mouth held firm, his emotions checked. "Others develop an abhorrence of it when a cannonball blows the brother in arms beside you to a red nothing, or when another man's lower jaw is shot off though he still lives, and his eyes beg you to shoot him." His voice had the scratch of iron on ice. "That is equally the effect of five corpses hanging from one beam in an unfinished building."

Of all the replies he might have made – that they fought a war here as surely as armies fought the greater War in the East, that he had never wanted to place the noose around the neck of any man, nor would willingly be a party to it again – Dan chose none of them. Perhaps Davis might come to a different opinion, given time. Perhaps not. Certainly he would hear nothing Dan could say at the moment.

"I came to discuss the Charley Baer case, Your Honor. If you have a moment."

19.

After supper, perched on the edge of the bed she shared with Dan'l, Martha put up her hair, still damp from her afternoon bath. Her fingers pinned up her hair every day of her life, but now, with Dan'l and the young'uns waiting in the big room, they dropped pins and moved like sausages.

She peered into the shadowy wall mirror. A thought crawled from its web in a back corner of her mind and bit: All the respectable people and their wives would be there. Everyone. They'd scorn her for a drab. They'd wonder what on earth Dan'l had ever saw in the likes of her. They'd know she was no better'n she should be. They'd think she snapped her fingers at morality, appearin' in public thataway with Dan'l. They'd whisper behind their hands, over their tables tomorrow. She couldn't talk right, neither.

Her hands dropped to her lap, and her unpinned hair tumbled down her shoulders. The mirror slanted outward at the top, and her reflection stared down at her. "You," she whispered to the wide-eyed woman in the smoky glass. "You, paradin' in public as Dan'l Stark's wife, which you ain't and can't be, given McDowell is still alive someplace." She laid her face in her hands.

"Are you ready yet?" Dan'l tapped at the door. She knew by his voice he was gettin' impatient. He'd likely call her fears "vapors" and tell her not to be silly.

She wanted to holler go on without her, but her voice only squeaked.

He tapped again and this time looked in. "Why are you sitting in the dark? It's almost time to go. Light a lamp for petesake."

Kerosene was too dear to waste on seein' her hair, she wanted to tell him. Before she could muster a word, he took out his tinder box, stuck flint and steel for a spark, lighted a splinter, and put it to the wick. He didn't even snuff the candle after he replaced the lamp chimney.

"There. We don't want to be late." He closed the door, opened it again and put his head in. "They'll love you almost as much as I do." The door shut with a snap.

Walk in late, create a disturbance like she was the actress? Lord, no.

She yanked the brush out of her hair, swept the hair up, and jammed hair pins into it. Her fingers moved like they knew their business, and as a finishing touch, she snatched down a curl at either temple. Snuffing the candle and blowing out the lamp on a prayer, she lifted her chin, and joined them in the big room.

Not just her family. Jacob Himmelfarb, Dan'l's chain man in his surveying that Timmy shared a bachelor cabin with, he'd come, too, and raised his thin frame along with everyone else, so that she near shed tears at sight of them all standing up for her like a lady had come into the room.

Timmy, a bit red-faced, stretched his neck at the first starched collar he'd ever worn, something Dan'l must have put on him, along with the tidy bow tie holding it. "My." She looked him up and down, held back tears at him being so close to man-grown. "You look quite the gentleman." He blushed, and his lips opened up, but he couldn't bring out a sound.

Dotty pleated a handkerchief, twitched at a button on her bodice, rocked back on her heels and forward again. Martha thought she might really cry to see the woman ready to blossom, for Dotty would be a beauty some day.

Both children favored their father, being big-boned and blond. They looked more like Dan'l's young'uns than any flesh of hers.

Dan'l smiled. "Your children are very handsome," he said, "and my dear, you are beautiful."

Jacob beamed and made a series of short bows, uttering sounds she figured were in his native language, but sounded more like coughing: "Ach, ja, shern." For however long he'd been here, his English wasn't reliable, but she worked out he must be paying a compliment. It was Dan'l's approval she wanted, though, Dan'l's assurance that hill woman though she was and just learning how proper folks spoke and conducted theirselves, she wouldn't disgrace him.

He wasn't much for outright saying, but she was learning to read the smile in his eyes and the little nod that told her she'd done fine. Tears threatened so, she could do no more than smile at all of them. The flutter of putting on wraps and gathering handkerchiefs and lighting the lantern saved her from weeping outright. As Dan'l helped adjust her blue cloak over her shoulders, his fingers stroked the nape of her neck and a small flame ran down her spine to her tailbone.

He lighted their way through the mounds and trenches of thick snow while she held onto his free arm and Jacob and the young'uns followed.

At Wallace they joined crowds of cheerful people, all a-chatter, expecting a fine time. They greeted each other and her and Dan'l and the young'uns, calling back and forth: "A fine night, though still chilly." "Downright cold, you ask me."

"Do you think Miss Harper will sing 'The Battle Hymn of the Republic?'" An answer growled from the dark: "She better sing 'Dixie's Land' if she does."

"I want to hear 'Lorena,'" said a woman. A man's Southern voice, "That damn song makes boys quit the war." Martha recognized Fitch's belligerent tone and glanced around to spot him. He walked with Berry Woman on his arm, his head up, proud like he escorted a queen, daring them all to snub his Indian wife, or call him a squaw man. "And you?" came another voice, needle sharp. There was a silence, and Martha imagined Fitch raising his short arm. A woman, sounding desperate to stop this before it turned into an argument, said: "Let's have 'Oh, Susannah.'"

"Or 'I Dream of Jeanie with the Dark Brown Hair,'" said Dan'l, like he might speculate on the weather. Martha blushed. Sure enough they laughed, and someone called, "It's 'Light Brown Hair.'"

Even so far from the War, mentioning songs could work some folks up, Martha thought, but in a few more steps they were at the Hall. Dan'l blew out the lantern, hung it on one of the last vacant pegs. He removed his hat, careful not to disturb the bandage.

She had forgotten Slade until she saw him standing at the back with two or three friends. Her grip on Dan'l's arm tightened, and he patted her hand. "I see him," he said, exchanged friendly greetings with Slade, who glanced at the bandage and bowed to her, as gentleman-like as though he'd never terrified her just yesterday, or nigh to killed Dan'l today. They made their way along, Dan'l stopping to exchange pleasant words with near everyone, as far as Martha could tell. He introduced her and the young'uns to everyone they met, so that Martha, wanting only to sit lost among the crowd and wait quietly, understood what a prize horse must feel like at a show. Except, she told herself, he said, "My wife, Martha Stark," so many times she near believed in it. At last, they found seats in the middle of a bench most of the way to the front.

They made quite a company, too, herself sitting between Dotty and Dan'l, with Timmy on Dotty's other hand, and Jacob next to Timmy. She took a little pride in the way they disposed themselves along the bench, but thought it a bit odd that Jacob and Timmy had entered the row first, before the females, until she realized the men had put her and the young'uns between them.

"You expecting trouble?" she whispered to Dan'l.

"No." He smiled and squeezed her hand, but his eyes were watchful. "He knows how to behave when ladies are present."

Ladies. He meant her, too. Martha let her shoulders relax. The new dress, the cost of the cloth and thread, the time spent taking a pattern and sewing it up – it was all worth it. She needn't have worried so.

Dotty whispered a question to Timmy, who leaned around his mother and sister to ask Dan'l. Behind her, Martha felt a bustle and shuffle of booted feet, a knee nudged her back, and she heard a whispered, "Beg pardon, Ma'am," that carried a prickly odor of sweat, liquor, and black powder. Meek as anything, Slade and one of his pals, the same Bill Fairweather that first discovered gold in Alder Gulch, took seats behind them.

Adjusting her blue cloak about her shoulders, Dan'l said, "This should be a good performance, don't you think, Slade? Miss Harper is renowned for her singing. My wife has been looking forward to this for weeks."

Slade mumbled something that was lost in a gurgling as he took a drink from a bottle. Martha felt Dan'l stiffen, like he came alert, and she thought he might not enjoy the evening as much with Slade behind them, drinking. When she glanced up at him, though, she saw nothing in his calm profile to alarm her. He smiled and squeezed her hand.

Across the front of the stage, someone had placed a row of lanterns. A small boy ran along turning each one up, the piano player came out with a bow, and then Miss Harper swept from the back of the stage to greet them. Martha was lost in the songs, the dances, the music. She was happy. It was only a woman singing and dancing with three other people in a revue, and the piano had two wrong keys, but somehow they made a kind of – she groped for the word – magic.

At the interval, she left her cloak on the bench as a token for their seats, and stood at the back where men clustered at the bar. A thin, dark man with intense eyes and a pretty woman with hair a few shades lighter than her own, walked over as Dan came back with his whiskey and her cider. Martha took the hot cider and felt her heart speed up as the men presented their wives: Mr. and Mrs. Wilbur Sanders. Harriet Sanders. Martha had heard of her. She came from a family so wealthy that she had brought a Brussels carpet out from Ohio. Her husband was the nephew of the Chief Justice of Idaho Territory, the same as had gone to talk to President Lincoln.

Martha's hard-won grammar deserted her, and she stood as tongue-tied as a Hottentot, scolding herself to say something, to be pleasant. Dotty stood to one side, her eyes huge and taking in every detail of Mrs. Sanders's wine-colored dress. Martha suspected it was made of silk. Her own dress became drab and dull in comparison. She introduced Dotty, and to her surprise the child responded politely as one accustomed to meeting cultured people every day.

The men drew apart, talked in low voices, and Martha heard Slade's name.

"Miss Harper," said Mrs. Sanders, "has a fine voice, don't you think?"

"Yes," said Martha. "Her notes ring true all through her range."

The other woman's eyes brightened. "Can you sing?"

"Mama sings beautifully," Dotty said. "She sings low."

Martha shook her head. "Don't you be exaggerating, you hear?"

"Some of us are starting a choir. We can always use another – alto? Contralto?"

"One of those," Martha said. "I'm not just sure which." It did not matter. When they took their places afterwards, she was sure her feet were not quite on the floor because Mrs. Sanders had invited her to join her choir. To make music with other people, to join in music-making. It had been her deepest joy before Sam McDowell smashed her dulcimer. She might never have another one, but now she could sing with other people. Make a joyful noise unto the Lord.

"Take it off!"

The song stumbled and broke on the piano's discord. Miss Harper stood alone on the stage in her ballet dress. Her fan dropped to the floor.

Slade shouted, "Show us your legs."

Women screamed. Martha in her outrage turned to Dan'l, the beautiful evening in torn bits around her feet.

"Take it all off! Show us your tits," Slade bellowed. Martha drew Dotty to her, wrapped them both in the blue cloak and clapped a hand over Dotty's exposed ear.

The actress burst into tears.

Slade, on his feet now, laughed. Fairweather echoed him: "Show us your tits."

"Do something," Martha hissed at Dan, who had already risen to his feet and was stepping across the bench to stand between her and Dotty and the center of the commotion.

Other men rushed at Slade and Fairweather, surrounded them.

Bumped and pushed, Martha held fast to Dotty, shielded her against the shoving and grunting behind them.

Then everything quieted, as if a storm rolled on to another place, and over the receding grumble of men, Dan said, "We'll see you safely home, you and the youngsters."

Jacob echoed, "Ja. We all go home now."

"That – that —" Timothy sputtered. "Ain't you going to do nothing about him?" He pointed his chin toward the stage. Someone had brought out a chair for Miss Harper, and a blanket. She sat weeping and shuddering on the chair, only her curls visible as she sobbed into the coarse wool while her impresario demanded apologies and compensation for the gross insult heaped upon her. "That poor creature. What about her?"

Around the impresario, the pianist, and his songbird gathered the owner of the hall and other men, their voices hushed, hands making damping motions.

Martha began to say that she would gladly tend to Miss Harper, but Dan'l said, "They will settle the business. Our first responsibility is to ensure the safety of your mother and sister. We're going home."

Against the firmness in his voice, and the flint in his eyes, and the set of his mouth, Martha did not argue as Jacob collected the lantern. The man who ushered them out of the Hall was not her Dan'l. He was someone she had not seen before. The Vigilante prosecutor.

20.

"She never got to sing 'Lorena,'" a woman said, her voice full of unshed tears. Another woman sniffed, "That horrible Slade. He ruined it for everybody."

"He oughta be horse-whipped," said a man.

The cold pinched Martha's nose. Trudging along, one arm in the crook of Dan'l's elbow and the other around Dotty's shoulders, she was hard put not to use some of the words she had learned from Sam McDowell. Men, she thought, were lucky. They could give free expression to their feelings.

"Why does he hate us so?" asked Dotty. "What did we ever do to him?"

"Is the drink." Jacob walked behind them with Timmy, his speech as uncertain as his steps. "Ja. Is the drink. When he work has, he is good man. When he has the drink...." Jacob shrugged, like he didn't have anything more to say. After a polite moment, conversation went on around him, but Dan'l waited. Sometimes Jacob had to pause and translate his thought into English from his own language, German or Yiddish or a mix of the two. "It is – how do you say? – almost, he has the devil in a bottle, and it escapes when he the drink takes."

"But knowing that," Martha said, "why does he take that first drink?"

A man spoke up. "I knew a man took arsenic. At first it was just an experiment, and he liked it so he did it again. Then it was like it took hold of him. He had to have more, even though his stomach hurt worse and worse." No one spoke. Only their breathing made clouds in the lantern light, and their steps scratched and slid on the crackling ice. They had all seen for themselves what drink did to Joe Slade. The voice said, "He's probably dead by now. Leastways, I hope he is. He suffered something awful, but couldn't stop."

"Slade can choose not to drink," Dan'l said. He sounded like he'd bit into a rotten apple and had spit it out, but the bitter taste stayed behind.

"Oooh." Feet scrambled, and a man said, "There, now, my dear, that was close."

"I don't think it's that way," said the arsenic-eater's friend. "It's like it gets a grip and don't let go of some folks. I think Slade's devil has got him and he can't get loose."

"Maybe if he looked up a rope, that would cure him." A man's voice, deep and growling.

"No! It would be too late, then," Dan'l said. "His friends want him to reform. All he has to do is to go home. Stop drinking."

"Look how he brought in those supplies," a woman said, "Why, just think. Hundreds of oxen, and all them wagons, with no roads."

Dotty whispered, "Mam, you're holding on too tight." Martha loosened her grip on the child's shoulders. Sturdy though she was, she was no one to lean on.

A Southern said, "Slade had to forge his own route, find passes through the mountains, locate fords on all the rivers, blaze trails. Not to mention the land's all fought over by the I don't know how many tribes of Indians."

"And he didn't lose even one ox," said Martha.

"That's Slade," said a man, sounding high and strained, like he was strung too tight. "Everything in his makeup for a genuine hero, and then he does something like this. He goes on these binges, and is like to wreck the whole town. It's getting as bad as before."

Martha shuddered. She'd always been on the look-out for stray bullets then, when even the former sheriff himself had put many a man in the Recovery, then bragged about shooting them.

Dan'l murmured, "We'll be home soon."

"I don't get it. It's like he wants to destroy himself," the tight-strung man said.

Another man spoke like he had too big a chaw in his mouth. "I'd be willing to help him do it. Before he kills someone."

Two or three women gasped, and Martha felt cold air at the back of her throat. She heard spitting, and Martha thought of yellow-brown, rank-smelling tobacco staining the snow.

"Or because he feels like it," the man said.

Beside her, Dan'l was silent.

At the house, instead of going on his way to the cabin, Timmy followed them in, Jacob trailing after him. While Dan'l lighted a lamp, and before they had taken off their wraps, the boy demanded, "Do something, can't you?"

"What can we do?" Dan'l looked about as exasperated as Martha had ever seen him. "This isn't like that business in the winter, not by a long shot."

"Why not?" Timmy doubled his fists at his sides and thrust out his head, looking so like his Pap in a temper it scared her. "You have to wait before he kills someone? Maybe you?" The boy took a breath. "I heard he near killed you again this afternoon, you and X Beidler and

Mr. Kiskadden. You been close twice now, how close d'you have to get before you-all do something?"

"Because he didn't kill anyone. He didn't want to kill anyone. He backed off." Dan'l's cheeks had spots of red in them; him being blond, the blood showed easy under his skin.

"And if'n he kills you, even not meaning to, who'll help Ma and Dotty then?" The boy's voice rose. "It ain't just you no more. You got us. And there's everyone else, all the miners and storekeepers have got someone at home to look out for."

"The law says —"

Timmy shouted, "The goddam law could get us killed."

"You will not curse in front of your mother and sister," roared Dan'l, a vein bulging across his forehead. "Apologize at once."

The big room was silent except for their breathing. Dotty chewed on a knuckle, her eyes huge and dark in her ashen face. Timmy took a step backward like he might have done when he'd spoke up to his Pap, only McDowell would've laid him out by now.

Instead, Dan'l stood as straight as a fence post and glared at Timmy until he mumbled, "Sorry, Ma'am. You, too, Dotty." On his own, he added, "I won't do it again."

Martha nodded and smiled at him, letting him know he was forgiven.

Dan'l said, "The law is the only thing between us and anarchy. You remember what it was like before?" He kept his voice steady and quiet, a reasonable man talking to another reasonable man instead of a boy, and only the stiffness in his shoulders, told how he had himself reined in, testified to his anger. That and the quick pulse beating at his jaw. "The law says we can't punish a person for what they might do, only for what we can prove beyond reasonable doubt they have done. If we were to hang Slade for any other reason, we'd be no better than the road agents."

The boy said nothing, but he was not giving in either, though he leaned forward from the hips, listening like he tried to catch something behind what Dan'l said.

With a sideways glance at Dan'l, Jacob said, "In winter, was different. Then ruffians ruled. What they said, men killed every day –" he shrugged "– ja. No one safe. All the time fights, shooting. On the trails, robbery. Murder." One sharp elbow poked out toward Dan'l. "What they did, now roughs are frightened. Murder stopped. Is peaceful place."

"Except for Slade," said Tim. "What's the difference with Slade? He comes into town whenever he needs a drink and he raises h–" a glance bouncing from Martha to Dan'l "– he raises Cain. Scares people, wrecks businesses, him and his pals are no better'n the roughs. You'll let him go on until he kills somebody. What he did to Mr. Dorris today? He was ready to kill the poor man."

Dan'l lowered his voice until she almost couldn't hear him. "Did your father ever whip you on general principles? Because you might do something?"

Timmy backed away from Dan'l until he bumped a kitchen chair behind him, and dropped onto it. More times than she wanted to think of – even once being too much – McDowell had thumped the boy, batting her away like a mosquito. He'd tried to protect himself, screaming, I ain't done nothing, and McDowell hitting him again, That's for what you're thinking of doing, what you're gonna do.

She went to him and wrapped her arms around him. Her boy. Her baby. Her first. When the outriders come to take whatever they had for the rich man's war, he'd drawn a bead on them with a long gun at an upstairs window and shouted them off the place in his child's voice, him being just thirteen and his voice not broke. Somehow, God be praised, it had struck them funny. They'd done as he told them and left after taking the chickens and helping themselves out of the storehouse and the creamery. All in all, she figured they got off mighty lucky.

Like he didn't see what memories his words raised up, Dan'l went on, "The law tells us we can't do that. We can't punish a person for what they have not done. Slade has been drunk and disorderly, he caused damage, he has intimidated people, he has been obscene in a public place, he has threatened people with a loaded pistol. We don't have a jail to put him in, and short of that, he has not committed a crime we can – try him for."

The young'uns might not have understood the hitch in his voice, at least Dotty might not, Martha wasn't sure about Timothy, but she knew what Dan'l meant, and by the anxiety etched plain in the lines on his face, so did Jacob. He meant that Slade had done nothing the Vigilantes could get involved in. Because the Vigilantes had only one punishment. If a man did something bad enough to appear before them, he was either innocent or guilty of murder and they'd hang him, just like they did the men in the winter. Some they had pursued all the way to Hell Gate, 200 miles over the Continental Divide through two feet and more of snow. Wags joked that the Vigilantes would go to Hell and back after a guilty man.

Only it was no joke. Seeing Dan'l lost in thought the way he was now, she wondered if Hell was a place they came back from.

21.

The bedsprings' squeak woke Martha from a dream of Slade on stage, laughing, while the actress wept. The men's laughter was real enough; she heard it as though muffled, like someone had stuffed a handkerchief in their mouths. She heard Dan'l pad quick and light across the floor, dip a drink of water from the clean water bucket, and tiptoe fast with long strides back into their bedroom, so his bare feet would not touch the cold floor more than need be. His side of the bed sank, and he was beside her again, shivering through his flannel nightshirt.

She sidled close to warm him, loving the way his body curved against her own. He pulled her hand across his chest and held it fast.

From closer outside, like they were in Con Orem's saloon across the street, men's laughter and shouting broke in on them, even through the closed windows and chinked walls. She remembered that Mr. Orem closed his saloon at two o'clock, and anyway he'd never tolerate Slade's habit of destroying things.

"Damn Slade," she thought she heard him whisper. She rubbed her nose between his shoulder blades and felt the little bones in his spine. "Are you worried about Slade?"

He yawned, his back muscles moving against her. "Yes."

Martha said, "He must have a powerful rage in him."

Dan'l turned over to face her. "I don't know. If so, it comes out only when he drinks." One eye gleamed at her out of the dark. "Why do you say that?"

"He's like, uh, McDowell when he drinks. Mad at the world. Wanting to hit anything in his way. Maybe it's the War, do you think?"

"The Mexican War was almost twenty years ago. He came west a couple of years before Fort Sumter fell."

"Maybe it's because he isn't 'Slade of the Overland' no more. Any more."

Dan'l turned over on his back. "It was drink that caused the Overland to let him go. He and his men destroyed the Army sutler's stores at Fort Halleck, like he destroyed Dorris's business this morning." He yawned and stretched, and his feet pulled the covers down past his shoulders, and Martha's. "He was intoxicated then, too."

She pulled the quilts up again. "Come summer I'll add another foot or so to these quilts. They are too short for you." Settled with only her face outside the covers, she went on, "I don't understand why he drinks, then. He has to know it'll land him in trouble." For that matter, Martha could not understand why McDowell drank, but in McDowell's case the drink only made his bad temper worse. It did not change him from one man to another, like with Slade.

"Why does any man drink to excess? Because it's hard to stop once you pass a certain point." Dan'l's silent laugh vibrated to her through the bed. "When I was a boy, maybe fifteen or sixteen, one night I drank some of my father's whiskey. I got tipsy. The next night, my grandfather made me drink until I was sick. Then he made me clean it up. That's how I learned to stop when my lips turned numb."

She giggled, too, and they were silent for a while.

"I'll pray for that," said Martha.

"He has to stop. We can't go on this way. People are running out of patience."

"He must crave it something fierce."

"I guess. I don't understand that myself."

"I do. I get to craving things when I'm in the family way, and then I can't hardly think for wanting them so much. Like tomatoes, or anything sour or salty. Maybe that's how Slade craves drink."

"Yes, but the difference is you don't go rampaging through town destroying people's livelihoods."

At the mental picture of herself, seven or eight months pregnant, waving a Colt revolver, robbing the grocers of their canned sardines, Martha had to laugh. After a second or two, she felt the bed shaking as Dan'l joined in.

A while later, he murmured, "Nonetheless, tomorrow we'll have to stop Slade. Somehow."

She lay for a time listening to Slade's noise from outside. Virginia City, its name more ambition than fact, had one main thoroughfare, Wallace, one street parallel to it on either side, and two cross streets. Slade and his men could not get far enough away for their noise not to be heard. She thought about Mrs. Slade, how she could hold her head up with her husband taking on so. Martha still felt like she trailed every one of McDowell's misdeeds, his every empty bottle, behind her like tin cans tied to a dog's tail. And like the dog, she would never run fast enough to be rid of them.

22.

Flying high overhead, an eagle screamed, dove at him, and as it came nearer, it had a woman's face, and the woman shrieked, a high, off- key D-sharp. Dan sat bolt upright out of a restless sleep. Martha lay peacefully snoring beside him, her thick dark braid lying over her shoulder. The woman screamed again. Women. Fully awake, he sorted out more than one woman screaming on Wallace Street.

He rolled out of bed, his heels landing, thump, on the cold wood floor.

Alarm and sleep thickened Martha's voice. "What's happening? You all right? The child?" She flung back the covers.

"Everything's fine. Something's happening down on Wallace. I'm going to take a look." He tucked his shirt into his trousers, buttoned them, hurried on swift stocking feet to the front door, pulled on his boots, put on his coat and hat. Slinging the rifle over his shoulder, he lifted the bar, pulled the latch, and stepped out into the raucous night.

The noises told him what was happening before he turned the corner and saw. Deep-throated laughter, whoops, and howls countered women screaming, glass breaking, wood splintering. At Fancy Annie's, scraps of sheets and torn blankets floated down from the second story, and feathers like snow leaked from torn pillows shaken out of second-story windows.

143

Hair streaming behind them, women, clutching bits of clothing about themselves, fled barefoot into the street. Dan glimpsed an exposed breast, the curve of a naked buttock. A man grabbed a woman and hauled her back inside, shouting, "I got mine!"

Slade, bottle upended to his mouth, swayed on his feet, hollered something Dan did not quite catch, but which sounded like, "Drinks on me, boys!"

From up and down the street, men came out of their stores, carrying shotguns and rifles. Dan roared, "Stop this at once!" Amid the horror at the attack on the brothel, he knew a rising fear: One trigger pulled in earnest would start a war. Other voices shouted, "Stop! Stop, goddammit! Stop, you sonsabitches!"

The ferment rolled on, carried on laughter greased by liquor farther up Wallace, leaving their destruction behind. Two grinning men ran out of Fancy Annie's, buttoning their trousers, and disappeared into the group following Slade. As they lurched whooping up the street, Dan saw that Slade's following had grown. Where there had been five or six men, now there were nine, maybe ten. God damn it! He swore to himself. Some men of the town —

"That bastard," said a woman close behind his left shoulder. "That fucking son of a bitch."

Turning, Dan found Helen Troy glaring at him out of one eye. The other had swollen shut. Her hair fell around her shoulders, and her dress was ripped. Shivering, she clutched its remnants about her. He held the rifle between his knees and stripped off his coat to put it around her shoulders. For the first time he realized saw how small she was, not much taller than Martha, who stood, they reckoned, five feet one in her bare feet. "Thank you," she said, but the shivering did not stop.

"You need some of your own medicine," Dan said. Around them, sober men moved wrecked items into the saloon. In the morning the women would see what could be salvaged. He gave her his arm, and after a moment, she laid her hand on it and leaned on him as he helped her inside. Turning upright a wooden chair with only one broken leg, he helped her to sit on it.

"Place looks like a bomb hit it," she murmured. Tears leaked out of her eyes, even the injured one, colored in shades of purple and green. Leaning forward, she wiped them on her skirt.

A thin girl, limping, brought her a fringed shawl. "I found this, Miss Troy."

"Thank you, Eileen." Helen Troy rose, and Dan took the coat back, slung the rifle on his shoulder once again. She put on the shawl, which Dan saw was made of heavy silk, embroidered with big peony blossoms in pink, red, and white against a green background.

"Yes'm. I brung this, too." From a large pocket in her skirt, she took a flask and gave it to the madam, watching enviously while her employer took a large drink. At no time did she so much as glance at Dan, who felt her watching him from the corners of her eyes. "Ma'am," Eileen said, "if'n gentlemen come tonight, I think some of us is already pretty hard-used."

Helen Troy reached up a patted the child's cheek. "Here." She offered the flask. "You look like you could use something —" Appearing to understand at last what the youngster meant, her other hand went to her mouth. "No."

The girl's eyes filled. She nodded, and the tears ran down her face. A thin child, her breasts had hardly bloomed. How old was she, Dan wondered. Helen Troy lifted up her arms and enfolded the girl onto her lap, into the shawl, as Dan had seen Martha take Dotty into her own warmth. More than once.

I got mine. Dan recalled the screaming woman dragged into the saloon. The ugly word took shape in his mind. Rape. He knew why Eileen limped, why bruises colored her bare upper arms, why a dark knot appeared on her jaw.

He thought of a man big as himself, forcing this waif, his strength against the girl's pathetic attempt to defend herself, fend off the man, being hit, strong hands pulling her knees apart, finding the place, inserting himself, and the girl's screams and ineffective batting and kicking fueling the man's pleasure, his glee that she wept in terror as he rode her into hell. He knew how that might be, he imagined it, and it shook him, tightened his grip on the rifle. He felt the blood surge in his veins, beat in his temple, set the scalp cut to throbbing. What man could do that? By God, he didn't need telling that McDowell had taken Martha. Never mind that they were married, that in law he could use her as he pleased, any man was a disgrace to manhood if he would force a woman. Let alone this youngster.

Or Dotty. Blessed little Dotty, not much older than this one, with her innocent delight in "pretties" as she called them, already drawing men's looks with her budding figure and her blonde hair, as women speculated about Timothy, barely sixteen, a big blond boy with widening shoulders and an embarrassing child's squeak to his voice. They took after their father in looks, Martha had said. Not in disposition, thank God.

Miss Troy's good eye glared at him over the waif's head. "She was training to be a cook. A cook, damn it. She's hardly got her monthlies yet." The other eye was swelling as he watched.

"What help do you need?" he asked.

She shook her head, gestured out at the room where a few townsmen were trying to sort through the wreckage. "We'll have help with this. I'll need you tomorrow. I'm gonna get Slade, and I want you to help."

Enthroned among the ruin of her business, wearing the brightly colored shawl, one eye swollen shut, she glared out of the good eye. "I'll sue that son of a bitch for everything he's got."

"Yes," Dan said. "Come see me in the morning."

As he walked away, she called after him, "I won't be fobbed off with Beni's ears. Legal tender, indeed, the bastard. He's got two ranches, that big herd of dairy cows. I'll ruin him sure as he's ruined me."

At home, he barred the door, laid the rifle across its pegs and hung up his coat. Leaving his boots by the front door, he padded into the bedroom and undressed. When he slid under the covers in his longjohns and socks, teeth chattering partly from the cold and partly from reaction and in-held anger, Martha put her hand on his shoulder. He turned to her.

"Slade and his bunch attacked the Shebang and Fancy Annie's," he whispered. "They've ruined both Moll Featherlegs and Helen Troy." She stroked his side. "We can't be sure it was just Slade's men. There may have been some others involved. I doubt we'll ever know for sure." Her hand rested on his hip.

"I heard screaming," she said, her mouth on his ear.

"Yes. It was bad."

Her hand reached for the lower buttons in his underwear.

He took hold of her hand. "They made me ashamed of my sex."

She freed her hand to work on the first button. "You got no call to be ashamed of nothin'."

23.

Maria jolted awake. Beside her, Jemmy fought the blankets, thrashing and kicking. One hard little heel caught her in the midriff, and gasping, she lost her grip on him. He rolled toward the fire, burned down to glowing embers. Breathless still, she snatched him back.

Holding the struggling child, she crooned to him between breaths, "Don't cry, little baby, don't cry, your mama's here, don't cry little boy, don't cry." Bit by bit, he quieted. She felt his breathing slow as he relaxed. She smoothed his black hair and kissed the tear-stained cheeks. "Mama," he said without opening his eyes.

"Shhhh, I'm here. You're safe."

He slept.

She knew his nightmares by now. When he screamed, "Fire," he saw flames leaping against the black sky to lick the snowflakes drifting down, and when he cried out, "Mama," he relived her long, black hair burning, as she ran from the house in flames. He whimpered when he found his little sister's frozen body in the dawn snow.

Though she done her best always to comfort him, he still sometimes lived that night over in his sleep. It was Joe's fault, too. The men he'd sent to recover Overland property had got drunk, fought with Jemmy's father, killed him and his Indian wife and burned down their cabin. Their little daughters, asleep when Joe's riders came, had run into the night clad in just their night-dresses and frozen to death, but Jemmy had survived. She imagined those drunken men on horseback, whooping and shooting, silhouetted in the flames, and falling embers blackening the snow stained red.

Joe, you have a lot to answer for. Maria spoke to him in her mind as she tucked the quilts around Jemmy. Damn you, Joe, you promised to come home, you promised to take me to see Kate Harper. You promised, Joe. Damn it, you promised. You promised me, you promised Jemmy you'd make it up to him, be his father. You like the whiskey better'n us? Better'n me?

Damn it, Joe, come home. Come home.

VIRGINIA CITY

MARCH 10, 1864

24.

Carrying the empty milk pail in one hand and a
lighted lantern in the other, Dan stepped over
the mudsill into the unsettling wind. The dog
whined to come along, so he set down the pail and put
the lantern in it to free his hands and untie the dog. Picking up lantern and pail again, he set off down Jackson.
Canary bounded here and there, his yellow coat visible
in the early morning twilight. Hardly anyone was about,
though candlelight flickered in a few windows. As he
noticed the quiet, the wind switched about and carried
men's rowdy laughter to him.

Slade. Dan cleared his throat and spat.

He paused while the veins in his neck swelled, and
the drum pounded in his head. He took hold of his temper as he might the reins on a panicked horse, to check
its headlong flight, wrapping the lines around his fist,

either to stop it or be carried into destruction. The dog came back and sat at his feet and whined.

"He didn't do it to them, did he?" Dan asked the yellow dog. "He just drank and laughed while the women screamed. But he did wreck Dorris's store, and who's to say last night wasn't revenge for Miss Troy making him leave yesterday? Drunk or sober, damn him, he's responsible for that young girl's rape. And for any others. By God, the sober man is responsible for the drunk."

Having made that speech, if only to a dog, he felt his breath coming even, the drumbeat fading to a manageable level. "Let's get our milk," he said. The dog grinned and bounced up, wagging his tail.

By now, Dan figured, Slade had not slept for more than twenty-four hours. How long could he go without sleep? He could surely not last much longer. Perhaps he would collapse from sheer fatigue and his friends could load him in a wagon and take him home.

On Wallace, the breeze snapped at his face, as if to warn him that winter had not yet surrendered to longer days. Canary jumped and skipped, squatted to do his business, leaped up and ran about on doggy errands of his own, lifting his leg every so often. Down the slope, a wagon drawn by one horse turned onto Wallace and plodded up toward them. Milk cans clanked together. Dan quickened his steps.

Slade waited with his pals outside the Nugget saloon.

Two doors down, Fancy Annie's windows were all dark.

"Milk. That's what I want. Come here, damn you. I'm thirsty." Slade's great booming laugh followed.

"Thirsty as a baby," shouted one of his pals. The others took it up as a kind of chorus: "Baby's thirsty. Baby's thirsty."

The driver stopped his horse in front of them, greeted them with a smile. Setting the brake, he wrapped the reins around it. Slade straddled a back wagon wheel, one foot on the boardwalk and the other on the axle. The milkman climbed over the driver's seat into the wagon bed, where he poured milk from a large bucket into a gallon can and handed it to him.

Slade took the can. As he lifted it toward his mouth, he leaned back, tilting it to drink. Bracing its feet, the horse shook itself, rattling the harness, jangling the trace chains, jiggling the wagon. Slade lost his balance and nearly fell. The milk splashed down his chin, onto his shirt front. His followers laughed to see it, bending over and slapping their thighs.

The milkman looked from Slade to his friends, as if uncertain whether to laugh or not, a smile twitching at the corners of his mouth, until his own merriment, bubbling up from his belly, burst out in a guffaw.

Slade poured the rest of the milk over the man's head. His men laughed louder, and Slade threw back his head and bayed his delight to the sky. "Who's laughing now?" he chortled. Dropping the can and stepping onto the boardwalk, he crouched, placed his hands against the wagon body, and shoved. Two or three of his men helped.

Dan hurried as fast as he could toward them, Canary bouncing among the ruts and mounds, tongue out, his doggy grin aping the glee on the men's faces.

The milkman jumped clear. Over went the wagon, buckets and cans and milk spilling into the street, pooling in icy ruts and running down crusted mounds of snow.

Milk dripping from his hat onto his shoulders, running down his beard and onto his chest, the milkman stood rigid, fists doubled at his sides. He stared at his work's ruin, the overturned wagon, the puddles of milk, as if he could not believe in it. His face, Dan saw as he closed in on the scene, reddened as Slade's laughter boomed out over his friends' gleeful howls. Struggling to stay upright against the twisted shafts, the horse whinnied. Yet even as he pitied the milkman, and cursed the loss of milk needed for his family, Dan had to tamp down his own laughter at both milk-drenched men. The others' wheezing laughter reminded him of a broken pump organ. Turning away, he pretended a coughing fit.

The milkman held out his hand to Slade, palm up. "You owe me two dollars in dust for all that milk."

Slade spat in his palm and pulled his pistol part way from his belt as the other man snatched back his hand.

"Hey," shouted Dan. "You've spilled enough milk, Slade."

The malevolent stare swiped across him, returned, and settled. Walking fast toward Slade, his face hot and stiff against the chill rising into his bones, Dan thought, That's three. You're using up your chances, you son of a bitch. You want to add murder to the charges of rape, malicious mischief, destruction of property? Not mine you won't. Not today.

He raised his pail. "My family needed that milk, Slade." Beside him, the dog growled.

The malice looking out of Slade's narrowed eyes vanished. "Aw, Dan, you have a good family. My little Jemmy is a good lad, too. My dear wife takes care of him like he was her own." He let the hammer of his pistol down easy, put it in his belt. Mischief lighted his face. "I bet it won't be long before you've a child of your own." As Dan thought, say one word about Martha and they'll wipe you up with the milk, Slade lifted his chin and shouted, "Not like some." Raising thumb and forefinger, he held them slightly apart and bellowed his song: "Oh, a pecker this small is a worrisome thing …." " Flinging an arm across Bill Fairweather's shoulders, waving his other hand as if directing a choir, he led his troupe up Wallace, the obscene chorus echoing from walls on both sides of the wide street.

Dan set the lantern in his pail on the board walk. The dog lapped at a puddle of milk. The milkman swiped his trembling fingers at his coat. "My God. That was Slade?" His words tumbled from his mouth so fast they slurred. "I heard he was up to his devilment, but I thought this early – what a mess. Look at this. He dumped it all, just for pure devilment." He pulled out a handkerchief, a square foot of checkered cloth, and wiped the back of his neck. "Ugh. My wife won't get this out till summer."

He meant, Dan knew, that with only one heavy coat to wear, he either must go coatless while she washed and hung all his clothes near the stove to dry, or stink of sour milk.

"Let's get this wagon up," Dan said.

Men came out of their stores, hair on end from their disturbed sleep, and took hold where they could. The bartender emerged from the Nugget, shaking his head and telling everyone he'd be glad to be shut of Slade.

The milkman took hold of his horse's bridle to steady the animal as Dan counted to three, and in one heave they righted the vehicle and set to work helping the milkman reload his empty pails and buckets and cans.

A woman wailed, "Look what he's done. There'll be no milk for my babies today. What am I to do?"

"Get canned milk," a man suggested.

"That's too dear. I ain't got that kind of money."

"My babies need milk, too," said a man. "Tell you what, I'll advance you dust for today's milk. You can pay me back when your man can work his claim again."

Someone cursed Slade, and another man snapped, "Damn it, Slade's a good man. If it hadn't been for him, we'd be starving by now without the supplies he brought in."

"When he's sober, he's a good man," said the first man. "Trouble is, these days he's drunk more often than not. Can't nobody make him quit drinking? Can't his wife make him stop? Him and his boys, they're as bad as the roughs."

Someone muttered, "Thanks to Slade, no milk to-day."

"I'll have milk tomorrow," the milkman said. "My cows are freshening right along. He raised the wagon's tailgate and hooked the chains to hold it shut. "What I'd like to know is when are the Vigilantes going to do something about him? I mean, I ask you, what good are they anyway, they can't make Slade let up?"

One or two people looked toward Dan, who kept his face noncommittal as he picked up his lantern and blew out the candle, then set it back in the bucket.

Someone chimed in, "Yeah, Stark, why haven't you-all stopped Slade?"

For a second before the milkman wiped his sleeve across his face, Dan caught a look of fear. Had he thought speaking against the Vigilantes would get him hanged? If we did that, Dan told himself, we'd hang half the men in the Gulch. "How many of you will agree to be taxed to build a jail?" Dan retorted. "Slade's friends are doing everything we can to persuade him to go home and sober up, but until we have a good stout jail to lock him up and keep him until he's sober, that's all we can do."

"I best be getting back." Raising his voice, the milkman said, "I'll have milk tomorrow." With that, he turned the horse and wagon in the street, empty buckets and cans rattling and jangling, and drove down toward the creek and Main Street.

When the clatter had died away some, another voice chimed in, "What good would a jail do? He'd sober up, get out and next thing you know, he'll be drinking again."

"That's right," said another. "He's got to stop drinking permanent. We can't take much more of his shenanigans."

"I ain't voting for no jail tax," said a man. "Now that travel's safe, soon's the snow melts out of the passes, I ain't spending another minute in this godforsaken hole."

A woman shrilled, "I'm gonna sue that bastard for what he done to my place and my girls. He's damn well bankrupted me, is what he's done. By God, Slade ain't good for business. You hearing me, Mr. Stark?"

Damn it, thought Dan. A fine thing when whores hollered at him in public. He lifted his hat, as if she were as fine a lady as Mrs. Sanders. "I've said I'll take your case, Miss Troy."

"I say you oughta hang him." A high, hectoring voice hollered from well back in the crowd.

Feeling a pressure against his leg, Dan looked down. Canary sat close beside him and slightly in front. He bent and patted the dog.

"No!" "The hell with that." "Hang him for what?" "Aw, shut up." As voices rose, people drew aside and left the speaker marooned in a space, a medium-sized man who took a fighter's stance. He squared his shoulders and lifted his chin, though he shivered in a threadbare coat so dirt-crusted its original color could not be seen. His plaid trousers were torn at the knees. Dan recognized him as one of Virginia City's ne'er do wells, who had drifted in on the tide of humanity following the gold strike, and stayed to cadge what he could without working.

Canary growled.

"Do you know the difference between hanging and lynching?" Dan demanded, in the trial voice that had reached a thousand men in the open air and won a murderer's conviction. The other man shook his head, but Dan did not need his answer. "Hanging executes a person found guilty of a capital crime on the evidence. Lynching acts without evidence, whether the victim is a murderer or not. Slade has not committed murder. Or any other capital crime," he added, spacing the words.

Someone coughed, and people shifted their feet. The man who wanted to hang Slade looked down, scuffed the toe of his boot in the snow.

"There will be no hanging," Dan said.

Several men nodded. One asked, "What can we do, then? We can't make a living if he's wrecking us every week or so."

Someone near the back of the group said, "Why don't y'all lock him in a storeroom?"

Another voice shouted, "Sure. We'll lock him in your storeroom, and you can hold off Fairweather and them other boys when they come to get him. They'll treat you just like they did poor old Dorris."

"Short of Slade swearing off drink," said Helen Troy, "I don't see there's any stopping him. Hire a tough bartender like Tomlinson and his Navy Colt."

"That's a good way to get killed," said a man.

"Tomlinson cleared them all out, what I hear," said a third man. "You was there, right, Stark?"

"That's right, " said Dan. "But as for stopping Slade, like I said, we need a jail to put him in, or any other drunk until they sober up and come to trial. If we jail Slade often enough, sooner or later, he'll come to his senses. Remember that when the County Commissioners ask you to vote for a jail tax."

The man with the high, sneering voice spoke: "I say you're scared of him, just like us."

Canary growled, stood up. Dan grabbed him by the loose skin on the back of his neck. Before the hot words crowding into his mouth could escape, Helen Troy pointed at the man. "Listen to me, you little shit. I ain't seen you walk up to Slade with a loaded gun looking at you. And where was you last night when him and his boys destroyed my place and raped my girls? Did you put a stop to it? No. Dan Stark did. He brought that repeatin' rifle and he'd a used it, too."

The man snickered. "You can't rape a whore. There's no crime there." Several other men nodded, and a few laughed outright.

"Oh?" Helen Troy yelled at them. "You want to look at their black eyes, their cut lips? Their bruised limbs? What son of a bitch gets his pleasure from hurtin' women? You?"

They muttered some, but no one argued with her. Let anyone, Dan said to himself, let anyone at all say one word about how you can't damage damaged goods, and so help me God, I'll let the dog go.

"If Slade's pistol hadn't misfired, we might have us a couple of funerals today." Not a shred of mirth remained as she said, "Maybe his'n, and then the Vigilantes would have reason and evidence a-plenty to hang

Slade." She stared at the speaker until he studied the ground as if weighing up the dirty snow for its gold. "You want the Vigilantes to hang Slade? Go ahead. Give them a reason. We wouldn't miss you a-tall."

What was the world coming to? Dan asked himself as he walked home, Canary alert and watchful by his side. He'd been called a coward in public and defended by a whore. Nonetheless, he owed her one. He wouldn't charge her for suing Slade. He'd take the case pro bono and his fee would come out of Slade's hide. And he didn't mean Beni's ears.

25.

Canary barked and would not stop. Startled, Martha sat back on her heels, leaving the scrub brush on the floor. She heard a woman's voice call, "Miz Stark, Miz Stark. I need to talk to you." What on earth? Martha asked herself.

"Can you call off the dog, please?"

As Martha rocked back and stood up, the voice took on desperation: "Please!" Thinking she looked a sight, her hair coming down, sleeves rolled up, dirty water splotches all over her best apron, she opened the door. Part way down the path, out of range of the dog's rope, a slattern hunched against the chilly breeze.

"Canary, hush up, now." The dog paid her no mind. Martha went to him and held his rope in one hand while she cupped her other hand around his mouth. "Hush. No." Just like Dan'l had taught her. It worked. When she let go of him, he stood quiet, only a vibration in his throat, and the way he crowded her knee, told her he still retained his suspicions of this visitor. Rightfully so, in Martha's opinion.

"How do, Miz Stevens." Martha did not like Isabelle Stevens, not so much on account she was one of the most soiled of the soiled doves in the town, but she was a mean one. Having a son of her own, and having raised him mostly herself, his Pap being a no-account, Martha allowed as to how Miz Stevens' boy had to come by his surly nature honest, so to speak.

Isabelle Stevens said, "I'm afeared of that there dog."

Martha said, "Is there something I can do for you? Your boy sick again?"

"No, no, he ain't. We had terrible trouble last night."

"Yes, my husband told me. I'm right sorry for it."

"Your – husband – is a decent man." A sly gleam in the Stevens woman's eye, the bare hesitation around the word, husband, told Martha how easily the woman could put her in her place – just above the brothel women, or the crib girls. Don't get high and mighty with me, she was saying, you're no better'n me, being a kept woman yourself.

Maybe seeing how Martha's temper showed itself, though she said nothing and moved hardly a muscle, the Stevens woman went on in a hurry. "There's two or three needin' some doctorin', needin' it bad. Miss Troy said I was to come get you."

"Wait here," Martha said. "I won't be a minute." She hurried into the house to set aside her floor scrubbing and put on a clean, old apron, her thoughts all at sixes and sevens. Rape. A word so foul she could hardly think it, let alone use it. It was far worse than a coarse expression like 'astride,' which was never spoke, leastways not by respectable folks. It was what Dan'l had been so angry about last night, that made him ashamed.

She put together in a small satchel all the medicaments she thought she would need, and a packet of her finest needles and threads for stitching up torn flesh, same as after birthing a baby. At the door, reaching to put on her blue wool cloak, she stopped. Was this proper? Her going off to tend these injured women, these dregs of the town? Was it right? What would folks think, and her already halfway to being one of them women, by most reckonings, living with a man not her husband, who couldn't be on account she had a live husband someplace. Maybe.

Her glance found the Bible on the reading table, and a voice spoke in her mind clear as could be: Visit the sick.

There, then. Putting on her cloak, she took up the satchel and left the house.

26.

She would not watch for him, Maria vowed, because looking for him, going out to the road and shading her eyes against the brightness that was not quite a sunny day but only a lighter gray, and darker where shadows formed on the snow, that would just make him stay longer. Yet, feeding the horses in the corral, and their two cows in the barn, her body kept a lookout though she kept her eyes away from the road. She listened for the clop of Copperbottom's hooves, but all she heard was the other horses eating their hay. Her tall black thoroughbred, Billy Bay, put his head over the fence for the usual withered apple she brought him. She had forgotten it, and cuffed his nose away. When he jerked back with an indignant stare and ears turned backward, she said, "I've got more important things to think of than an apple for a horse." He pulled his head back on the other side of the rail fence, and went to bully one of the work horses away from his hay.

When she went in to fix their breakfast, Jemmy followed her. As she cut a thick slice of bread and wove it onto the toasting fork, he took dishes and forks and knives to the table and laid them as she had taught him to do, this time even remembering which side to lay the fork and knife on. He said, "Why not go 'n get him? Bring him on home? He'll get into trouble, he stays too long."

She tried a smile that fooled no one, least of all the boy. "No, he'll be all right. Ain't nothing can hurt Slade of the Overland."

Jemmy shook his head. "They's Vigilantes down there. They made rules to stop hijinks like his'n."

"They're his friends. Besides, he wouldn't thank us for spoiling his fun, you know." She thrust the toasting fork into the fire, wishing the cold lump in her stomach would warm, melt, and disappear.

"If you was to go, he'd listen. He minds what you say." His jaw set, and his lower lip thrust out.

"Drinking men don't think about anything but the drink when it's on them like it gets on him." How could she tell a child what she knew of a drunk? Joe loved her, she knew that. When the drink took him over, though, it changed Joe Slade, almost like he turned into a different man, and wasn't himself no more. When that Joe Slade came out, she could almost believe he was the man his reputation made him out to be, a dangerous killer who'd murdered more men than the Vigilantes hung.

"The toast is burning," he said.

Sure enough. Maria snatched the fork back and blew the smoke away. Pulling the blackened bread from the fork, she gave it to Jemmy and cut another slice. "Toast this slice, and I'll scrape this one."

"All right. I won't burn it either." He glanced at her from under his eyebrows, half fearful, half teasing.

Thinking she heard a horse on the road, she went to the door. Nothing. It must have been one of the horses in the corral. No riders at all on the empty road toward Virginia City.

Shoulders sagging, she went back in and closed the door behind her. When they'd come here, she'd had high hopes they could live peaceable, make a new start in a beautiful country rich in gold. No use to have hope with a drinking man, she thought, until he quits drinking. And maybe not even then.

27.

Dan felt the bandage under his fingertips. Wishing he could yank it off and give the wound a good scratch, he pulled his hand away. He stretched his arms up and yawned. His eyes were hot and dry from the strain of an hour's writing by candlelight in chalk on a slate, but paper was too scarce to use for drafts, and he would have to use black powder to make more ink. He had found no good solution to Charley Baer's problem; perhaps there wasn't one. Any way he looked at it, even pleading that Charley didn't know about the larger diameter of the head would not do the trick. Besides, Dan thought both he and his partner had tried to cheat on the water rules. He stared at the slate.

Hard upon a quick tap, the door to his office rasped open, and before the voice, before the first tip of a wide-brimmed hat, the odor preceded the woman, a scent compounded of lavender overlaying dried sweat and another female odor he refused to identify. He rose to his feet.

"Mr. Stark?"

Helen Troy came all the way in now, her hand extended in a business-like way – his business, not hers. Before she spoke, he knew Helen Troy had come to make good her threat to sue Slade. Her eye, several shades of deep purple merging into black, was still swollen shut, and she moved stiffly. He offered her the visitor's box in front of his desk, apologizing for it not being a chair with a back, but she managed a smile and a half nod to acknowledge his effort. As if she were Queen Victoria taking her throne, she sat straight-backed, adjusting her hoopskirt, peeling off her gloves and laying them in her lap, on top of her netted purse. She wore her extravagantly plumed hat at a defiant angle. A brave hat, he thought, surprised at himself for thinking so.

"How are you?" He slid the desk top aside to open the left-hand box and brought out a glass and the bottle of scotch whiskey. Her eyes widened when he showed her the label. "How's Eileen?" he asked, pouring a shot for each of them.

"Good God, you wasting that on me?"

He stopped pouring to frown at her in mock irritation. "I'll waste it on whom I wish. Even myself at times."

A smile shone in her eye, followed by tears, and she reached into her bosom for a handkerchief.

He rose to hand her the glass and waited while she blew her nose and put away the soiled cloth before she took the glass. Reseating himself, he watched her slug down the scotch. As she coughed and grabbed for the handkerchief again, he corked the bottle and put it back in the box.

Waiting for her to stop coughing, he fought with himself. Much as he wanted to punish Slade for his attacks on the town, for the rape of Eileen, he did not – double did not – want to be a whore's lawyer. Yet, remembering the winter's trial, and a witness broken because one of her whores had known where and how he had come to overhear a crucial piece of evidence, Dan saw Miss Troy as if silhouetted in torchlight flaming against the night, heard the shouted threats against his life. No matter that they had known nothing of it, he owed these women something. No matter that Slade's victims were whores, they had not earned such beatings. Eileen had not invited her rape. You can't rape a whore, came the voice from earlier this morning.

Just like you can't beat up a pugilist, came the retort. Reaching for his slate, he wrote that down. When the fighter is not in the ring, beating him up is assault and battery.

No matter that Slade himself had kept his prick where it belonged, in his pants, he had led his men on that spree. Not had he made any attempt, that Dan had seen, to control any of them. Guilt by association, by God. As one robber is guilty of murder when his partner kills someone during the course of the robbery, so Slade, being present during a rape, was also guilty of rape.

"I think I can make that stick," he said.

"What?" she asked. "Make what stick?"

"Beg your pardon, I was thinking out loud. Let's begin again." Seeing she looked mystified, he asked, "How may I be of service to you?" As his voice died away, his stomach writhed with embarrassment, the question so nearly one she might ask her own customer, if she still entertained in that way, having other women to do that part, like the owner of a grist mill, except these women ground out pleasure of a sort. He squeezed his thigh muscle hard as he could to shut off that line of thought. Neither she nor any whores here had ever known his custom. Nor would they, now that he had married Martha.

"Hell, why do you ask? You know what I want. I want to sue Joe Slade. I want to punish him. That – that hell-raiser, you know what he did last night. Or his men.

What's the difference? The bastard's bankrupted me. Raped three of my girls." She sat, back straight, her hands twisting on the handle of her purse. No tears now. The one bloodshot eye glared fierce as an eagle's sighting prey.

"Do you have a bill of damages?"

"Bill of damages?" she screeched. "He's near to bankrupted me, damn it. And you're asking if I have a goddam bill of damages? Hell, no. He smashed my place, and someone made off with a poke of gold I had sitting on a shelf under the bar. Damn him! I want to sue, and I'll take Beni's ears and his, too, believe you me. The son of a bitch."

"A bill of damages is a place to start." He began to tell her that she could also sue for loss of business and if that were not enough he could think of more reasons to convict Slade of wanton damage, disturbing the peace, being drunk and disorderly, and vandalism. Rape. He did not get the chance.

"How do we get him for rape?" The dam on her temper broke. Her stream of rage ran in full flood, so that she shook, every loose hair, bit of cloth, each plume on the extravagant broken hat. "He and his pals wrecked the place, and some bastards attacked the girls. You saw Eileen. We don't know what all they did to them, or which ones did it. Slade don't attack women, and not Bill Fairweather, neither. Them others, though. Slade opened the door, and the devil come in."

She told him precisely how many kinds of bastard Joe Slade was. Pinned behind the desk against the single board wall at his back, he could only listen and hope she would run out of steam at last. He imagined people in the store hearing this, while she damned Slade in a vocabulary of invective that would have done a steve-dore proud. Or an Army private.

"What about his wife? Their adopted son? They're innocent in all this. Ruining him would ruin them." He meant to be sure she understood the consequences of a lawsuit, that she would have an idea where a jury's sympathies might lie. Not with raped prostitutes, but with Mrs. Slade and the child, Jemmy.

She misunderstood him, and jumped up. Leaning over the desk, she shouted at him. He smelled rotten teeth and whiskey, and down the front of her dress saw sweat and powder had caked in the skin between her breasts.

"I don't see you-all doing a goddam thing about him," she yelled. "You-all, you so-called Vigilantes, you're no damn good, you'll just stand by and watch him ruin them as wants to make an honest living. Attacking defenseless women. Look what he done to Dorris, and now me, and my girls. We ain't the last ones by no means. He done this just last week, he's been doing it for months, taking the goddam town, and you-all just standing by and letting him do it." She poured her rage over him, and so much fury in a small body. "You-all hanged them boys, and Club Foot George who never harmed a fly, and you ain't done damn all about Slade. What are you doing to protect us? Ain't we got a right to earn a living same as them others?"

She raised her umbrella as if to sweep everything off his desk, and Dan snatched up the slate and ink bottle.

"Mark my words," she said, "the whole town's mighty sick of these shenanigans every time he comes to town. Whatever he's punishing us for, we didn't do it to him."

Yanking the door open, she spoke in a loud voice that even so was several notches quieter than she had used to flay Dan: "What are you-all sniggering at? Ain't you never heard a few home truths?"

Dan reached the doorway and called out to her as she stalked away, her heels beating on the planks. "I'll take your case, Miss Troy."

She stopped several feet away, and turned toward him. Chin high, she frowned at him. "You're sure, now?"

"Yes. We'll go to Judge Davis now. Let me get my coat."

The customary group of idle men, miners whose claims lay under the snow and ice and vendors of various merchandise waiting out the winter until the miners had dust to spend, sat warming themselves at the round black iron stove. As one, they rose to their feet and cheered him.

28.

"You don't want to be seen walking up the street with me." Helen Troy raised her face to look at Dan from under the brim of her flamboyant, ostrich-plumed hat. In the daylight, it looked worse than it had in candlelight. She pulled her shawl closer around her shoulders, and shivered a little in the sharp wind. "I'll see you in court." Half-turned to go into the door of her establishment, she said, "Thank you for taking the case."

"You're welcome." He did not stay to watch her go in. A sense of urgency seized him, an unexplainable feeling that he had to hurry for some reason, though there was nothing he could think of out of the ordinary. And he was tired. Lord, how tired, but overriding the weariness this feeling that he must lose no time spurred him. He quickened his stride up the street toward a clot of men outside a saloon doorway.

They craned and jostled to see inside, but no one spoke. A man broke out of the crowd, his face bleak; he shook his head at Dan, but said nothing. The crowd's odd silence made Dan think he had gone deaf. He could not hear the normal saloon sounds, tinny piano music or out-of-tune fiddling, boots thumping. Nor the talk and laughter of men whiling away winter over a card game, a drink or two. As he drew nearer, he heard the onlookers' whispered curses, a muttered question, "Can't someone stop him?" Inside the saloon, grunts and sounds, a hard thwack and squish as though someone struck a watermelon, the rind cracking, a fist smashing into soft flesh. As he shoved through the crowd, men turned pain-filled faces toward him, the faces of men who did not want to see what fixed them to the place, yet they could not bring themselves to leave.

Slade was beating two of his friends. One of them crumpled to his knees. Slade's hard fist to the other man's midsection doubled him over, but he stayed on his feet, gagging and retching as Slade drew back his fist to land another blow.

By God, Dan said to himself, this is what a mad dog is like. No one dared intervene between Slade and his intent.

Slade's fist drove into the man's mouth, snapped his head to the side. Blood spurted.

"No!" Dan hollered. Startled, Slade turned. The malign stranger glared out of his eyes.

Making his voice reasonable, Dan spoke as if inviting Slade for a drink. "Stop. You don't want to kill them, do you?" The Spencer weighed on his shoulder, but he could not touch it. He held his hands in front of his hips, palm out; by themselves they dared Slade's malignant force to do its worst, to use his famous skill with the pistol against him. It's a poker game, he thought, holding his smile, concentrating on keeping his hands steady, while all the time knowing that his hole card was his own skill with the Spencer, that he held his hands in position to swing it off his shoulder, cock, and fire the first chambered shot before Slade's pals could think of retribution.

He smiled at Slade, and pictured himself in his New York office, endlessly practicing, as he willed the imaginary deer not to escape.

The man on the floor rolled over, pushed himself to his hands and knees, found a chair. Putting both hands on the seat, he shuffled his knees closer, grabbed an arm, and crawled into it.

No one helped him. He slumped to the side, one arm dangling toward the floor, the other lying limp in his lap. He groaned.

Slade's other men carried their pistols loose in their belts. As Dan spoke, they set their beer glasses, the shot glasses, on the table and got to their feet. Fools, thought Dan. Did they not understand the other Slade could turn on one of them as easily as he did these men? What quality in the man led others to follow him blindly, slavishly? But Slade's rule by fear caused men to lower their voices to a whisper when they repeated the dreadful tales of his cruelty, how he had shot a man's dog as it lay sleeping in the shade, and just last week he had cut off a mule's ear as it stood dozing at a hitching rail. If that were not enough, there were always Jules Beni's ears. Conclusive proof of what Slade could do when drunk.

When the devil escaped its bottle and entered Slade.

Even as he held Slade's stare, the malignant stranger gave way and Slade appeared to see his two men as if for the first time.

"Dear God." He pulled a handkerchief from his hip pocket, dabbed at the blood flowing from the corner of his man's mouth. "I'm sorry. Good God, I'm so sorry, Harding, old fellow." He wiped at blood, his hands gentle as a mother's whose child is hurt.

Muttering rippled around the crowd outside as X Beidler, closely followed by Fitch, shoved through and into the saloon.

Stopping just inside the door to let his eyes adjust to the gloom, Beidler said, "For God's sake, Slade, what was it this time?"

Fitch looked down at the man on the floor and massaged his stump, his face nearly hidden by his downturned hatbrim and the full beard. "Christ, Slade, your own men. Your own."

From outside, someone called: "Here comes the doc."

The man in the chair groaned.

"Will he be all right?" Slade gave his handkerchief to Harding, who held it to his mouth, and knelt beside the chair. "We'll have you fixed up in no time, no time at all."

The doctor jogged into the saloon. "Damn it, Slade, what is it this time?" He stooped over the man in the chair. "Get me some light. I can't see a goddam thing." He put his bag down, sank to his knees, and held out a hand for a candle.

A rat emerged from a crack between the floorboards and scurried over the doctor's calves, disappeared into another crack. "Son of a bitch!" shouted the doctor. It was a small saloon, the floor made of newly sawn planks, and as they had dried and shrank over the winter, cracks between them had widened.

Peering through the gloom at the doctor and the other men, Dan realized this felt like Tuesday, when he had helped to take the muleskinner to Dr. Byam's house. Only two days ago. How much more of this would they have to endure before Slade gave in and went home? And when would he be back, Slade and his devil?

"Do you need help getting him to the Recovery?" Another thought crossed Dan's mind. "I don't want my wife tending men there any more."

The doctor rolled back the injured man's eyelid, felt along his ribs. "We won't need to move him there. He'll be all right in an hour or two." Standing up, he dusted the baggy knees of his trousers. "Your wife wouldn't be available to tend him, anyway. She's already looking after the victims at Fancy Annie's."

As Dan stared at him, absorbing this news, wondering why Helen Troy had not told him, feeling his face growing warmer and the pounding beginning in his head, he heard Fitch, behind him, upbraiding Slade.

"Damn it, Slade, you can't go on beating up men this way, or there'll be bad trouble ahead. Just go on home and sober up." Fitch flung his short arm outward.

Slade, perhaps thinking that Fitch meant to strike him, caught the arm and raised it high, bringing himself so close to Fitch that their coat buttons nearly touched. "No man tells me what to do. No man, do you hear me?" He drew back his fist, as though to strike Fitch, whose jaw muscles tightened as he raised his own doubled fist.

"You'd hit a one-armed man, Slade?" Dan tried to make his voice neutral, hoped he would not have to use the Spencer for leverage over Slade, not with so many other men ready to back up their leader. Slade's pal Bill Fairweather moved in close to Slade. The hairs rose on the back of Dan's neck, as two more of Slade's pals moved in on each side and slightly behind him, hands on the pistols in their belts.

The silence stretched out brittle and hot as blown glass.

Slade laughed, let go of Fitch's arm, and stepped back a pace or two. "You're one man with balls, Stark. Hell, no, I won't hit a cripple."

A vein bulged across Fitch's forehead. His mouth worked, collecting tobacco juice.

If he spits that mess into Slade's face, it'll all be over. Dan held his breath.

Turning his head a degree or two, Fitch spat. The ugly stream landed in a gob close enough to Slade's boot to make Fitch's point without touching it. Turning on his heel, Fitch stalked out of the saloon.

Slade laughed. "I'm thirsty, God damn it." He flung an arm around Harding's shoulders. "I'll buy you a drink to show how sorry I am." He strode forward to the bar, and the men who had come back into the saloon now that it was safe, moved aside for him.

29.

Outside, the crowd had broken up, men moving on about their business, shaking their heads, talking about Slade's latest outrage, asking how he could beat up his own men, or why they stayed on with him seeing how he treated them when drunk. Dan rubbed a hand over his face. He had always kept Slade at arm's length, not understanding why, when the man was so affable and winning in his ways. Now he knew. The bristles on his cheeks reminded him that he'd forgotten to shave this morning, perhaps yesterday morning as well, and his beard felt as scratchy as his throat, as if bristles grew there, too. About to step off the boardwalk and cross the street to Pfouts & Russell's store, he heard his name. X and Kiskadden had come out of the saloon.

"Walk with us a bit," X said. "We thought we might look in on Dorris."

"And talk this situation over," said Kiskadden. "Maybe if we put our heads together we can figure a way to —" He shook his head. "I'm blamed if I can see a way to make him go home."

They walked up Jackson, as if by agreement taking the long way round to Dorris's store, though their reason proved false because none of them could offer a way out of this situation. Slade had to give up and go home, Dan said to himself. That was the crux of it.

They turned the corner and walked up Idaho to Van Buren. There, below Dorris's place, Fitch stood talking to Sheriff Fox. As the three men joined them, Fox was counting Slade's misdeeds on his fingers. "He's broken up saloons, bankrupted poor Dorris, and now he's beaten up two of his own men. He's making the town a perfect bear garden. If we let him go on, we'll be a laughing stock."

Like Fox already was, thought Dan, after Slade's song about him, as if the gossip about him and his wife weren't humiliating enough. She had left him for another man, then returned to Fox's bed and board with a sack of gold from her paramour. Then, with Fox's help, she had left on a stage and taken the gold with her to – to where? What was her ultimate destination, anyway? Would she ever return to Fox? Or would she just keep going with her nest egg? He said, "They've also bankrupted Fancy Annie's. Helen Troy came to me to file suit against Slade for what they did last night."

X said, "They wrecked the Shebang, too. Moll Featherlegs is bankrupt."

"Three businesses bankrupted, then, not to mention the damage to a few saloons here and in Nevada," said Fitch. "The bastard will kill someone pretty soon unless we stop him."

"Did they attack the women at the Shebang like they did at Fancy Annie's?" Dan asked.

"I don't know about that." Fox swallowed, coughed, and turned his head to spit. "Damn them, they did enough. I wouldn't be surprised."

Fitch snorted. "You can't rape a whore," he said. "They get paid for it. If it gets rough, well, they have to know the risks going in. It's part of the territory."

"I can't believe he'd do that," Kiskadden said. "Not Slade. He loves his wife. He wouldn't go to a whore, or have anything to do with one. He's like you, Stark. He's, he's – temperate in his habits."

"Not in his drinking," Dan said. "There's no temperance there at all."

Kiskadden held out his hands as though to plead with them. "The Troy woman must —"

"There's no sign Slade did anything but stand back," said X, "and let his men have their fun. That's the problem. He brings that bunch into town, gets drunk with them, and what he doesn't do, he lets them do."

"Them and some wasters like Bill Fairweather." Fox's voice rose higher in pitch to a complaining whine that grated on Dan's ears like a fiddle out of tune. "I tell you, what devilment Slade don't get up to, Fairweather does. And him the richest man in the Gulch."

Kiskadden had been looking past their shoulders toward Wallace. "Watch it. He's coming this way. Slade, I mean."

The men waited without speaking. Dan thought about Fairweather, one of the discoverers of Alder Creek gold. He had panned the creek for a little "tobacco money" and found a strike so rich there seemed no end to it. Even after the flood of prospectors, miners and suppliers into the Gulch, his claim would make him millions, but he seemed not to care. Grinding his toe at a lump of frozen snowmelt, Dan shared Fox's frustration. How was it that a man would value the poison in a bottle over the immeasurable wealth in his hand?

By his steady pace, Slade looked as sober as a parson, but when their circle opened to include him, Dan saw the alcohol blush on his cheeks, and the tiny veins a fine red mesh in his eyes. He stank of bad whiskey.

Swaying on his feet, he said, "Christ, I'm sorry. God forgive me, I don't know what got into me. My men are good men, all of them. Those two, especially. They said something, and I – I don't know …." His voice trailed off. Tears shone in his eyes, spilled over, ran down his cheeks. "How could I have done that?" He stripped off his leather gloves, studied the swollen knuckles, and flexed his hands, tightening them into fists, stretching out his fingers. "What gets into me? That's not me. Dear God, how could I?" He wiped his face with his bare hand, pinched a thumb and forefinger over the bridge of his nose. He put his gloves on, and put his hands in his pockets, and squirmed inside his coat, as though his body itched. His feet could not find purchase on the slippery ground. He pulled his hands out of his pockets, pulled off the gloves and unbuttoned his coat, drew the gloves on again.

All the time, he repeated, "What made me do that? How could I?"

Dan thought, Slade feels his crimes. He's suffering remorse. Exchanging a look with X, he dared to hope that perhaps now they could convince Slade to go home. When he tried to speak, his lips felt stiff, as if they did not want to let the words out. "You look done in. Maybe it's time to go home and get some rest." In his ears, the concern for Slade rang false, like an actor's lines badly learned.

"Yeah," Fox said, "You can go home and sober up. Stop this goddam drinking before someone gets hurt bad."

"Or they die," said Fitch.

Irritation flared in Slade's face, and his eyes narrowed. When Kiskadden put his hand out as though to touch Slade's arm, he took a half step back. Kiskadden's hand fell to his side. "Think of Mrs. Slade. Think of Jemmy. You have a family. Think of them."

"Yes," X said. "Your wife will be waiting and wondering what's happened to you."

Not so, Dan said to himself. Poor Mrs. Slade would know what was happening. She would know her husband was drinking and raising hell. Why didn't she make him stop? He remembered the ancient Greek play; the wives had withheld their favors until their husbands stopped making war and peace reigned. Had Mrs. Slade thought of that?

Slade said, "Oh, yes. My dear wife. Yes, yes, you're right. I'll do that. I'll go home. Dear Maria. She is the light of my life, don't you know." As he spoke, they all walked with him down and around the corner to his horse, standing tied in front of a saloon, head drooping.

"Have you fed or watered the poor beast?" asked X. "Or unsaddled him since you rode down here?"

"Unsaddled him? Yes, yes, indeed. We shared a stall last night for a little nap. When we get home, I'll give him grain and a rubdown. Rest him. He's a good boy, old Copperbottom." He patted the horse's shoulder. Dan unwrapped the reins from the hitching rail, and gave them to Slade, who fumbled with them a minute before he had them sorted out, one on each side of the animal's neck. Taking both reins in his left hand along with a handful of mane, he twisted the left stirrup around. "God, my head aches." The horse sighed and shifted his feet the better to take Slade's weight as he put his foot in the stirrup.

Dan held his hands behind his back, the rifle stock hard against his wrists, and crossed his fingers. Would this be it? Had they truly persuaded Slade to go home? He didn't know how many false starts they could tolerate. Especially Fox, who waited and watched Slade out of narrowed eyes.

X stood at the animal's head, petting him, scratching his blaze.

Slade swung aboard. "You fellows are right. I'll just go on home." As he reined the horse around to ride away, laughter burst from a saloon, along with a few notes on a fiddle.

Bill Fairweather came out laughing. "You going home already, Slade? It's early yet, and there's a party on."

Slade whooped. "Hell, yes. Let's have ourselves some fun."

Kiskadden called after him: "No, Slade, think of your wife. Think of –"

The malevolent stranger looked out of Slade's eyes, all humor gone. "No one gives orders to Slade of the Overland." Flipping his middle finger at them, he reined the horse around, and booted the animal up Wallace. "Last one to the garbage dump is a horse's ass!" His remaining friends rushed from the saloon and jumped onto their horses. They followed him, hollering at the top of their voices, firing their pistols in the air.

Men leaped out of the way, scurried for cover. Merchants locked their doors and drew the shades, and turned the "Open" signs to "Closed."

They watched him go, by a nod, a glance, a furrow between the eyes, and part of a shrug they read each other's minds, each man muttering curses that were close to prayer: Christ almighty what do we do now? X's mustache drooped at the ends. Dan felt his shoulders sag as though a hundredweight barrel had settled on them. Fitch's brows came together. Kiskadden blinked rapidly, and tears shone in his eyes. Fox took off his hat and ran his fingers through his hair, resettled the hat on his head.

Fitch said, "We're running out of options." Even he, Dan thought, could not bring himself to say the dreaded word. Not now, though he had used it freely enough earlier.

"No," said X and Dan together. Dan said, "There's the court."

"Yes, yes," Kiskadden said. "He respects the court. It has always worked before."

The ends of X's mustache lifted, and hope gleamed in his dark eyes. "He likes Alex Davis."

"I'll get a warrant for both him and Fairweather," said Fox.

"I don't know. I think we should get a consensus." Fitch stared at Dan, daring him to disagree.

Damn you, Dan told him silently, you hope to get a consensus to use the rope, to treat them like the five on the hill. "Nothing can be done without a quorum of the Executive Committee," he reminded them. Even if they found nine members, Williams and Lott and others being in Nevada, they could get no consensus to treat Slade as a murderer. He might be a murderer, his reputation screamed murder as much as Beni's ears, but he had killed no one during his time in the Gulch. Only Fitch thought of the ultimate punishment now.

"All right," X said, "let's go. We'll meet behind Pfouts's store. Get as many of the Executive Committee as you can. Fast. We have to stop him quick."

Dan said, "I have to meet Helen Troy in court. You boys go on without me."

X planted himself in Dan's path. Feet spread, fists on his hips, nearly a foot shorter than Dan, he was an implacable obstacle. "What do you mean you have to meet her in court? With what we have to do?"

"She's suing Slade for ruining her and for what his men did to her girls. I took the case. We'll show Slade in court that wrecking this town doesn't pay."

30.

Seeing Dan'l pelting her way, Martha stopped short, her skirts whipping about her ankles, and waited for him to stumble to a stop beside her. "You should not be out here," he said. "What are you thinking?" He seized her upper arm, hauled her like a rag doll toward opposite board walk.

She judged it better to go along with his greater strength, seeing's how it was where she'd been headed anyhow. "Whyever not? I'm on my way to see if Miz Hudson has a tincture of —"

"Slade is worse than – What? I've been told – You really are tending those, those —"

When he could not say the word, on account honest women weren't supposed to know it or any words like it, she cut him off. "I am tending the women Slade's men – hurt." She could not speak the word, rape, even to Dan'l.

They reached the board walk, but he did not let loose, or slow down one notch. The jewelry store and the stores in Kiskadden's Stone Block were closed, she noted as he dragged her along.

"I know what they are, but the good Lord, He didn't call me to help only the decent folks."

They stopped in front of the Eatery, and he pounded his fist once on the door. About to bring it down again on the wood, he paused, stared at her.

"He come eating and drinking with sinners, after all," she said.

"Good God," he said, "what sort of woman have I chosen to spend my life with?"

A woman's shrill high voice yelled curse words. Spun off her feet, her face buried in his coat, Martha twisted herself in the grip of his left arm. "I can't breathe," she gasped. He let go a notch, enough so she could turn her head and breathe, and see.

Across from them, by the vacant corner, Helen Troy screamed at Slade, who sat his horse with a bottle in his hand. "You hear me, Joseph Slade? You hear me? I'll get you for what you and your men done to me and mine! Damn you to hell, you son of a bitch, you won't have even one bead left on that fancy suit when I get done with you."

Dan'l pounded twice more on the Eatery door.

Something evil peered out of Slade's eyes. Martha come near as a non-Papist could to crossing herself, and she wished she knew some gesture that would shield her from that demon in Slade. Behind her, the door opened. Albert came out and stood aside. As he looked beyond Dan'l across the street at Slade, his deep black color turned a shade lighter.

Dan'l thrust her into the Eatery, into safety behind its log walls. Martha did not protest. She had come as close as she had never wanted to seeing the devil, like reaching to pet a friendly kitten only to have it change into a cat-amount and bare its teeth. God help Helen Troy facing down Slade, and her only an outraged madam in a plumed hat and hoop swinging in the wind.

Dan'l said, "Stay with Mrs. Hudson until I come for you. We'll settle Slade's hash this very afternoon."

Albert closed and barred the door, turning the log cabin into a miniature fort. Not until some minutes after Lydia had settled her on the back bench close to the stove, could Martha stop trembling. She warmed her cheek on a mug of ersatz coffee. "Mr. Slade, he looked like —" The word would not be spoken. Trying again, she said, "I ain't never — Like he had a —"

"A devil, Miz Stark, begging your pardon," said Albert.

"Yes. Like that." Martha sipped at the sweet thick brew that comforted her mouth.

"That Slade," harrumphed Lydia. "He has a devil, all right, but it lives in a bottle. If he would quit taking strong drink, he would be a decent man. But when he takes a drink he lets the devil out."

From where she had been resting in her soft chair that stood in a corner behind the stove, Tabby said, "It be the ruin of him someday."

"I do hope not." Without consciously deciding, Martha prayed for Joseph Slade and for Dan'l, who had gone out to fight Slade's devil.

31.

"Slade makes bleeding cowards of us all."
Fitch's jaws worked hard on the new
chaw, the muscles knotting and loosening
so that his comment slurred past the stuff. "The son of a
bitch." He crouched behind a freight wagon parked behind Pfouts and Russell's store.

Dan leaned against the wagon and pretended to con-
sider the nags at the bottom of the draw in the Elephant
Corral. They snuffled along the ground, looking for remnants of the hay they'd been fed that morning. Waiting
for X to bring the others, he wished to hell this meeting
– if that's what it would be – would start so he could get
on with Helen Troy's business. A knife-edged wind
scraped along the back of his neck, and he shivered as if
an owl had flown over his head.

They met here, instead of in Kiskadden's upper room
or gathering in Pfouts's store, because they did not want
either Kiskadden or Alex Davis to know the Vigilantes
were meeting about Slade.

He raised up to his full height to look over the wagon,
uphill. No sign of Slade – thank God – but no sign of
anyone else, either. Leaning on the wagon again, he said,
"Damn. I need to be in court."

"You are," said Fitch.

"Like hell. This is no court. It's not the Tribunal, either." He stopped. Why was he telling Fitch something

he already knew? The Vigilante Tribunal needed a quorum of the Executive Committee – nine men, out of seventeen.

"Close enough, if need be," Fitch said.

The raw breeze ruffled the horses' winter coats as they lipped along the ground, searching for fodder. Two of the animals looked toward the men, ears pricked. Fitch rose to his feet. "Here comes X and the Mayor." He muttered under his breath and spat tobacco juice.

"What have you got against Pfouts?" Dan asked.

"He's from Missouri, too, but he's never had the balls to fight."

"He was in Texas by then, wasn't he?"

Fitch grumbled something around the chaw that sounded like "no excuse."

"Oh," Dan said, "you think he should have gone back to fight and die for the Cause?" Dangerous, he knew, but he did not feel like controlling the sneer on his lip and in his voice.

"What d'you know? You're a rich goddam Yankee that bought a substitute." Fitch matched him contempt for contempt.

Before Dan could snap that the Southerner had no right to talk about rich, having owned a cotton plantation and a hundred slaves, Pfouts and X joined them. Pfouts walked up by Fitch's side, while X, holding his shotgun in the crook of his elbow, came to stand by Dan. We're lining up North and South, Dan said to himself.

"We sent for Williams," X said. "He'll be here soon."

Fitch said, "X, you still think you can talk him into going home?"

Beidler shook his head. "He ain't listening." He looked at Dan. "Like you said, we're running out of options." He seemed to stare at the horses in the corral, but his eyes were unfocused.

Dan looked over the wagon bed. "Here's Sanders." Wilbur Sanders, his blue greatcoat an insult to all Confederate sympathizers, walked down the steep slope, his every step an agile dance to keep his footing. He joined them with a general nod of greeting. "Williams is not far behind me."

Sure enough, as he spoke Dan heard a horse's hooves clopping on the frosty slope. James Williams riding, and Jeremiah Fox walking beside him, one hand grasping the piggin strings on Williams's saddle skirt. The two joined the others, and dismounting, Williams holding the reins as though expecting to ride straight back to Nevada City. Glancing around, he thought, Slade unites us all. Union and Confederate, proslavery and abolitionist, and every shade of political opinion in between, we're here to decide: What to do about Slade?

"We have to stop Slade," said Pfouts. "The question is how." He turned his head this way and that, looking each man in the eye, gathering their agreement, inviting their ideas.

"Same way we stopped them others." Fitch pointed his thumb toward the hill beyond Daylight Creek.

Before he finished, most of them were shaking their heads, No.

Looking at Sheriff Fox, Pfouts answered Fitch. "That's out of the question. If we did that, people would say that we acted because of gross insults to Jeremiah and me."

"That's right." The Sheriff nodded, but a glint in his eye made Dan wonder how sincere he might be. Certainly, Slade did not like him, but he did like Pfouts, who had defended him and pleaded with him to stop drinking whenever he went on one of these sprees. Then why, Dan asked himself, did he publicly humiliate and ridicule both men, one his friend and the other – Fox – whom he disliked?

"We don't use the rope to settle personal scores," Dan said.

"We can't even seem to do so." Sanders tilted his head toward the hill rising the other side of Daylight Creek. "We already have enough against us, with their friends howling murder every chance they get."

Dan shuddered, hoped the icy blade drawn up his spine might be taken for a shiver in the raw wind. It didn't have to be this way, said the voice from his nightmares, and he'd said, You should've chosen differently. Aloud, he said, across the others' muttered agreement, "We can't be seen to go easy on him because he's a friend to some of us, either."

"Right," said Sanders. "It has to be one law for everyone."

Williams said, "It's a crying shame. He's a good man, saving the drink. But when the drink takes over, it's like the devil comes in on him."

"You couldn't ask for a better friend when he's sober," said Beidler.

Did no one think of the insult to the actress, the bankruptcies, the injured men and women? Dan wondered. What kind of friend was a man attacked his friends and allowed rape, even of whores? When men were so inebriated, could they tell the difference between whores and honest women? Between our wives and daughters – Christ!

As if the light had changed, the clouds drawing apart and letting through a shaft of sunlight, Dan saw everything differently. What an ass he was. Despite the danger to Martha just night before last, he'd been thinking like a single man, not a married man with a wife and youngsters to watch over. He was a father, albeit a stepfather. He had a duty their own father had never stood up for. If something should happen to either Dotty or Timothy – unthinkable. That so far they were safe merely testified to dumb luck.

"Damn it, we have to get control of Slade."

"You're right," said Fox. "We're past putting his sprees down to hijinks and boys will be boys, damn it. When he's on a bender, people go in fear of their lives, like they" – a nod toward the hill – "ran things."

"There's no question," Dan said, "that people shouldn't have to dodge stray balls when they come to town." A thought struck him, and his stomach clenched. Are we assembling evidence? Are we talking ourselves into using the noose? It can't come to that. Yet Slade posed a danger they had to deal with or go back to those days.

Sanders said, "My little boys run all over town, along with other children. A bullet could strike any one of them at any time."

Christ, thought Dan. "My stepdaughter goes back and forth to school, and down to Cover street to play with little Sheehan girl." "Do we have to wait for a little one to catch a bullet?" demanded Fitch. "Or the whole town to catch fire when he shoots out a lantern in a saloon? He's got to be stopped."

"We agree on that," said Sanders. "Until we can establish a true legal system, complete with duly constituted courts and a jail, we have the obligation to protect the people. Ourselves included."

"On the other hand," Dan said, "we can't hang a man for drunk and disorderly or endangering public peace. Those aren't capital crimes."

Sanders nodded. "True enough."

"He does respect the court, though," Williams said.

"Yes," said Beidler. "He likes Davis, and respects him, too. He'll do what Davis tells him."

Looking satisfied for the first time since Slade had begun to sing about him, Fox said, "All right. I'll ask the Judge for a warrant. Two warrants. One for Slade and one for Fairweather. What Slade doesn't get up to, Bill does."

Pfouts looked around for their opinions, but even Fitch was silent, though his jaws worked the chaw as though it would be his last. "All right, then. Have Judge Davis write out an arrest warrant and serve it on him, Jeremiah."

"I'd like witnesses to what happens." The Sheriff glanced from one to the other. "How about Stark and Fitch?"

Dan shook his head. "I have other business to tend to. Helen Troy asked me to represent her in a suit against Slade for demolishing her place and mistreating her employees." It was as near as he could come to saying Slade's men had raped her girls.

"I'll help," Fitch said, "but what if this doesn't work?" He waited a second. "What then?"

In a thick silence, they consulted with each other: a quarter nod, shoulders set straighter, a foot squared with the other, a mouth tightened in a resolute line.

Pfouts said, "We'll cross that bridge when we come to it. If we do."

32.

D an escorted Helen Troy through Pfouts's store, ducking low-hanging horse collars, holding the rifle stock so that it did not knock against the display cases, or upset the careful arrays of miners' pans and hammers or ladies' kid gloves. Paris Pfouts, warming his posterior at the stove in a back corner by the door into the court room, nodded to Dan and ignored his client. Pfouts did not approve of fancy women. "Everyone's in the courtroom," he said, tilting his head to his left, toward the door.

Dan halted. "Everyone?"

"Indeed so." Pfouts's Missouri accent, its vowels resonating through his nose and flavored with overtones of a low-slung Texas drawl, made Dan think of prickly pear mixed into thick sourdough pancakes. "Your client has many friends, it would appear."

Though Pfouts would not look at her, Dan heard Helen Troy gasp. As he ushered her through the back door, she put her palms to her bruised face and her shoulders shook. Looking down, he could not see her expression; the ridiculous hat hid her face from his view. But in the courtroom, perhaps twenty men – mostly miners and a few men of substance, as well as some Dan thought wasters and ne'er-do-wells – applauded when she appeared in the doorway.

Judge Alex Davis sat on the raised platform, perhaps six inches off the floor, bent over the table that served for a bench. He wrote on a paper in the light of a candle at his left elbow, but looked up when they came in. Seizing his gavel, he banged it once on a wood block near his right hand. "Silence!" His whip-crack voice stopped the noise once. By a nod he acknowledged their arrival, and went back to writing while Fox, holding his hat, waited in front of him. At a smaller table sat the clerk, a young lawyer who had taken notes at the first trial in December.

Walking in after the Troy woman, Dan said to himself, we have both the judge and the jury pool assembled and waiting. Now all we need is the defendant.

Judge Davis was still writing, when heavy boots sounded in the store. Everyone looked toward the doorway. The Judge dipped his pen in the inkwell. The footsteps stomped closer. Dan heard Paris Pfouts say, "Hello, Mr. Fairweather." His right hand sought the Spencer's stock, and he looked for a clear place to stand should he have to take it from his shoulder.

Bill Fairweather hardly paused in the doorway, but stalked to the judge's bench and stopped beside Fox. Ignoring the Acting Sheriff, he said, "I heard you're writing up warrants for my arrest and Joe Slade's. That them?"

"Yes." Dipping his pen again, Judge Davis looked up, his expression pleasant and calm, and went back to his writing.

Watch out. Even as the warning formed in Dan's mouth, and he took a step toward the bench, trying to get clear of the people around him, he heard more heavy steps in the store coming toward them. Fairweather snatched the papers from under the Judge's pen. "You ain't gonna arrest me for nothin', Goddammit!"

His hand on the rifle stock, Dan ground his teeth. He could not get clear. Trapped among the shifting onlookers, pressed back toward a wall as they sought to get as far away as possible, he had no shot, though here was the provocation he had been waiting for. He could not bring the rifle to bear without an innocent person coming in the sights – his or Fairweather's. Without a clear field, he could not cover Fairweather.

Joseph Slade stopped just inside the doorway, and some of his taller friends looked past him into the courtroom.

Fairweather ripped the papers to pieces, threw the shreds on the floor, and ground them under his boot. "Take that for your Goddam warrant!" shouted Fairweather.

Slade whooped and slapped his knee. "You tell 'em, Bill. Attaboy! Give 'em hell."

Fairweather shouted at Davis, "You and your Goddam pissant court can go to hell and take your fucking warrants with you."

"Go on, Bill, I'm with you!" Slade clapped his hands and laughed, his glee echoing off the walls. He rocked on his heels, and for a moment Dan thought he might fall backward, but he rocked onto his toes and pulled out his pistol. As if they had waited for a signal, Slade's friends pulled theirs, metal hissing against leather and cloth, and hammers cocking with a ratchet clatter as the weapons cleared their throats, ready to speak.

Fairweather sneered, "That warrant is no damn good, and you know it. This ain't a proper court. It's a trumped-up deal, that's what it is, a set up by the gol-durned Vigilantes. "

"That warrant was proper," said Davis, getting down from the bench. "Entirely proper, and this is a court of law." A thin man who loved to run and commonly won any footrace he entered, Judge Davis's face seemed fleshless, the bones covered only with skin. Or perhaps that was the effect of near starvation on his long, poverty-stricken walk West.

Facing Slade, he spoke as one reasonable man to another, his voice soothing and calm. "You don't want me killed, do you?" he asked Slade, as if asking about the possibility of snow, as if the pistol's single eye did not glare at him. "Go home, Slade. Your wife will be worried to death wondering where you are and what you're doing while she's up there all alone with just the boy, and –" His murmur smoothed the sharp edges of their hasty anger.

"You don't really want to cause a commotion, do you? No, you're a reasonable man, and an honest man, and you can surely see that the law must be upheld. If you'll just go home and get some rest and talk to your wife...."

Slade let down the hammer and pocketed the weapon. "The hell with you, and the hell with this pissant court." He shoved past Fox, a motionless statue of himself, and walked to the door, two or three of his men sidling out before him, another waiting to follow, protecting his leader from men like Dan, who gripped the rifle stock, though trapped behind other men with no clear sightway, and made cautious by his duty to safeguard his client, not to endanger her.

Tension sang high in Dan's ears, like a piano string tightened nearly to breaking.

At the doorway, Slade turned back to answer the Judge. His voice differed from his normal manner of speaking; it growled in his throat, and malice lighted his face. "You know, Alex, you're a damn good man. Much too good to be associated with this petty little volunteer court. You better tell them to go to hell. A thing like this ain't worth your time." He wiped his buckskin sleeve across his mouth. "Damn, I'm thirsty."

With that, he was gone. The courtroom was quiet, everyone listening to the men tramping away, until the bell over Pfouts's front door clanged. Postures eased, hands drifted a little away from sagging coat pockets where pistols rode, and Dan allowed his grip on the rifle stock to loosen, though he did not let go.

A clamor of men speaking at once, congratulating each other on a narrow escape, the tide of relief rising to anger and cursing around him, but he felt his own thoughts had turned a bell jar over on him, trapping him inside them no matter how he beat his wings to get out, away from them. He saw what had to come next, yet there must be a way to avoid it, or everyone stood in mortal danger of their lives, their souls. Remembering Slade's raucous, triumphant laughter fading toward the front door, he could have wept for the pity of it all. He said, to the lingering smell of Slade's presence in this room, Damn you, damn you, why could you not have stood down? Why could you not have accepted the warrant and gone home as we have begged you to do these three days? Why bring us to this pass?

"Hey!" A high-pitched, scratchy voice shattered his inward silence, and a babble of words broke over him. "You hearing me?" Helen Troy glared up at him from her uninjured eye. "Can we do business with this here court, after that?"

Judge Davis took the bench again, and gaveled for order, each blow a hard, sharp knock that vibrated through Dan's teeth. Fox, his face dark and swollen as if from a beating, shouted, "Order! Order, damn you! Quiet down."

Could anyone have confidence again in Fox's abilities as sheriff? Or had he shown his true stripes when Davis got down off the bench under the glare of Slade's pistol and smoothed the situation over while Fox, whose job it properly was, stood by?

"What about my suit?" demanded Helen Troy. "Damn it, I want that bastard's hide."

Whispering, he answered her from the weight and force of his conviction that everyone now stood in mortal danger. "Not now, I think. Perhaps tomorrow. At the moment, there's some other unfinished business I have to tend to."

The glare left her eye, and he had an uneasy sense that she understood him, that she knew what his unfinished business might be.

33.

Outside, the clouds pressed down on the tops of the nearer mountains and hid the taller peaks farther off. Dark junipers spiked through the snow. They cast no shadow under an invisible sun. The flat light smoothed out the contours of the ground, and masked the angle of the sun. The wind gusted from this direction or that, blowing one clammy breath down his neck, another up his sleeve, yet another almost knocking his hat off from behind.

The wind carried Slade's laughter, his men's whoops and pistol shots, their horses' hoofbeats, from somewhere up Van Buren, then from Alder Creek, or Daylight Creek, below and behind Pfouts's store. All along Wallace, and up Jackson as far as Dan could see, the town stood still, except for a few pedestrians, men only, but no women. They walked with a special alertness, on guard against slipping, or a pistol ball's ricochet.

"He owns the town now." X walked up to stand beside Dan.

"Yes." Dan added, "For the moment. Fox rode down to Nevada to get Williams and Lott." He shifted the weight of the rifle on his shoulder, wondering if the time would ever come when a man did not think it wise to go armed about the town.

206 | CAROL BUCHANAN

The pedestrians he had been watching walked toward him as he waited outside Pfouts's store. "It won't be long now," he said to X.

"Do you think we can avoid it?"

"I hope to God." Feeling close to tears, Dan swallowed. "I hope to God we can."

His face hidden under his hat, X said, "So do I. God, so do —" His voice broke.

They waited for the others without saying more.

34.

The bell over the door to Pfouts and Russell's store jangled over Dan's head each time a man joined the meeting until he felt like climbing onto a window ledge and ripping the damn thing down. To do it, though, he'd have to walk over Beidler, who had perched one haunch on the sill. His fists in his pockets tightened and relaxed, tightened again. The rifle hung on his shoulder like a weight of guilt. Why had they not been able to stop Slade? Damn him, that instead of leaving when he promised, he had to take one more drink.

The Executive Committee were all present, Williams and Lott having ridden up from Nevada, and others from up and down the Gulch. Paris Pfouts tightened his lower lip and whistled. "This meeting will now come to order. We all know what we're here for." Pfouts had taken up a position midway toward the back of the room, and across from Dan. "Bill Fairweather and Joe Slade today defied the People's Court at gunpoint. Dan Stark was in the court and saw it all. I only heard most of it because I was out here." He gestured toward Dan, who wished to God he were somewhere else, and not in this crowded store, helping to decide yet again to end a man's life.

His account was brief, cut to the essentials: Fairweather had torn the warrants out of Judge Davis's hands as he wrote them, while Slade egged him on with drawn pistol, and cries of "Go on, Bill, I'm with you," and "By God, Bill, I wouldn't let any pissant little court tell me what to do." When he had finished, he closed his mouth and hoped he would not have to say another word.

Up and down the room rolled the angry comments: "The son of a bitch." "God damn that Slade." "That bastard." "No respect, damn his hide."

Fitch, standing across the aisle, leaned his short arm on the glass top of a display case in front of him. "Do you think after that we can send him peaceably home?"

Pfouts said, "Quiet, everybody, quiet, I say."

A restless shiver ran up and down the room, as if men reined in their tempers as Williams had controlled the injured mule.

Dan remembered the gleam in Slade's eyes as he left the court, the triumphant lift to his chin when he said the Vigilantes were all played out. He heard Slade's war cry: No one gives orders to Slade of the Overland. Damn you, Slade, that you have brought us to this. "No. I think he wants to rule the Gulch as he ruled the Central Division, and he won't stop until he does."

Beidler, at Dan's left, made a sound like a groan, low and cut short. He stood up, then resettled himself on the other haunch. His odor, compounded of his own old sweat and long-unwashed clothing sharpened by cold outside air, assaulted Dan's nostrils.

Wilbur Sanders leaned against the wall to his right, his jaw muscles tense under his close-trimmed beard, his dark eyes seeming to glow. "We have to protect the court," he said. "Without it, we have no means of enforcing such laws as we have put in place."

Unless, Dan thought, the Idaho Legislature has drawn up a civil or criminal code.

Sanders said, "Until we know if we're in Idaho Territory or Montana, until we have codes of law, and a properly constituted judicial system, the People's Court is all that shields honest people from thieves and murderers."

Massaging the end of his short arm, Fitch stood up straight. "Besides which, if we don't hang Slade, he becomes the de facto ruler of Alder Gulch, and we're worse off than we were in December. The roughs will come back, and they'll come for vengeance."

No man, Dan reckoned, had to have a picture drawn of what life would be like. In a country without any code of law, where millions in gold lay in the streams, and only strength of character restrained men, they needed this volunteer court to be the dam holding back men's willingness to murder for gold. If they allowed Slade to breach that damn, ruffians would rule and murder would be tolerated as before. No one would be safe, least of all the men in this room. We would – I would – all be marked for murder, he reminded himself.

Beidler kicked his heel against the wall below the window ledge, making a dull drum beat that caught Dan's pulse and echoed in his scalp. "It's Slade or us," said Beidler.

Dan glanced at X, and away, embarrassed and feeling like a voyeur because he had caught a glimpse of a man's soul, naked and quivering in pain that the tough little man thought he hid from view. Slade, with whom he had 'communed as a friend,' whom he had warned repeatedly over the past three months, these last three days.

"None of us wants to do this," said Dan.

A shuffle of feet, a long indrawn breath, one or two men crossed themselves. Beidler rose from his perch, and Sanders braced himself. Dan drew himself up, but he could see only Pfouts's right shoulder, the store was so crowded with men bent on – bent on what? Hanging Slade? No. Defending the court and its judge.

Pfouts said, "Regrettable as this is, we know what we have to do. We cannot let Slade and the roughs have the upper hand."

"For God's sake," Dan said, "before we go to that, give us time to persuade him."

"Dammit, you've had time! Months. He ain't gonna change." Fitch's short arm stabbed into his palm. "We've tried it your way, you and Davis, and Pfouts, and look where it got us. Here. He has us by the balls, and if we don't do something, it'll only get worse. How many times do we have to say it?"

His shout died away. The wind hissed through a crack in the window caulking behind Beidler. Someone cracked his knuckles.

Williams said, "Sanders, we know damn well the roughs have to respect the Court or we're all dead and the Gulch has no protection. Without us being willing to use the rope, no one's safe." He looked at his rope-scarred hands.

"We have only one choice," said John Lott. He stood in the aisle, part way toward the stove. "Hang him or don't hang him. If we don't hang him, he wins. If we do, everyone will know we mean business."

"That's right." "You tell 'em, John." "That's so." Men nodded their heads, their mumbled agreement running about the room.

Dan raised his voice over the others. "Even so, he has done nothing to justify hanging him. There is no capital crime here."

Fitch's lip curled. "You mean we can't hang him unless he kills somebody."

"That's how the law works, generally, yes," Sanders said.

A man spoke from the back of the room. "You want to be the one to let Slade kill him so we can keep to the letter of the law?"

"Just so you understand what this means," Dan said.

"We know what it means," said Williams. "God knows none of us want to do this. Sober, Slade's as decent as they come. But drunk, he's a demon."

"Sometimes there are necessary examples," said Lott. "Everything we've done is at risk now. Do we put everyone in danger because some of us like this man when he's sober?"

Williams scratched his chin. "I think we've talked this thing to death."

"Damn right," said Fitch.

Pfouts said, "I agree. Let's have a voice vote. All in favor of hanging Slade?"

He could see nothing else to do, but he had never hated a decision as much as this one. He joined his vote to the others': "Aye."

"Opposed?"

Silence.

For Dan the silence held a note of disbelief. We have just voted to condemn our friend, thought Dan. Our fellow Vigilante. But who had they condemned? The kind, sober, honest man who could not abide theft or the drunken thief who called Beni's ears payment for his rampages? The man who supported our aims and our work, or the devil who would overthrow good order and bring back anarchy, the breeding ground of crime?

Damn you, Slade, forcing this on us. For pitting our friendship against our duty.

"Very well, then." Pfouts looked at each of them in turn, holding each man as if reading his mind, making sure each would stand firm.

For God's said, we've always stuck by our decisions, Dan told him silently. Do you think we'll weasel out now? An echo of the recent past whispered in his memory: It didn't have to be this way. True, he answered now as he had then. You could have made a different choice, picked different friends. Damn you, Slade, you could have gone home.

35.

"This is a hell of a thing." Dan walked out of the store with Williams and X Beidler. The three men crossed Wallace to Williams's horse, waiting at the hitching rail.

"Damn right." X's eyes showed red around the rims, with black circles beneath them, and his cheeks appeared to have sunk in. He looked how Dan felt.

Williams hooked the stirrup on the saddle horn while he tightened the cinch. "I still have to get the opinion of the Nevada group. The final decision is theirs. If they agree, you can expect to see us in about three hours."

As if, Dan thought. As if it were not a foregone conclusion, as if the Nevada Vigilantes, at least the core members who had signed the oath of secrecy and loyalty, would not follow where "Cap" Williams led.

"When they hear how he treated the court, they'll agree," Dan said.

"Yes." Williams dropped the single syllable among them. John Lott had mounted his horse and ridden a few paces farther down Wallace, where he stopped to wait, but Williams lowered his voice and turned to his companions, making a small circle of secrecy. "I figure it'll take about three hours to round the boys up, get a consensus, and get back here. If Slade goes home in the meantime, well and good. But he has to understand he's

214 | CAROL BUCHANAN

out of options. If he goes on another bender, the sentence holds. He's got to quit this horseshit."

Dan tugged up his coat collar, flexed his shoulder under the rifle's weight. He was tired of carrying it, weary of thinking he'd need it. "Three hours, huh?"

"About that, I figure." Williams tugged on the cinch. "Come on, you hardheaded cayuse." He jabbed his thumb into the horse's barrel, and the animal let out its breath. As Williams took up the slack, and fastened the strap, Dan watched hope light up X's face.

"We could still talk him into going home." Beidler stood straighter, glanced around as if looking for Slade. "Let's get to work."

Untying the horse, Williams twisted the stirrup and put his foot in it, facing the horse's hindquarters. "Here he comes." He gathered the reins and swung aboard, ready to ride off on his errand, but waiting with Dan and X while Slade and his pals trotted toward them. "Slade, you'd better go home. Your time's about run out."

Slade laughed. "Hell, Cap, no one talks that way to Slade of the Overland."

"I'm telling you for the last time. Go home. We're out of patience."

A few men passing by paused to listen, perhaps to hope as Dan hoped, that Slade at last would yield and spare them his death.

"Who? You Vigilantes?" Slade's upper lip curled. "A bunch of toothless wolves, you ask me. If those boys last winter had a real man as a leader, they'd rule the roost. Instead, they had that nance, Plummer." Laughing, he nudged the tired horse forward, his entourage following.

Williams nudged his horse and rode down the slope to the river. He did not look back, and Dan knew they had just seen Williams's last try at saving Slade's life.

He meant what he said. He always did. Yet they still had the three hours.

"All right," Beidler said. "Let's see if Jim Kiskadden can help."

All along the street men clustered together in small groups, talking and gesturing. The word was going out that something was afoot, that the Vigilantes had met. Dan heard one man say, "He ain't done nothing to deserve hanging." Another man retorted, "You'd change your mind if it was your place they wrecked. Ask Dorris what he thinks, or Charley Baer down in Nevada, or Helen Troy." "Yeah," said a third man, "or …"

Their voices faded in Dan's wake, but a few steps on, a man in deep discussion with some others glanced up, saw them, and signaled to his friends. The group fell silent as Dan and Beidler walked by. Not until they had left the group several feet behind them did Dan hear a faint mutter of talk, though the wind teased the words away.

They found Kiskadden standing at a row of shelves near the back of his store. He tapped the end of a pencil along the edge, and counted in fours. Not until he had finished and made a note on a pad did he acknowledge them. "What's wrong? What's happened? Is it Slade?"

X slid his eyes sideways up at Dan. "You might say so. We just had a meeting, and it ain't good for Slade." X swallowed. "We're prepared to act, Jim. He's about run out of time."

For a second or two, Kiskadden stared at them, his mouth open, the blood coming and going from his face. Pencil and pad slid out of his grasp and clattered onto the floor. "Oh, dear God." He put a knuckle to his mouth. "You can't mean that." He took his hand away, and Dan saw the indentations of his teeth.

When they said nothing, only stared back at him, his eyes filled with tears. "Not Joe. Why, he hasn't done anything — You can't do it."

"It'll take some time to round everybody up," Dan said. "We think we still have about three hours. Can you help? Persuade him to go home while he can."

X added, "He doesn't hear us, but maybe you still have some leverage with him."

Behind them the door hinges squeaked, and a gust of air brought an odor compounded of liquor, stale sweat, and cured leather. Before he turned around, Dan knew it was Slade.

His pale deerskin suit was soiled at the elbows and knees to a dark brown, the beaded flowers along the sleeves broken in places. Dan had no greeting for him; he held silent, wishing he could find a way to make Slade comprehend his plight, scare him out of his cocksure certainty into knowing that so far from again being Slade of the Overland and ruling over Alder Gulch as he had ruled the Central Division, his time was nearly up. He held his useless tongue that could form no words he had not already used. Something in Dan's face – in all their faces, perhaps – caused Slade to peer from one man to the other, his round green eyes inquiring. Perhaps this was the other Slade; perhaps he had left his devil behind in some saloon.

Kiskadden stepped out in front of Beidler. "Joe, for God's sake, go home. Now. Ride over the hill. That ain't a lot to ask, is it? Please, do it. Just go. They mean business."

"They do, do they? All right." One corner of Slade's mouth curled upward, and a glint shone from his narrowed eyelids. "I'll go. But I came to ask a favor, Jim. Could I borrow your derringer? Alex Davis has my pistol, and I don't dare go around naked this way." After all, he did not say, but they well understood, that there could be another Jules Beni waiting to ambush him. He smiled in his most engaging way, weaving a little where he stood, in a drunken certainty that his friends would grant him this favor, that they understood a man in his position could not go unarmed where so many other men carried their weapons hidden and in plain sight.

As Dan himself did, and Beidler, whose pistol rode his belt an inch or two from the buckle.

Kiskadden felt in his coat pocket for the derringer and handed the fat little weapon to Slade. A double-bar-reled .41 caliber, Dan saw. Small, but no toy.

Handing it over, Kiskadden said, "Promise me you'll go home now. Your time's running out. Go home, Joe, for God's sake, go home."

Slade peered at them, at Kiskadden, near to pleading with him, and at Dan and X, standing behind Kiskadden and saying nothing.

"You talking about the Vigilantes?" He laughed. "Hell, they're all played out. I told these fellows and Williams so just now."

X said, "It may appear so, but you'll find out in about three hours."

"What do you mean?" Slade stared at Beidler as though trying to read something behind his words.

X said nothing, while Dan, equally silent, crossed his fingers in his coat pocket and hoped Slade would just do what they asked and ride home with no more talk, no more questions, just go away and spare them from what they had resolved to do. He cursed the oath of secrecy he had taken in December, that bound him in chains of honor to reveal nothing of what was said in their meet-ings, nothing of what was said among themselves aside from meetings, never to betray the others. Beidler, out of friendship to Slade, had said as much as could be said.

Slade looked from one to the other, a deep furrow showing between his eyes as he tried to understand what they were telling him, at last coming to some conclusion.

Dan gripped the rifle stock, held onto the solid shape of it, and hoped to Christ that days and nights of steady drinking had not robbed him of the power to recognize the fate now stalking him, that he could hear what they had not said and just go home before it was too late.

36.

That hope drove all three them out of Kiskadden's in Slade's wake, and almost Dan dared to breathe easy when Slade mounted his jaded horse and hauled the animal's head around, away from the snow-piled boardwalk, but instead of turning on Jackson, toward the road out of town, he steered Copperbottom up Wallace. What route was he taking homeward?

"Where's he going?" X asked.

Dan looked around. "And where's Fairweather and the rest of them?"

Kiskadden said, "Bill? His friends locked him in my storeroom. After what he pulled in court, they're taking no chances."

Meaning, of course, they were taking no chances on having him hanged. "Oh, shit," Dan said. "Where the hell is Slade headed? Damn him, he's not leaving town." Unaware of how he put his feet, or how they carried him forward, he walked on with the other two in Slade's wake. His head throbbed, and the pulse beat in his temples – had it ever stopped? It was worse than before although the cut had to be well on the way to healing.

"Why not do that with Slade?" Kiskadden kicked a chuck of ice, toppling it off a crusted snowdrift and breaking it in countless shards that flew like glass splinters.

"Because he is Slade," Dan said, "and locking him in a storeroom won't stop this." This was Slade of the Overland, who has to be in charge of his destiny, or was that a fancy way of saying that that they couldn't treat Slade like one of the boys, that he was more than that, and they wanted him to save his life and his pride by choosing his own way? Or, more simply, locking him up would not end the cycle of danger to us all, but make him more liable to take revenge the minute he's let loose.

Wary of the rough ice underfoot, he felt his feet come under him as he walked. "That wouldn't work with Slade," he said. "He'd get out, and then he'd get drunk and come after us for locking him up. He'd be worse than ever."

"How do you know that?" demanded Kiskadden. "Damn it, how can you say that?"

"Beni's ears," Dan said.

"He waited a long time for that," Kiskadden said. "Almost two years. Besides, I don't believe he would ever torture someone. He's not that sort. He's a good man."

X said, "Except when he's drinking. Then the devil gets into him, and there's hell to pay."

"Christ, no!" Kiskadden stopped in his tracks. Dan walked on with X a couple of steps before he understood what Kiskadden meant, and broke into a heedless run, leaving both his companions behind.

Slade, instead of riding on, dismounted in front of a store, and went in.

Sliding, stumbling, Dan leaped onto the boardwalk in time to hear Slade say to Judge Davis, "I guess the damn Vigilantes are after me. You know anything about this?"

"No, I'm not aware of anything like that. Why don't you go home and get some rest? We can talk later."

Judge Davis did not smile, but he looked friendly at Slade, before he turned back to listen to the store owner tell how he knew some goods had been pilfered.

How the motion went, how the thing went between one split second and the next, Dan did not know, but the derringer appeared in Slade's hand, both barrels pressed against Davis's forehead. The Judge, as if the cold steel making pale rings on his skin were merely a slight nuisance, or less than that, ignored Slade. "Can you recall what's missing? Or how many?"

Speechless, the man goggled at him, his mouth opening and closing.

Dan swung the rifle off his shoulder, cocked it. As he shouted, "Stop!" and lifted it to sight down the long barrel to Slade's head, another man, who stood closer to them, drew both of his pistols and trained them on Slade.

"Slade," the man said, "put the damn derringer on the counter and back off. If you go on as you are now, you'll be hanged before sunset."

"If I don't shoot you first," Dan called.

Startled, Slade put up the derringer, let the hammers down easy, the slow soft clicks of steel ratcheting into harmlessness. Seeming to take in what he had done for the first time, he removed his hat, put on his most respectful face, a child's mask for Hallowe'en. "Ah, hell. Let's quit this. I apologize, Judge. You know me, I was just joking." His wide-eyed, innocent expression lay claim to the benevolence other men have for hijinks – boys will be boys, after all.

Dan was not amused. This was no hijinks, no joke, for a man rising forty to put a gun to another man's head, moreover one who had always befriended him, who even now waited, smiling, for Slade to put the derringer in his hand. Not until the Judge's fingers closed around the little weapon did he let the rifle's hammer down and hold the long gun in the crook of his elbow, looking at the floor. He would not sling it again until Slade went home.

Memories – Martha's terror, the injured muleskinner, the gun misfiring at himself, Dorris weeping over his ruined store, the injured whores sobbing, Helen Troy's black eye, Harding's bloody mouth – overlay each other in Dan's mind like sheets of translucent foolscap, and rising above all Slade's gleeful laugh. Who was the real Slade, that one raising the bottle to his lips, or this man who now acted with contrition and humility?

Slade put out his right hand. "You know I was only kidding. I'm a great kidder, you know, I didn't mean nothing by it. You know I like you, Alex, I'd never hurt you."

Judge Davis extended his hand carefully, Dan thought, unsure whether Slade might bite. "I accept your apology." The two men's hands touched, clasped, let go.

Judge Davis said, "Now, Slade, go home. Get on your horse and ride out of here."

"I'll go home when I'm good and ready." Slade's chin jutted out at Davis. "No one orders Slade around." He stepped past Davis and came toward Dan, standing just inside the doorway.

I could drop him where he stands, Dan thought, and I might if I could bear the thought of killing an unarmed man as I would kill a deer. With Slade a few steps away, Dan stepped aside and followed him out the door, closing it behind them.

As Slade swung aboard his horse, Kiskadden said, "Give my best to your lovely wife, Joe."

Forefinger touching his hat, Slade beamed down at them. "I'll be seeing you boys."

Dan watched him ride down Wallace, willed him, pleaded with him to turn up Jackson, to take the road out of town, ride over the ridge toward home. Go home. You know what will happen if you don't. Go home. Go home, for God's sake, just go home.

37.

Of course she hadn't bided at the Eatery like Dan'l had told her to. The streets were safe to cross if a body knew where Slade was, and Martha could place him by the whooping and hollering and pistol shots that made her flesh cringe. Lydia didn't have enough of the Arnica, but she had all three kinds of wormwood – sagebrush and silver sage and plain sage. Lucky they all grew together around here. She'd use any of them for poultices, and she could use a bit of the sagebrush in a tea, too, as long as she was careful, on account it was strong enough to be dangerous. A tea would help with injuries to the women's inward parts. She wished she knew better what to do, but she had never thought to encounter such a thing as this.

With Albert there, she couldn't come right out and ask Lydia, either. A husband had to know some things about a woman, but another man, never. And a darky, to boot, about white women – unthinkable.

Lydia bound up the medicaments in separate deer hide pokes. "How are thy patients?"

"They'll be a sight better when I can use these, thank you very much." Martha, so wanting to ask her questions, hesitated. How could she say it, when she hated even to think a word like that, or admit it even to herself that she knew it or what it meant.

Bringing the candle closer to them both, Lydia peered at her and whispered, "Thee has aught else to say?"

Martha breathed the word, her lips exaggerating the shapes of its sounds. Rape.

Lydia blew out a puff of air, and the corners of her mouth turned down. Shaking her head, she took back the pouch with the silver sage in it and filled it up to the brim. "How many?" Martha held up three fingers. Two women violated, and a third hardly more'n a child. Maybe Dotty's are or a little younger. Figuring the pouch full would treat all of the women's injuries, she started to thank Lydia, but here she added half of another poke to be sure.

"Thank you," said Martha.

Lydia took her hand. "I am happy thee are tending to the poor creatures. They are no less God's own than you or I. Bless you. Let me know what more I can do to help."

By the look of her, Tabby wasn't about to share Lydia's opinion. As the black woman brought the wooden spoon to her lips for a taste, her face had a decided prune-like aspect, tight and folded in on itself like maybe the venison was off.

Outside, some men were going about some mighty important business, while others stood talking amongst themselves. They paid her little mind, raising their hats to her as she passed by and walked up Jackson like she was going home. The town was quiet, which she thought was odd. Feeling a spurt of joy well into her thoughts, she realized that Slade must have gone home at last. "Thank you, Lord," she whispered as she hurried along, head down to see where she put her feet. For the sake of what few shreds of reputation she might have left, she was minded to cut behind Dan'l's house and across the yards to go in the back door to Fancy Annie's.

As long as she was so close to home, she thought she'd stop there a moment and be sure Dotty was home safe from school. Slade might have gone home, but his men could still be around, and the child knew better than to go off by herself when Slade's men were hoorahing the town.

The house struck cold when Martha opened the door. No one had stirred up the fire since morning. The child was not at home. Dropping the pokes, Martha spun on her heel and dashed out the door, slamming it behind her. Where could the child be? The dog set to barking, jumped at the end of his rope. Untying him, wrapping the end around her hand, Martha trotted after him as he strained at the loop around his neck. "Find Dotty," she begged. "If anyone can find her, you can. Find Dotty."

38.

I nstead of riding straight on toward the inevitable left turn up Jackson, Slade angled his horse toward another saloon, dismounted, and went inside for a drink. Dan, Beidler, and Kiskadden kept track of his erratic journey from that place to another, while a clock ticked on in Dan's mind, and his jaw muscled ached from gritting his teeth. At last it looked like Slade would yield and ride out of both. He mounted his horse again, rode down Wallace Street. In front of Pfouts and Russell and stopped. Swinging his right leg over the cantle, and kicking his left foot free, he dropped to the ground, staggered on a slippery patch, and regained his balance in one fluid motion.

"No!" Before his single cry finished, Dan jumped across a snowdrift and ran to intercept Slade. Damn him, he muttered to himself, damn him, damn him. He has to go home. Now. We're running out of time. The couriers had reached Summit and Nevada City, and they'd had time for their meetings, time to explain what was afoot, to take a vote and be even now on their way back. Slade acted as if he had all the time in the world to do one more task, try one more time to get the upper hand on everyone. For Christ's sake, go home. Get back on that horse and go home. Why was that such a difficult task, when his life was at stake? Or did he not believe it?

Slade stood inside the door, talking to Judge Davis. "You know me, you know I wouldn't hurt you. Hell, you and me's pals. I like you. You're a good man, even if a little misguided, and I wouldn't hurt a hair on your head."

Mindful of the discussions, though he couldn't know – and why couldn't he, Dan asked himself – as if everyone in town had to know that Slade's time might be running out, that the Vigilantes had given him all the time they could or would and it was draining out fast, like Alder Creek itself, running under the ice.

"Yes, I do know that," said Davis. "I understand that. I know you like me. Go on home and get some rest. We can talk again." The Judge was urging Slade out the door, and for a wonder, Slade, smiling, walked past Dan and remounted his horse, reined it away into the street toward Jackson, just one or two doors away now.

A dog barked, tearing Dan's attention away from Slade, and there by the Eatery, Martha stood talking to two men – no, Jacob Himmelfarb and a boy, his own stepson, Timothy. Dan sprinted across and slipped on a patch of watery ice to fetch up hard against the Eatery's log wall. Ignoring the other two, he said to Martha, "Didn't I tell you to stay in? Why are you out?"

She bridled at him, and amid the fire in her he read fear. "I can't find the child. School's out by now, but she's not to home. I went home to look for her and she's not there."

"Good God," he said. "Where could she be? Now of all times, where is she?"

"What do you mean?" asked Jacob. " 'Where could she be?' Daniel, what is happening?"

"Maybe nothing, but you should all just wait in the Eatery until I come for you. Do you understand? Just wait there."

Jacob and Timothy spoke together, but it was Jacob's deeper tones that won out, and for once his English did not fail him. "We can not wait while we do not know where the child might be. We cannot. She we must find. Forthwith."

"Yes," Dan said. "Forthwith. Or sooner." A rider across the street, partway up Jackson, distracted him. Slade turned his horse around, and plodded back, his face troubled. "God, no. Christ, no. No. Don't come back, Slade. For Christ's sake, go home." Turning his back on his family, he stepped atop a pile of hard-packed snow and from there recalled himself enough to say, "I have to try to stop this. Please, find Dotty and then wait in the Eatery until I come."

39.

Voices mumbled amid the trudge and squash of many boots in the silence of the ice-bound creek. The Nevada men. Always the ones to pursue justice to the end no matter where the chase led them, because they had sworn an oath, perhaps twenty-five or so of them, on their sacred honor they had pledged themselves. Looking downhill, he laid his hand on the stock of his rifle, swung it off his shoulder, ready to cock. Even as the rifle came to rest in the crook of his elbow, he whispered, "Damn it, Slade, go home."

His glance swept the street, where men and a few women came out of the saloons. Martha hurried down Jackson toward Daylight Creek and Cover Street, where the Elephant Corral stood. He wanted to shout, Get away from there! Don't go near the Elephant Corral.

From behind him, Fitch asked, "What are they doing down there?"

"They can't find my step-daughter." He did not say that he should be looking for her, too, but for this – this duty, this God-damned dreadful duty.

"Why the hell did Slade come back?" He wanted to seize Slade, shake him till his brains rattled into a new arrangement: Damn it, Slade, go home. Why do you force this on us? For Chrissake, you know us, you've ridden with us, some of us helped you build your house

— Why, Slade? Why don't you believe us when you well know what we're capable of?

He ran toward Pfouts's store, where Slade talked to Judge Davis, held Davis's hand and pumped it up and down, said how much he held His Honor in high regard, and woudn't have hurt him for the world, he hoped the Judge understood that. "Will you forgive me?" asked Slade, his thick, strong hand wrapped round Davis's long slender fingers.

"Of course," said Davis, "of course I forgive you. Now, go on, go home, it's all right. We're friends. You're forgiven." Yet he looked pale, as if he must hear the tramp of many boots outside, the low mutter of voices like thunder approaching from afar, only the thunder was not so far off now. Just inside the door, Dan leaned back on his heels to look down Wallace in time for the parade from Nevada City to turn the corner by the Leviathan Hall. God almighty, there must be a hundred men, more, maybe two hundred or more, and men came from the buildings lining Wallace to join them. The Nevada men had come armed, carried their rifles and shotguns, and Jim Williams and John Lott walked at their head. The Nevada men had signed an oath of loyalty to each other, and if they reached Slade before he rode away, it would all be over.

"Christ almighty, Joe, go. Get on your horse and ride out before it's too late." He knew by the set of Slade's jaw, the bloodshot glare, that he talked to Slade's devil, that the contrite Slade, the man who begged forgiveness had stepped aside in favor of this man, whom other men did not rule; he ruled them. Just ask Jules Beni. Tough men yielded to Slade.

"No." Slade rocked a little. He was unsteady, but not enough, Dan thought, not enough to pass out here and now and awaken sober in such pain as to make him swear off drink forever. Was there nothing to save them from this?

Word like fever had spread. Men came from the saloons, the stores, their cabins, to find out: Had the Vigilantes lost patience at last? Would they hang a man for disturbing the peace? For all the outrages to the peace? Would Slade die today? Or would they back down at the last, put the fear of God into Slade and let him go, knowing what his fate would be if he took the town again? Dan read their minds, saw in their eyes the avid shine of men at a dogfight. "Let him go." "Hang him." "Make him pay." Their shouts pelted Dan as he stood in the doorway. "You can't do this!" "He don't deserve hangin'!"

Reading their unholy glee, he stepped farther into the store and shut the door behind him, somewhat muffling the shouts and yells from the street.

"I need to know you forgive me," Slade told Davis. "I can't just ride off and leave this between us. I like you, though I don't care much for that fellow Fox, but you're a good man, and a good friend, and I like you." He held the Judge's hand, implored him as if Alex were God, who had the power to forgive sins, and would forgive Slade, wash him clean.

Davis covered Slade's hand with his own. "Yes, I do forgive you. It's all right. We're friends. You can go home with a clear conscience. I like you, too. Now go. Dear God, go." Davis spoke as if in prayer, but to the Almighty or to Slade, Dan could not tell. "Go home while there is still time." He pointed to the door.

Moving out of Slade's path, Dan looked out the window. He could not see the men tramping up Wallace, but the horse, Copperbottom, head up, watched them. The gelding swiveled his ears, listening to something only a horse could hear amid the rough slog of miners' boots; nervous, sidestepping one way and the other, the animal pawed the ground, stamped a rear hoof, as if adding its silent voice to those demanding Slade go home.

Slade emerged as from a dream, his eyes focused on Davis's face, and he tilted his head to hear something in the voices and boots. As if realizing for the first time the danger he had courted for three days, he looked past Davis's shoulder at the door.

"Go now," Dan said, "while you still can. They're coming for you and they mean business." As Slade lingered, begging Davis's forgiveness yet again, and Pfouts stood behind a display case with his arms folded across his chest, he gathered his breath to shout loud enough to penetrate whatever illusion of disbelief held Slade in place, but it was already almost too late. The Nevada City men, joined by miners up and down the Gulch, several hundred strong it seemed, had reached Fancy Annie's. Only a couple hundred yards more, and they would be here.

Williams led. "Cap" Williams, the Vigilantes' Executive Officer, whom the people of the wagon train had elected Captain over Slade while he slept off a drunk. Williams, the salt in Slade's wounded reputation.

40.

Slipping, scrambling for her footing, Martha rushed down the hill to the corner of Cover Street and Jackson, where Daylight Creek burbled through the ford's broken ice. The Elephant Corral stood on that corner, and downstream was the Sheehans' cabin, where the child sometimes went after school for help with her lessons, Molly Sheehan being much of an age but years ahead of Dotty in her schooling.

She stubbed her toe on a snow-covered rock and came near to falling, losing her grip on Canary's rope. She hardly noticed Jacob's hand at her elbow steadying her, as the dog, trailing his rope, raced uphill toward home. Shuddering, she picked up her pace as the two of them turned the corner, past the wickiup where Fitch and Berry Woman lived, and headed downstream. Seeing a man toss a rope over the crosspiece in the gate to the corral, she shuddered. Dear God, was Dan'l mixed up in a hanging? Again? Not Slade. Not Slade. They must be intending to scare him good, that's all.

But in her heart she knew it was not so. The Vigilantes never scared someone straight; when they brought out the rope they meant to use it. Not Slade. Never on him, they liked him.

About a hundred yards ahead, a young girl fled away, half stumbling along the beaten trail of packed snow, the soles of her boots flicking snow upward with every step.

Molly Sheehan, running home. She met Timmy, stopped for a few words, then bolted for home while Timmy jogged toward them shaking his head as Martha and Jacob waited. Behind them, the grumble of men's voices was louder, like they argued amongst themselves. Where, oh dear God, where was the child? Martha clutched the folds of her cloak, pulled it tighter around her.

Timmy, panting, trotted up to them. "The Professor kept school later on account of all the goings-on. He didn't want the young'uns getting mixed up in this. He let them go when he thought the coast might be clear. Made them promise to run straight home."

Oh, Lord. Martha closed her eyes. Here she'd run after the child, worried herself sick, and in the meantime maybe Dotty bided safe at home. She opened her eyes, looked into her son's anxious face. "The dog. He got loose and ran uphill, toward Idaho Street. I made sure she was at Sheehans'." She gulped back a sound partway between a laugh and a sob. "Canary knew where she was. She was coming home from school."

Men shouted, now and then one rising over the others, like they all quarreled with each other and no two agreeing but a rumble of voices yelling, like a squall coming nearer, that they had to take shelter from or be caught in. Dan'l wouldn't like them being out in it, on account he'd feel he needed to protect them, and he couldn't be thinking about them now, him being part of this, this horror. Would they hang Slade after all, even though he'd done nothing to hang a man for?

Jacob said, "You could not know. Now we have no more time."

"Let's go back to the Eatery, like Dan'l said." Martha picked up her skirts heavy from the wet, soaked almost to her knees. "We can wait there for him."

With Jacob ahead and Timmy close behind in case she fell again, they hustled up the slope to Wallace and the safety of log walls lest some hotheads took a notion to shoot off their weapons. What if Slade's pals took a notion to save him? They'd have war between the Vigilantes and the roughs, just like the roughs had promised all these weeks on account of their friends up on the hill, and others hung at Hell Gate. Dear God, don't let that be. Oh, Dan'l, keep him safe, Lord.

Albert opened the door to them, held it wide for them to walk in.

"Come thee in where it's warm," called Lydia.

Martha sank down on the back bench, but Timmy stayed in front with Albert and Jacob. He would take turns with them to see outside, so's they would know something of what was happening. For her part, she did not want to know; she had seen too much and needed to adjust her mind around the thought that — "Oh, Lydia," she burst out. "I think they're a-fixin' to hang Mister Slade."

41.

"They're almost here," said Dan. "Damn it, go before you've run out time."

Slade rushed to the window, peered out. "Yes, I'll go now." He dashed out the door, half-stumbling, caught himself, and stopped altogether at the sight of the Nevada City men tramping up the street. His jaw dropped, and he stared wide-eyed, as if he could not believe what he saw.

Sanders came out of a store, hat brim low on his forehead, hands in his pockets. He watched where he walked, intent as it seemed on keeping his footing.

Slade's irises widened into black pools. "Save me, Sanders, you're a friend of mine. Goddammit, you can't let this happen."

When Sanders kept walking, Slade cried out, "Sanders, I've always been straight with you. Get me out of this. Help me now."

His plea added another layer to the foolscap overlay in Dan's memory – Plummer: Sanders, I've always been friendly to you. Save me now. I beg you. Save me. But no amount of banked good will could balance the account of public terrorism.

Pausing, Sanders faced Slade, his cheekbones prominent in his face, as if the skin were stretched over them. "I'm sorry. I'm truly sorry, but if you won't save yourself, there is nothing I can do for you." Turning in that abrupt military manner, as if on parade, he walked away.

Dan heard an echo: Sanders telling Plummer, I'm sorry. There is nothing I can do for you now. Without speaking, Sanders shouldered his way through the restless, muttering crowd, crossed Wallace, and walked away, turned the corner uphill on Jackson and was gone from sight.

"You heard them," said Dan. "Get on that horse and go home."

"No," Slade screamed. "You can't do this. You know me. I was just joking. You're my friends. Save me." His fingers dug into Dan's arm. "Save me, Stark. Davis, I've always been decent to you, save me now." Tears flowed down his cheeks.

Kiskadden shouted at Dan. "Don't let them do this. God almighty, stop."

Dan shook him away. "Only Slade can stop it now." Why in God's name could Kiskadden not see it? If they stopped, if they simply let Slade go now, he won. He would know, everyone would know, that the Vigilantes would not hang Slade, who was a friend to some of them. Slade must save his own life. If he mounted his horse and rode home he could yet live. If not —

Weeping, Slade clung to Dan's arm, and Dan could not shake him off.

In the midst of his terror, his head came up. He dropped Dan's arm. "Davis. He'll save me!" With that, he rushed back into Pfouts's store, trailing Kiskadden's shout behind him: "Noooo!"

42.

ollowing Slade into Pfouts and Russell, Dan resumed his place at the front window where he could look for the Nevada contingent and still keep a watch over Slade. He was not sure what that meant, only that he had to be where he could act – but to do what? The slog and trudge of hundreds of boots, carrying men bent on hanging Slade, blended into a ragged thunder rumbling ever closer. Good God, must this happen? Would they hang Slade? Saving his own life still lay in Slade's power; he could yet get on the horse and ride out of town. But only for a minute more.

"I apologize. I'm so sorry. Do I have your forgiveness?" Slade, apologizing for the fifth time by Dan's count, seized Davis's hand and bowing to him as the Judge tried to pry his fingers loose, murmuring as to a nervous horse, "Yes, yes, I accept your apology, I forgive you, it's all right, but go home. Now. You've not a minute to lose. You're in danger. Please, I beg you, get on your horse and go home."

"Danger?" As if he had not seen the men walking up the street, Slade sounded puzzled. "From what? I haven't done anything." Dan heard a lightness come into his voice. "Besides, you forgive me. They can't do anything to me now that you've forgiven me."

Turning his back to them, the rifle resting in the crook of his elbow, Dan thought, No, you've done nothing.

Nothing but damage property, bankrupt businesses, commit assault and battery, and suborn rape, besides destroying our ability to keep the peace by holding up the Judge who accepts your apology and begs you to leave before you are hanged. Not one of Slade's crimes and misdemeanors was tantamount to a hanging offense, he knew, but heat bloomed in his neck, and the drum beat quickened in his veins. How could they save Slade, when he would not save himself?

How long would you last as a forgiven man? How long before the craving for a drink resurrected that devil of yours that lives in the bottle?

Outside, the first of the Nevada men, came to a stop in front of the store. Williams and Lott conferred with Beidler and Kiskadden. The two leaders conferred with Beidler and Kiskadden. Beidler, as pale as though he faced his own death, pointed a visibly shaking finger at the window where Dan stood. When Williams and Lott turned to Dan, he nodded yes, Slade is here. This can't be happening, he thought. We cannot be about to hang this man, our friend and his devil.

In the aggregate, though – his train of thought continued on its track – taken altogether, would Slade's crimes add up to a hanging?

No. Even in the aggregate, in a normal society, Slade does not deserve this. He's right; he has done nothing to hang him for. Williams and the first phalanx of men walked up to the door. But if we let him live, we show yellow, we prove to everyone that we cannot maintain civic order and everything we've fought for and risked our souls for melts away like snow into the creek. The door slammed open, filled with rifle and shotgun barrels. Out of the midst of these Williams stepped into the store, his shotgun leveled at Slade.

Dan wheeled around, the Spencer looking at Slade across a display case, and cocked the hammer, the ratcheting click echoing in his blood.

"Joseph Slade," said Williams, "you're under arrest." He walked forward, and Dan gestured with the rifle for Slade to raise his hands. Williams patted his pockets, spread the sides of Slade's coat to be sure he was not armed.

"No!" shouted Davis. "You can't do this. Listen to me, you can't do it!"

"I've apologized," said Slade. "Alex understands. He's forgiven me." When Williams shook his head, Slade turned toward Pfouts. "Sir, you can get me out of this. Please, you can save me. Call them off. Tell them to stand down. They'll listen to you." Yelled, "Please!"

Pfouts said, "I can do nothing for you now. You had a hundred chances to reform, and you would not. You could have gone home any time these last three days, these last three hours, and you would not. It's over."

Outside, Kiskadden yelled so loud that Dan heard him and recognized his voice over the men's low muttering: "No! You can't do this!"

Over the crowd's grumbling Kiskadden's scream tore the air: "You can't do —"

Dan looked over his shoulder to see some of the Vigilantes step in front of Kiskadden, preventing anyone else from harming him if he tried to rescue Slade. No one could intercede now; Slade had made his own choice, to challenge them to the end.

Slade yelled, "Pfouts. Goddammit, Pfouts, you have to stop this. You can't let this happen."

Pfouts shouted, "I can do nothing for you, do you hear? Nothing." The last word was cold and hard enough to skate on.

Outside, Virginia men, fed up with Slade and his self-granted license to terrorize them, came out of the saloons and hurdy-gurdies. Merchants walked out of their stores and locked their doors to join in, to lend their weight to the proceedings. A few women, shivering in satin dresses, clutched their ostrich boas around their necks, and sheltered themselves as well as they could against the log walls of a saloon. Despite the cold, they laughed together, and their heads nodded up and down as they talked, like puppets in a play. They had come for their friends, injured by Slade's men; they had come for retribution. For vengeance.

Dan ground his teeth, and his knuckles whitened around the stock and on the trigger guard. Why could he not have sent Slade away at rifle point, knocked him unconscious and slung him like a sack of flour – or a dead man – over the back of his horse, but that was not how this was to end. Slade had not agreed to go home, to leave Virginia City in peace. Given the choice, he had chosen, damn him. How had he not seen his fate trudging closer every day, that every time he dismounted for one more drink, fate wound another loop on the hangman's knot?

His face blanched white as paper, blue eyes huge above sharp cheekbones, Judge Davis begged them. "Stop, you men. Slade has done nothing to hang him for. Stop, I say. Stop."

He might as well have tried to command Fate itself.

43.

Eyes dark in his blanched face, hair long as Dan's own flying, the fringes on his buckskin suit dancing as he twisted about, hands outstretched to this man and that, Slade sought friends, saviors, rescue from the death coming toward him. He pleaded for life even as they seized his arms and roped them to his sides, leaving his hands free in front.

"You may have one hour," said Williams, "to settle your affairs, make a will if you don't have one, write letters."

Slade flapped his hands in front of him. "How can I write with my hands tied so?"

"I'll help you," said Dan. "It will all be done as you wish, to leave your affairs in good order."

Slade could not settle to the task. He begged, wept, screamed that they could not kill him, he had done nothing to deserve this, he had done nothing, nothing, nothing. "I never harmed you," he sobbed. "Why are you doing this?"

"You cannot do this," Davis said, "you cannot. It's murder."

"My wife," Slade cried, "my wife. Let me see my wife." Bending over, he sobbed into his hands, his nose running. "I don't deserve her, oh God, I never deserved her, and will she now be a widow?"

"Then make a will," Dan said. "Don't leave her intestate."

Slade swung his fists, knocked the writing box out of Dan's hands. Pens, ink bottle, and paper spilled onto the floor, and Slade's boot came down on it all. The ink bottle broke, and black ink pooled across the planks, ran into the cracks between them. He bellowed, "You damned sons of bitches, you won't get away with murdering me."

Amid Slade's weeping, cursing them all, Dan murmured low as though to soothe a terrified child, the voice he had used to cajole his small sister's kitten out of a tree. As though he did not hear him, Slade wept, and screamed, and fell to his knees, walked around in a small circle on his knees, begged to be set free, to be maimed, punish him however they would but only let him live.

Davis said, "I could talk to them outside, couldn't I? If they quit this, will you quit it?"

Williams answered for them all. "You can try, but I doubt you will change their minds."

"I'll get up on that wagon and talk to them all at once." Davis started for the door.

"I wouldn't do that," Lott said. "The boys aren't in any mind to listen, and if you get up there, you'll make a mighty fine target of yourself." As Davis stared at him, perhaps not sure he had heard Lott right, perhaps thinking that he could be in as much danger as Slade himself for defending Slade, Lott nodded. "You can try, but mind what I say."

Williams added, "Keep off the wagon, or you'll be shot. They're not minded to respect anyone that wants to talk them out of this."

This he could do. Perhaps he could not save Slade, but he could make sure that Davis came to no harm. Dan followed him out, stood guard on the boardwalk while the Judge moved through the crowd of men, talking, pleading with them not to do what they had come to do, that he had forgiven Slade, and he knew Slade would never do anything like that again. His voice floated on the wind, scraps of words came back to Dan, who watched the crowd. Davis's words bounced off them; they stared at him grim-faced, their mouths drawn to tight lines half hidden in their beards, their shoulders stiff. They shook their heads. "No. We ain't backing down now. You ain't talking us out of this."

Charley Baer stepped in front of Davis, his burly shoulders and muscular arms, his barrel chest mountain-ous beside the Judge's leaner, longer build. "We tried it your way, damn it. Damn near three months we put up with him and his insults, his wrecking our businesses whenever he had a drop or two in him. He's attacked us time and again, and we never done nothing to him. Now stand aside and let us get it over." As Davis stood there, looking from man to man, seemingly unable to compre-hend what they were telling him, Charley added, "No disrespect to you, sir, you having the balls to come out here like this, we'd be obliged if you'd step aside."

Davis slumped, his head drooped. As he passed Dan and went into the store, tears ran down his face. Dan felt his own tears start. Damn it, he did not want to help hang Slade, whom he could have liked, did like when he was sober, in order to quash the devil.

"They would not listen." Weeping, Davis fumbled in his coat for a handkerchief. "I can do nothing more for you."

"You have to save me," shouted Slade. "You've for-given me, save me now."

"They would not listen. I did everything in my power." In one pocket, then another, Davis searched for his handkerchief, but could not find it, although Dan saw the edge of white cloth in the breast pocket of his waist-coat. He wiped his face with his hands, but the tears would not stop.

Fitch, who had come in behind Dan with Beidler, jerked a thumb toward the door. "Let's get this done." He was dry-eyed, his face hard as flint. He had been proven right, that after all they would hang Slade, but he did not gloat.

Spotting X Beidler, his great friend, Slade called out, "X, can you not help me? We've been friends, can you not help me now?"

His voice cracking, the little man shook his head. "I can do nothing for you now. I warned you, I told you countless times to go home, stop this rampaging, quit drinking. I've done all I could. I can't do any more."

"Damn you," Slade yelled as Williams and Fitch and Lott bundled him out the door. From the street, his voice came back to them, "Davis!" The A was long, drawn out. "Davis! Help!"

Davis, sobbing hard, turned back to his office. "I cannot watch him hang. I cannot be at his death. There is nothing more I can do to help him."

"None of us can help him now," Dan said, following the others out the door. "We've done everything possible to help him by stopping him, even after he grossly insulted you and the Court, put a loaded gun to your head. We can do no more." Inside himself, he cried, Oh, God, why could Slade not have heard us? Why did he not believe us? How did he think he could challenge us, knowing what we did in the winter, being a small part of it.

Christ almighty, Slade, why do you have to make us kill you?

His stomach roiled. Bile leaped into the back of his throat. He tasted the bitter gall and coughed. Beidler, walking beside him, stanching his own sudden flow of tears in his harsh wool sleeve, looked up at Dan and shook his head without speaking.

Slade screamed, "Let me go. I'll never touch another drop."

"Christ," said Beidler. "Can we do this? We were friends."

Dan said, "He can't die alone, without his friends." Immediately, he wanted to bite back the words, because Slade's friends were among those killing him. How the hell had it come to this?

Beidler wiped his face on a grubby handkerchief the size of a small tent. "You have it right." He blew his nose. "It is a sad business, and we can't let him die alone and friendless, even though...." He ended the thought with a shrug as he stuffed the handkerchief in his coat pocket.

People were coming from everywhere. A small boy ran up to Dan and tugged at his sleeve. "Mister, will you hang Slade? Will you? Like them fellas in the winter?" His eyes were bright, and he jumped up and down. "My Pa says if you don't hang him the roughs win, but his friends say Slade's gonna run the town."

"Go back to your father and tell him to keep you at home where you belong." Dan shook off the boy and walked on to catch Beidler and the others who were moving Slade down Wallace.

When he came closer, he heard Slade over the hub-bub of men calling out to each other, to Slade, to the rest of them. Everyone stopped, and Dan shouldered his way through the crowd. He and Beidler stood by Slade, close to Fitch, who gripped the rope around Slade's upper arms.

Slade clasped his hands together as if praying, unclasped them and flapped them at the men surrounding him, made fists, and punched at them. "I beg you, let me go."

Kiskadden came out of the crowd. "You can't do this." Plucking at Dan's arm, swinging from him to X and back again, between spasms of weeping, he said, "He's your friend, for God's sake, your friend." He sobbed. "Our friend."

Dan wanted to yell at him, Don't you think we know that? Don't you think we hate every second of this infernal task, that we want to murder the good man to be shut of the drunk who would drive us all back to lawlessness? He could not see Beidler's face, hidden under the hat brim, but he had no need to see it. It would be a mask like his own, to hide his horror at what they were about to do. There had to be law, or it would again be every man for himself, the strong preying on the weak. He clenched his jaws to keep the words down.

Kiskadden hauled at Fitch's short arm. "Damn you, stop this. You're murdering an innocent man. He has done nothing to be hanged for."

Disliking Slade as he did, Fitch roared, "Get away with you. We ain't hanging him for spitting in the street. If you can't see why, you can go to hell."

"You'll be damned, you know you will." Kiskadden, unarmed, shouldered aside and protesting every second, called, "Someone go for Mrs. Slade. She can save him." And to Dan, "See if you dare hang a man with his wife watching."

"No!" Beidler hollered. "Don't bring her into this."

Another friend of Slade's, seeing Copperbottom shifting about, eyes rolling, ears swiveling in all directions, but tied to the hitching rail, ran to the horse, tested the girth and tightened it a notch, untied the reins, and jumped into the saddle. Reining the animal around toward home, he kicked spurless heels into the horse's ribs. Copperbottom sprang forward, and in three strides leaped into a full gallop out of town. No one stopped him.

Dan thought, Why could that not have been Slade? Even ten minutes ago, he could have been free, but he would not go.

"Let's get this done," said Fitch.

All the fringes on Slade's coat shook. He tried to cover his face with his hands, but could not bring them up high enough. "No!" His cry rang out over the tromp and shuffle of their feet.

Galloping hoofbeats faded from their hearing. Dan looked up the winding road to the east. The horse yet galloped full out, head outstretched, each stride a leap over the rough road.

One of Slade's men in the crowd leveled his shotgun at them, cocked it. "Let him go," he yelled. "You murdering bastards, let him go." Other men took up the shout, their cries rising against the dull, low-lying clouds.

Dan pivoted, brought the Spencer to bear at the man, heard amidst the cries and shouts the ragged clicks of a hundred hammers being cocked as men brought their long guns to bear at Slade's would-be rescuer.

The frustrated savior threw his shotgun down and wept.

"Will no one save me?" Slade shrieked. The fringes on his buckskin trousers quivered. "Must I die now?"

254 | CAROL BUCHANAN

Turning from Dan to Beidler to other men, he folded his hands as if in prayer. "At least let me see my wife. At least do that for me. Let me say goodbye to my dear wife. They've gone for her. Don't let me die without seeing her."

Past his trembling, frantic pleading, Dan consulted in silence with them, and by the slight twitch of a head, a tightening of lips, read that they all agreed. Slade must die before his wife came. A strong, powerful, beautiful woman, there was hardly a man in town who would not feel like falling on his sword for Mrs. Slade. If she came, men would attempt a rescue, and there would be blood-shed. They could not do it.

"It won't be long now," muttered X. Fitch nodded, and holding one of Slade's arms while a third Vigilante held the other, they filed in uneven procession down the steep slope to the Elephant Corral.

44.

The day brightened, as if sunlight had broken through somewhere behind him, though clouds overhead spat wet snow, and the men cast weak shadows as they plodded downward. Walking behind and to one side of Slade and Fitch, he smelled Fitch's sour tobacco odor, the dank odor of long unwashing, and over it all, blocking the air, the sharp stink of – what? Dan sniffed, wiped his nose on his coat sleeve. Fear. No, more than fear. Terror.

The others had been terrified, or they showed bravado, cursed and damned their executioners, or mumbled long forgotten prayers – *Be with us at the hour of our death.*

Slade wept. His broken keening overlay their boots' ragged squash through the sludge on their soles. The wind swept his low mourning to Dan: "Maria. Maria. My dear, dear wife." Swirling past, it wafted snatches of talk to him from behind: "Plenty of chances ... show them ... mean business, can't be let to go on ... wouldn't reform." Someone laughed, "This'll reform him right enough."

Down on the left stood Fitch's wickiup, smoke rising from the smoke hole. How did Fitch like this execution so close to his dwelling? The Missourian did not so much by a turn of his head acknowledge his home. Where were Martha, Tim, Jacob? He yearned for them to be out of this, far away. And Dotty? Dear God that she should even know of such things. He thought of his small sister in New York, sheltered from all knowledge, as the whole family – he, too, had been until Father's — Breaking off the thought, he could not stop the memory of blood sliding across a polished mahogany desk top. Since then, death had been his constant companion, only his own avoiding him.

At the corner, as they swung toward the corral gate, Dan saw the rope dangling over the cross bar. The noose swung in the wind, and the backs of Dan's hands prickled. Heat rose in his face. Slade shrieked, "Will no one save me?"

Fitch and some other men walked Slade toward the packing crate under the noose. He stiffened his knees, dug his heels into the soft heavy snow, screamed, "No!" Charley Baer had strung the rope over the gate to the Elephant Corral, but now he was nowhere to be seen. Fitch and two other men helped Slade onto the box beneath the noose, where he stood trembling as if in a wind. He cried and wept and begged for someone to save him now. When someone attempted to put the noose over his neck, he ducked his head like a bull that did not want to be roped, but at last it was done, and the knot tightened behind his left ear. All the time he called for them to bring him some help. "Get Sanders," he shouted, "he'll help me. He likes me. He knows I've never done anything to deserve this."

A friend of his sprinted away, stumbled on the rough icy ground, picked himself up and ran on, up the hill. Slade called out for someone to bring Davis, and again someone left the crowd to run as best he could to find Davis. He held his side as he ran, and Dan realized it was Harding, whom Slade had beaten just a few hours ago.

Dan did not imagine that either Sanders or Davis would have anything to say that could make a difference now, but they waited, though Fitch grumbled and muttered at Slade's feet. What does it matter now? Dan wanted to yell at Fitch. When a man stood poised to die, what did it matter that he drew a few more breaths, that he gained precious seconds of life to feel the cold wind, the beating of his heart? We can do this for him, he said to himself. We can do this if it will ease his way across the divide.

In a matter of minutes, the courier to Sanders returned. He shook his head as he told them, "Sanders said he's sorry, but there is nothing he can do for you now."

"Oh, God!" shouted Slade. "Is there no one who can help me?"

The man holding the end of the rope began to take up the slack. A voice called, "Here comes Davis!"

Slade's face brightened in hope as Judge Davis came down the slope. Muttering and grumbling, men made way for him to walk through their midst. Standing at Slade's feet, he looked up at the tear-stained, bleary face above him. "Help me," Slade said. "You have to help me. Get me out of this. You know I've done nothing wrong, nothing to deserve this. Nothing1" The last was a shout that the wind shredded against the buildings, and carried across Daylight Creek to the hill beyond.

By his face, Dan knew Davis realized it was a lost cause. He had only come because he could not deny a man about to die, he would make one last ditch effort to satisfy himself if nothing else. The messenger came to stand with Dan and the other Vigilante leaders. He whispered, "The Judge said he'd come only if we waited to hang Slade until after he'd gone."

Slade cried out, "You can plead for me, Judge. Dear God, you defended Ives. Tell them. I'm no Ives."

"I don't know what I can do, but I'll try." Judge Davis held up his hands to the grim men around him, still the talk and the catcalls and the shouts went on so that Dan thought no one could hear him from more than a few feet away. "Hear me, all of you. Do not do this thing. He committed the outrage to my court – " Someone hollered above the rest, "Let's get on with this," but the Judge went on, "– but that was only a drunken prank. You know Joseph Slade is a decent man –"

Someone shouted, "When sober, but he's never sober."

Was any of this getting through? Was there any sign of a rescue? Dan caught sight of Jacob standing at the edge of the crowd. Why was he here? Where were Martha, Dotty, Tim? God forbid they saw any of what happened here. Tears flowed down Beidler's face, and he was not alone as several openly wept. One man broke away from the group of Vigilantes and walked a few steps away before he collapsed against the rail fence, his face in the crook of his elbow, his back shaking with sobs.

The sound of a rifle being cocked split the crowd, left one man in a space leveling his long gun. "Let him go," he bellowed. "He's done nothing to be hanged for. You murdering bastards." Tears flowed down his cheeks and his hands shook, the barrel wobbling up and down, side to side.

Christ! If it went off, anyone might be killed. Dan brought the Spencer to his shoulder, peered down the sights, cocked it. Too many men behind the would-be rescuer, around him, rifles and shotguns and pistols drawn on the man, several would die if one did, their balls and pellets passing easily through the rescuer, into other flesh. Including his own. His own. To steady the rifle, Dan told himself, Just a deer, this is deer fever, just deer fever, he'd had deer and men in his sights before, just a deer.

The rescuer lowered the hammer, the muzzle sank toward the ground, and he flung away, sobbing. A nod or two among the Vigilantes, and two or three followed him to make sure he would not try again.

"I can do no more," said Judge Davis. "I must go now." Bringing out a handkerchief, he wiped his eyes and nose. "I'm sorry, Joseph. I – I must go."

Pivoting on his heel, stumbling almost to one knee, he blundered away.

A flash of motion near the crest of the mountain caught Dan's eye.

"There comes Mrs. Slade," he muttered to Fitch. "For God's sake let's get this over with."

45.

The log walls would stop pistol balls, and maybe rifle balls, but they could not stop the sounds from outside, the commotion of men shouting, boots by the hundred pounding toward them. A horse whinnied.

Timothy said, "I'm going out there."

"No." Martha heard her voice sharp as broken glass, but her son said, "You can't stop me."

Lydia snapped, "Are you so all-fired bent on watching a man be killed? You want to look on murder? Shame on you. For shame."

Martha could not read his expression in the gloom, but by the sliver of daylight from the window slit, she knew he had put his head up, just like always when he was a mind to take his own way on his own. He said, "I seen the others, in the winter, when I fetched Dan'l for you. I've seen dead men."

Albert could stop him. Bless his heart, Albert was big and strong enough to stop even as big a boy as Timmy was getting to be, but she didn't ask him. Tim would make his own decision and have to abide by it the same as all of them. It would be awful out there, where a man would die. She would not stop him, but neither would she say he could go. Albert stood aside, and Tim raised the bar, lifted the latch, and sidled out, leaving Albert to barricade them again. Too late, Martha asked herself,

Should she have forbidden him? Had he waited for her to tell him no so he could obey and spare himself whatever he might see?

She bent her head to pray, but could not think what to pray for: Slade's rescue, Dan'l's change of mind, Mrs. Slade? Or all of them? She put away thought, and waited.

Albert stayed by the door, while the three women huddled together on the bench.

Outside Slade screamed his wife's name, long and drawing out each syllable. "Maria. Maria. Mareee—"

46.

Hoofbeats. The dog rose from his bed near the stove, and walked stiff-legged to the door. Maria's hands, in the basin of soapy water, washing the bigger mixing bowl, stopped. She listened. A ragged drum, two and two, coming closer. The fur along the dog's spine rose. He lowered his head, growled. Hope rose in her throat, choking her, and she rushed outside to look for Joe. Shivering, hugging her body against the cold wind, she waited. Beside her, the dog barked, and kept on barking, wagged his tail, growling, the wind ruffling his long thick fur.

Jemmy came running from the barn to stand with her. "Is it Slade? Is it Joe?"

"Maybe." Maria seized his hand. After a few seconds, he pulled it away. "You're hurting me."

The familiar blaze in the coppery face, but the rider was – was not Joe. Another man on Joe's horse, and Copperbottom was all lathered up, foam dripping from his mouth, foam on his chest. The rider pulled the horse to a stop, jumped off. The horse hung his head, his sides heaving, gasping for air. Joe would never ride him that hard, run him up a mountain.

The rider seized her shoulders. She looked up into his eyes, and something inside her cracked apart like thick ice over black water. "He's dead?"

"No. Not yet. They're fixing to hang him. Go. I'll look after things here."

Turning on her heel, she dashed into the house, changed from her house shoes to her riding boots, strapped her pistol belt around her waist, threw on her coat, grabbed up the rifle, ammunition pouch and powder horn. A dry-eyed Jemmy followed her about, ran with her to the corral, where the man had saddled Billy Bay, who would not take the bit from a stranger. While the man fastened the saddle scabbard under the right stirrup and slipped the rifle in, she bridled the horse. She knelt to hug Jemmy, called him her brave boy, said she'd be back soon. The man boosted her into the saddle, opened the gate and stood aside as they went through at a lope.

She turned the thoroughbred toward the ridge, and they plunged up it in Copperbottom's tracks. At the top she paused to scan the ground for the shortest way down the mountain. The useless road, a rocky track, twisted back and forth, its snow-piled, rutted surface no better than the ground around it. Going by it would take too long. As if aiming a rifle, she drew a bead on the town below and kicked the horse.

Thoroughbred that he was, born for speed and pent up too many days in the corral, he vaulted into a dead run around snow-piled boulders, mounded sagebrush, and stiff junipers as high as his withers. His hooves missed badger holes buried under snow. Maria left him to it; so he carried her to the town as fast as possible, he could pick his own route. She crouched low, and his black mane whipped her face, the saddle rocked at his every stride, the horn pounded her stomach, and she had only one thought in time with the horse's hoofbeats. Save my Joe. Save my Joe.

47.

They had done this twenty-four times. They knew how to hang a man with speed, efficiency, dispatch.

"My wife," Slade sobbed. "My dear wife. Maria." He stood on the box, his head drooping. The breeze ruffled his hair, ballooned his trouser legs.

Dan stood, the Spencer ready on his arm, where he could see the crowd and Slade and the wild rider galloping down the mountain. What the hell, he asked himself, what the hell are we doing? How did we come to this? Why did he not go home? Around him the crowd waited, and he caught a few phrases from mumbled prayers: "Lord deliver him," "be with us now and," "God damn stranglers, at it again," and "receive the soul," while other men sobbed, men he did not think had any feeling except for easy women and marked cards.

Here and there, he caught a few avid looks from men who loved to watch someone else die, and he wondered if their enjoyment might someday lead them to stand where Slade now stood.

Slade cried out, "Save me! Will no one save me?"

Someone hollered, "You've had this coming for years!" Men cheered that; others booed. In silence, Dan answered him, Slade, damn you, why did you not ride home? You could have saved yourself a hundred times in the last three days. You didn't believe us when we told you, when Beidler said you had three hours. He looked around for Beidler, who stood with a face like grief itself, dry-eyed and bloodless under the stubble beard, the mustache hiding his mouth. Someone shouted, "Let's get this over with before she gets here." Kiskadden's tears streamed down his cheeks.

The rider was halfway down the mountain. Dan talked to the horse, don't stumble, don't stumble with her, don't fall. The black horse galloped in a wide turn, so that Dan saw long hair streaming behind her, skirts flowing back along his flank, the saddle rocking. Valkyrie, he thought. She is a Valkyrie, like the old legend. Except that she rode to save her hero, not conduct him to Valhalla.

A man climbed onto the box, adjusted the noose, and jumped down, his boots squelching through a layer of ice into the mud below. He and three others seized the crate, and they eyed each other across it, between Slade's trembling legs.

Williams said, "Men, do your duty," and they snatched the box away.

"Mareee—" Slade fell. His last cry broke off as his neck snapped and his chin dropped to his chest. Feet kicking, his body swung and turned in the wind.

48.

The rider disappeared into a draw, and at the corner of Dan's eye, the dead man's kicking slowed; his feet twitched two or three times, and stopped. The crowd sighed long and drawn out, almost a moan. Slade's friends among them glared through their tears, and some shook their fists or swore at the "stranglers" who would "hang a decent man like Slade." Like the Ives trial, Dan thought, with Ives's pals casting threats in the dark, but that was all it had come to. So far. He kept the Spencer ready, in case Slade's friends tried to take their revenge, now that they had failed to save him.

Jim Kiskadden, dabbing at his eyes, barely able to speak, asked X, "Can't we get him down and decent before she gets here?" He jerked a thumb over his shoulder at the mountainside, where the rider crested the draw and whipped the horse to greater effort.

"Let's get him down quick, then," said X.

Fitch pulled the half hitch around the fence post free, paid out rope hand over hand to lower the corpse into waiting hands. Already the onlookers were dispersing, some to the saloons to quench their sorrows, others to go their somber ways back to Nevada, to Summit and camps between. No one celebrated this, but no one had celebrated the others either. Killing a man was never a good thing, Dan thought, letting the hammer on his rifle down easy. He slung the weapon onto his shoulder and raised his hands to help take the weight of Slade's body.

X and Williams jumped down, and they carried what had once been Joseph Slade up the slope to Wallace Street. Dan thought he heard hoofbeats, but when he concentrated, he caught only the sound of men's low mutterings, a woman's higher cry, "It's a damn shame," and many boots slogging away from them. They turned up Wallace, heading for the Virginia Hotel. Looking over his shoulder, Dan saw the small parade of grim-faced men guarding their backs. Someone said, "She's in the homestretch."

"Quick, oh God, hurry," Kiskadden urged them, but their faster sideways shuffle only increased the number of steps they took without helping them to greater speed. Around Dan men panted, muttered, "Don't drop him," and "Steady there." Kiskadden said, "Hurry. For God's sake, hurry." Someone growled, "We're hurrying, damn it. Can't you see that?" Dan imagined he heard hoof-beats, but it was only someone's boot heels. He held Slade's right shoulder, his fingers gripped the smooth soft deerhide, and beads dug into his knuckles. As funeral suits go, he thought, Slade's suit would do him proud. Would she have him buried in it?

An errant ray of sunlight caught the dull shine of Slade's open eyes. Startled, Dan asked himself: Did Slade live? Then clouds sailed on across the sun, were streaked with yellow glory that faded to dull gray. A few merchants lighted lamps in their windows, so that they carried the corpse through patches of mellow light past Pfouts and Russell, and others. Did Davis see them go by, or did he stay in his office and court room, weeping? At that, Dan felt a prickling at his own eyelids, and scolded himself, Not yet, not yet.

He glanced down at the corpse. Slade's face was grey-blue, his green eyes stared up at Dan, his swollen tongue protruded from purple lips. He would see this face in his nightmares.

"Hurry." Kiskadden ran ahead to open the door to the Virginia Hotel. The proprietor met them in the lobby and wordlessly showed them upstairs to a room with two double beds, a stool, and a vanity, besides the usual amenities of basin, pitcher, and chamber pot. They laid Slade's corpse on one of the beds as galloping hoofbeats sounded outside.

Kiskadden muttered, "Too late."

One of the men who had helped carry the body said, "This is Slade's last night in a hotel. Hope he enjoys it." Swift as a snake, X wheeled on him. "Get the fuck out of here," he hissed. The man raised his hands shoulder high and backed from the room.

Downstairs a woman screamed, "No! Oh, Joe! No!"

"Quick." Beidler tugged the hangman's knot loose while Dan untied the hands and coiled the rope. They would not let Mrs. Slade see her husband's body with the ropes still on it, but where could they hide them? He lifted Slade's head while Beidler slipped the noose over it. He smoothed Slade's hair, his hands gentle as a mother's, and closed the eyes. Light feet ran up the stairs, hesitated, bolted down the hallway, stumbled, came on.

X pointed at a dark corner of the room. "Toss them there." As the ropes fell into the corner, X stripped a blanket from the second bed and threw it to Dan, who dropped it over the small pile of rope. They straightened Slade's legs, folded his hands across his chest. Dan closed the eyes and retreated to a shadowy corner as

Mrs. Slade burst in and flung herself, screaming, across her husband's body.

She shrieked at them, "Why did you not shoot him? No dog's death should have come to such a man!"

"Go," Kiskadden whispered. "I'll look after her."

Dan murmured, "Don't let her come to harm."

"I won't," Kiskadden said. "Now, for God's sake just go. All of you. Get out of here."

49.

ocks, knees, and belly crusted with flung snow, the black horse waited, spraddle-leg-ged, head hanging low. White froth flecked his deep chest, steam rose from his quarters and neck, and he breathed hard through flared nostrils, his sides rising and falling. Down the street, Copperbottom stood at a hitching post, on hip cocked, ears splayed in every horse's pose of making the best of a long wait, only for this horse the wait would be eternal. His rider would never again swing up onto his back.

From inside the hotel, the woman's screams flayed the evening, and Dan knew she would not think of the animals. She will never forgive us for killing her husband, Dan thought, but the horses need tending. What those two thoughts had to do with each other, damned if he knew.

"The horses," he said to Beidler, who nodded and took Billy Boy's reins. Leading the black horse, they walked down to collect Copperbottom, who nickered at the black horse and came alongside willingly enough. Perhaps they both sensed that they were headed for rest and hay.

The town was quiet. Through saloon windows layered in smoke and grime, he saw men sitting at round tables and talking over their beers, but the fiddle players bowed over their instruments as if they could only hear

271

the music escaping from the sound boxes. He and Beidler walked on, their steps muffled by snow and covered by the horses' slow hoofbeats. Heads down, men hurried past them on their way to their own destinations.

Dan thought of the military funeral processions he had seen at home, the riderless led horse, the empty boots backwards in the stirrups. Did Beidler recall them, too, or had Bleeding Kansas been too much of a battlefield for pomp and ceremony? We should have drums to beat our way here, he told himself, but the only drum he heard came from the blood beating in his ears and throbbing in his scalp.

On Jackson, a young girl hurried down the street, intent on watching her footing, but when she heard the horses' slow tread, she halted and looked to see who this might be. Her hands went to her mouth, and she backed a step or two.

"Dotty?" To Beidler, "It's my stepdaughter." X took the reins from him, as Dan lengthened his stride toward her. "Where's your mother? Why are you not with her?" He had not gone more than two or three paces when she cried, "Dan'l! How could you do it? How could you hang Mr. Slade?"

50.

Inside the Eatery, Martha heard the squelch and tramp of boots, the low rumble of many men's voices trailing down Wallace Street, and knew they were going. They'd done what they'd come to do, God help them, and now were heading back to wherever they came from. But her young'uns was somewhere out there still, and she had to find them, make sure they was all right. The child – dear Lord, let the child have stayed to home after school.

Fumbling, she tied the sash of her cloak about her waist, aware that something changed the atmosphere in the restaurant, so it crackled like something frying too hot. She was afeared like she'd never been in here before. She had to get out quick.

Someone pounded on the door, and Albert let Timmy in, closed it, and dropped the bar.

The boy came down the aisle and dropped onto the back bench, his head in his hands, elbows propped on his knees. "They done it," he whispered.

"Who?" Her heart beat in her midsection, down where it shouldn't rightly be. She sat beside him, her arm around his broadening shoulders, and a prayer went up all on its own: Please, God, Dan'l wasn't one of them.

Timothy didn't take her meaning. "Those men. They come from everywhere in the Gulch, and they hung Mr. Slade. The Vigilantes said do it, so they done it. Must've

273

been three, four hundred of 'em. Maybe more. They come from all over the Gulch, and every one of them saying it was high time, and they wasn't going to put up with his trouble-making no more."

Outside, a high shriek rose to a long scream, and sank, only to rise again like winter's howling wind.

"Who can that be?"

Timmy said, "Poor Mrs. Slade. As they was hanging him, we saw her riding hell bent for leather down the mountain to rescue him." He shook his head. "I'll never forget it." Bending his head he pressed the heels of his hands into his eyes like he'd squeeze out the sights of the last few hours.

"Poor Mrs. Slade." Lydia bit off the end of every word. "The poor, poor woman, her husband murdered by those he thought were his friends. We must pray for her." She bowed her head, but Quaker-like, said nothing out loud.

Martha folded her hands in the sleeves of her cloak, but as she began to pray, the thought came that drink had widowed Mrs. Slade. The devil in the bottle had killed her man, no matter how his death had come about. She said, "Poor Mrs. Slade. Is there anything we might do for her, do you think?"

Lydia kept her eyes down as though to hold her place in her prayer. In the wobbling candlelight, her face looked to be set in hard, downward lines from her nose to the corners of her mouth. She squeezed every word from between tight lips, like a miser pouring dust from his poke. "Some of us may be able to bring her some comfort, later, but there will be nothing thee can do, thy Daniel being no doubt one of her husband's murderers."

A buzzing started in Martha's ears, as if a hive had settled there; it drowned what else Lydia said. How could she possibly think Dan'l would commit murder? Her being a Quaker and all, she didn't hold with violence no matter who did it, but to call him a murderer?

"Dan'l is no murderer," she said, as Timmy jumped to his feet.

"No!" the boy shouted, "You can't say that. You can't!"

A draft of cold air around her ankles, the sliding sound of the bar being lifted, told Martha the door opened, though she had not heard a knock. Small feet ran down the aisle. Martha rose to meet the child, who wrapped her arms around her Mam's waist, clinging to her and crying. "I couldn't find you. I couldn't find you and I was afeared – Mam, they hung Mr. Slade, and then Dan'l said you were here."

And there, behind her, was Dan'l. She couldn't tell his features against the fading daylight as he paused in the doorway, but she'd know the shape of him anywhere, even with that infernal rifle slung on his right shoulder, the barrel standing up by his ear. Albert said something, and he caught the toe of his boot on the mudsill, shook off Albert's hand at his elbow, and righted himself. That stumble caught at Martha's heart, because he was commonly a balanced man, but this business must have thrown him off. And then, when Albert closed the door behind him, he left his hat on, and that in itself told her how upset he was, him being so mannerly that he always took it off in the house.

He paused in the space between the benches for the front and back tables. "She was looking for you, so I escorted—" Sounding uncertain, not like her Dan'l at all, and she couldn't see him proper, with his face hidden that way in the shadows under his hat brim. She thought he might be hurt, but something told her what hurt him wouldn't show on his face like the cut on his head, so she closed her mouth and bided her time.

Before Albert could shut the door, Jacob walked in and spotted Dan'l right off. "Gott sei dank! It is you I see come in here."

"Yes, it's I." Dan'l's hat tilted as he looked down at his hands, turning them over like he saw them for the first time. She had to listen hard to catch what he said.

Beside her, Timmy shifted his feet like marching to nowhere and breathed hard through his mouth while Dotty sobbed against Martha's bosom.

Dan'l said, "She saw what happened. The Professor kept school late, and she and Molly Sheehan were on their way home from school when Slade —" He coughed, like something choked him.

Dotty yelled at him. In the candlelight, her cheeks shone wet. "He didn't deserve to hang! You killed him. He didn't do nothin' and you hung him anyway!"

"The child is right," said Lydia. "Thee knows Mr. Slade had done nothing that thee should hang him for. Thee murdered him."

"Do you all think so?" He spoke like asking how much snow they thought fell this winter.

In the silence, the room seemed full of people, thought Martha, waiting to hear what the others would say, defending Dan'l? When she opened her mouth to say Dan'l would never murder anyone, let alone Mr. Slade, who he'd quite liked at times, she knew she was too late.

He turned away, holding himself braced so straight it near brought her to tears, and she choked because one word stuck in her throat, hard as a stone, blocking all the others she needed to comfort him: Why? She didn't un-derstand why they had done it, why he might have been part of it, even though she knew he was not, and could never be party to murder.

Slade done something that even his best friends would not stop him from dying.

There had to be a good reason for Dan'l to be part of that. What was it? Why?

She tried again to ask, but the moment had passed. He said, "Very well. You can all think about this. We —" A cough interrupted him, and when it passed, he went on, "We pleaded with Slade to go home. We gave him every chance to save his life. Right up to the very minute before he was arrested, he could have got on his horse and ridden home. But he would not. We'll never know why not. He knew what would happen if he did not go home, because we told him. But he would not go home."

Jacob's question came like it was squeezed from him. "Ich verstehe nicht. It is – not, I do not understand – what he did? You did this –" his hands made a wringing motion like killing a chicken. Martha shuddered. "– because he would not go to home?"

"He held a gun to Judge Davis's head and said he'd hold him hostage, his freedom for the Judge's life. After he was disarmed, the Judge forgave him, but if we had let him go free, every criminal in the territory would know the Court was worthless, that it meant nothing and we would not enforce the law. They would know it was safe to come back. With Slade to lead them, it would have been worse than before. It —"

"Thee has no excuse," Lydia snapped. The candlelight caught the glimmer of a thousand trembling reflections from the jets sewn onto her dress. "Thee fought violence with violence then, and thee did it today. No matter what they might have done, when thee hanged those men, thee murdered them. Now thee have murdered Mr. Slade. Violence is never right."

Something tapped on wood, a tiny sound like a rapid rat-tat on a small drum. After a second, Martha realized Dan'l's fingernails beat on the rifle stock. When he answered Lydia, he said, "Perhaps you would be keen to turn a cheek and go to the cross, but I'm not prepared to put others in a situation of having to make that choice. Especially not the children."

He waited just a moment, not looking at Martha. "If anybody wants me, I'll be at the Idaho Street Livery taking care of Slade's horse." In silence, he walked to the door, brushing past Jacob, raised the latch and was gone.

51.

The horse had been ridden hard and gone largely untended for several days, and he buried his nose in the small pile of hay, scattering it about to suit himself. In between mouthfuls, he sucked from the buckets of water. After flattening his ears at first, a horse's usual response to food that warned others away from it, he let Dan tackle the grooming. A good horse, spunky but well mannered, though not a creature to drop your guard around, Dan found. As he brushed the caked mud and sweat from the thick winter coat, he murmured words to soothe this animal, who would not understand why a stranger worked on him instead of his usual rider: "Easy boy, sorry old Copperbottom, easy boy, sorry old Copperbottom, easy there, easy boy."

When he heard the small door open and shut, he went on working, bending into longer strokes, tracing the way the hair grew with his lead hand and following with the back hand. A woman's short steps shuffled toward him through the straw in the passageway. Martha.

His leading hand lost track of the hair growth, and he dropped the brush. He had hung a lantern on a two-penny nail on a post, and when she stood in the circle of lamplight, he was bent over, searching in the bedding straw hay for the brush. Straightening, he cursed himself for an imbecile, to present his posterior to her in that fashion, and the hammer in his head pounded its anvil beat. He seized a handful of the horse's mane to steady himself.

Copperbottom swung his head around to know who had stopped behind him. Dan brushed partway down a foreleg. He did not know what else to do, what to say to her, until he knew why she sought him out. Would she tell him it was over, that he could sleep tonight in the hay and look for a room in the morning? If she held with Lydia, her great friend, he did not see how they could go on.

He sneezed. And sneezed again. Setting the brush on the horse's back, he groped in his trousers pocket for a handkerchief, but found none. He'd hung his rifle, coat, and hat on another nail, and worked in shirtsleeves and waistcoat. In a coat pockets he found the soggy rag he'd used earlier, when there was no one but the horse to see him weep for Slade, and for the agony of what he'd done. He blew his nose, and when he replaced the handkerchief in his pocket, he could not keep her from saying her piece any longer.

"I'm sorry I didn't come sooner," she said. "There were the young'uns, and I thought you'd be home to supper."

She had expected him home for supper. She'd expected him home. In his relief he nearly wept again, but covered the weakness with the business of dusting himself off before he put on his coat. "I didn't think I was fit company. Besides, the horse needed a good brushing. He was soundly neglected the last few days."

They had come to it. He had to know, but could not think how to ask: Why did you not speak then? Do you think I committed murder? Because I did, but I can see no other way than the way we took.

She said, "I kept some supper for you. It's venison stew."

They had a joke about venison stew, and how one winter on it was enough, but he could not think of it now. "I don't know." He picked the brush off the horse's back and set it on a box in the passage where the hostler would find it in the morning. "What do you think about – about what happened today?"

"I know you'd never be a party to murder, but I don't understand why …." She stretched one hand out, he fingers spreading wide. "Mr. Slade was a good man when sober. Why could you not trust him to reform after the Judge forgave him?"

"He never promised to reform. Never said he'd stop drinking, and he wouldn't have stopped. The craving would come over him again, and he'd have to have it. We couldn't take the chance with so many lives." Watching her face, he knew she was not having it, and perhaps only one thing more could convince her. It meant breaking his oath of secrecy, telling her something they all understood and would never say aloud. He buttoned his coat. The oath, or her?

"He asked to join us, and we allowed it, thinking that he would help us in our cause. He was a great man on the Overland Route, a truly great man." God, what a waste of a life, Dan thought, swallowing to keep himself from shedding tears. "Honest to the bone, with a strong hatred of thieves and murderers. Williams thought well of him, if he would not drink. He abstained when they led that wagon train up. But we made a big mistake. He was no help. He would not abstain. Dealing with that gang, we needed every man in his right mind, but Slade could or would not limit his drinking or lay off altogether. Other men drank, but Slade turned into a demon.

We could not trust him even with so many honest people in danger. Either he wanted to hang everyone we suspected, or he sided with the roughs, depending on whether he liked them or not. We never knew which it would be. We kept our activities secret from him, as much as we could. If we had let him go now, we had no reason to believe we could have trusted him."

When she did not speak, he demanded, "God help me, do you think we – or I – would have done that if there had been any other way?"

"No. I don't, but some might," she said. "I know you'd never be party to murder."

"What about Mrs. Hudson?" He drove one fist into the other hand. "The idea of turning the Gulch over to the roughs, endangering everyone – you and the children – because violence is evil. It is evil, but I can't step aside just to keep my own soul clean."

"Is that how you see it?"

"Yes. Naturally, Fitch wanted to do what we did from the start. And others. There were plenty of them on the street this afternoon." He shivered.

"We'd best be going on home," said Martha.

When she said that, he wanted to dance, or sing, or skip down the passage. She was not telling him to find another place to live. It was not over between them. Despite everything, she wanted him. As he wanted her. To cover his feelings, he asked, as if he inquired about the weather, "Do you think the children will ever understand?"

"Timmy already does. It may take longer with Dotty."

"And you?" He put on his hat and hung the rifle on his shoulder. Taking up the lantern, he lighted their way out of the barn, making sure to shut the door.

"I wish you hadn't thought it was the only thing to do." As they walked up Idaho Street toward Jackson, Martha put her hand inside his elbow. "I was hoping and praying you-all could find another way. Knowing you, though, I figure if there'd been one, you'd have found it. And done it."

He put his arm around her shoulders and held her to him. He had not lost her, his good angel.

Historical Note

For a definitive biography of the life of Joseph A. Slade, please see *Death of a Gunfighter* by Dan Rottenberg. While I agree with him about the character of Slade, I disagree about why the Vigilantes hanged him.

Wilbur F. Sanders wrote in his unpublished account, "With great deliberation he locked horns with the Vigilance Committee, defied its authority…. The Committee was compelled to abdicate its functions or then and there vindicate its right to be and to do. An abandonment of its authority would have left the communities without adequate protection and subjected much of its membership to the vengeance of him and his sympathizers. His execution assured the existence and authority of the committee within its limitations to maintain quiet over this region."

Having just rid the region of a band of murderers and thieves, the Vigilantes could not surrender to Slade. The danger Sanders writes of was real.

For more information on the Vigilantes of Montana and on the legal situation in which historical people and fictional characters find themselves in my novels, as well as a complete list of the works I've consulted while researching the history of Montana during the Civil War years, please visit my website:

https://carol-buchanan.com

ABOUT THE AUTHOR

Carol enjoys talking to readers at book events.
With a PhD in English and history, she writes historical
fiction about the Vigilantes of Montana, who battled terror on
the roads during the Civil War, when gold, greed, and a
vacuum of law led to ruffians' rule and a tolerance for murder.
She teaches Montana's Vigilante History at Flathead Valley
Community College. Her Montana Vigilante series has earned
numerous awards, among them Spur and Spur Finalist
awards from the Western Writers of America, and the "Spirit
of Dorothy Johnson" award from the Whitefish Library
Association. A native Montanan, she is a member of the
Flathead High School class of 1958. She enjoys reading, hiking,
and watching movies with Richard, her husband of 40+ years,
owner/operator of Byte Savvy Computing Services in
Kalispell.
Follow her on Twitter (@CarolBuchananMT) and Facebook
(https://www.facebook.com/carolbuchananauthor/)
Or https://carol-buchanan.com

www.ingramcontent.com/pod-product-compliance
Lightning Source LLC
Chambersburg PA
CBHW030648020726
47493CB00006B/1928